Dangerous Memories

Dangerous Memories

Lisa J. Peck

This book is not an official publication of The Church of Jesus Christ of Latter-day Saints. All opinions expressed herein are the author's and are not necessarily those of the publisher's or of The Church of Jesus Christ of Latter-day Saints.

ISBN: 1-55517-389-6

Published by: Bonneville Books
Distributed by:

Cover design by Corinne A. Bischoff and Sheila Mortimer
Photography credited to Bower's Photography
Printed in the United States of America

A special thank you to my husband for his support and to my writer friends, who I'm deeply indebted to: Judy Anderson, Betty Briggs, Rebecca Crandall, Sandy Hirsche, Rachel Nunes, Linda Orvis, Carol Williams, and a special gratitude to Max Golightly, whose support and influence is still felt beyond the grave.

PROLOGUE

Twenty years had passed and Karen still couldn't remember all the details. They were blocked in her subconscious, and she wanted to keep it that way.

What she did recall was that the day had been sweltering hot as the dirty rays of light targeted the earth. She had waded through the muggy afternoon to the house of her best friend, Charissa.

They had planned to run on the California beach and perhaps snatch a cool drink afterward. When she strode up her friend's pathway, Karen's muscles instinctively tensed.

It was unusually quiet. Yesterday's free newspaper waited on the front steps to be thrown away. Reading information from the outside world had never been allowed in Charissa's home since her parents' divorce.

Karen swallowed the awkward lump that had risen in her throat before she tapped on the door. Straining to hear noise from inside, she almost felt the silence.

Perhaps Charissa had fallen asleep. She pressed the doorbell. The dong of the chimes seemed out of place against the stillness of the house. Karen's hand reached for the knob.

She hesitated as she calmed herself, knowing Charissa's mom had left hours before. Karen had seen her pulling onto North Street. Even knowing the mom wasn't there hadn't relieved her nervousness. The cold brass knob turned easily. Startled it wasn't locked, Karen shoved the door open.

Scattered mail laid strewn on the floor — not touched since the mail lady delivered it early that morning. Most of the letters were addressed to Charissa's mom in black handwriting. Karen couldn't resist staring at the notes. She made up her mind to find her friend.

"Charissa?" she called.

No answer.

Karen cleared her throat. The sound bounced off the walls. She couldn't bring herself to call for her friend again.

Tip-toeing through the kitchen and living room, she continued searching. No sign.

The house was unusually clean. Odd. Her heart pounded harder as she progressed through the hallway — each step more resistant than the last. Something whispered "be careful" in her mind. She crept to her friend's room, slowly pushing open the creaking door. Empty. She turned to the master bedroom. Chills raced through her as she inched open the door.

Karen's memory stopped there.

She'd been told over and over that she'd crept in and screamed at what she saw. Her screaming lasted until the neighbors rushed into the house and phoned the police. She still didn't remember what horror the room held, and she had no desire to. A freezing, evil, uncomfortable feeling surrounded the incident.

Two days later, they told her Charissa had been killed. Her murder was committed in the name of a cult under the direction of Charissa's mother.

The knowledge forced Karen to harbor fierce hatred for cults — all cults — even traditional religious organizations.

Chapter 1

Karen hurried to open the window. The kitchen had become stuffy since she learned her sister-in-law, Betsy, who lived upstairs, had joined one of those cults. Sweat bubbled on her forehead. She wiped it away with her sleeve. She turned a page of her cookbook, struggling for control.

Her whole family watched her as she pretended to be interested in cooking their supper. Finally she couldn't control herself any longer and she blurted out, "A Mormon!" Her mouth settled into a deep sneer. "You've got to be kidding. A cult!" She looked her sister-in-law, Betsy, straight in the face.

Karen's husband, always calm in emergencies, asked, "When did this baptism happen, Sis?"

"Today," Betsy said.

"Let me get this straight," Karen choked. "You woke this morning and decided, 'I'm going to become a Mormon?'" She flipped another page of the cookbook.

"Karen." George raised his thick eyebrows as he rested his back against the tan-tiled countertop by the oven. "The kids are here. Are you sure you want to discuss this in front of them?"

Trying to slow the pound of her exploding heart, Karen glanced at him. He was quick in reprimanding her. Didn't he know what this meant? Her teenage children watched her with blank expressions, but they had no clue of her repressed hatred...but George knew. He had held her for hours as she vented and sob through the pain that refused to go away, no matter —

"Actually, I'd been thinking about joining for a couple of weeks while I took their lessons." Betsy's hand with its two inch-nails waved as she talked. During the pause in her explanation, she stared at Karen.

Had she no heart? Karen wondered, looking away.

Betsy continued her spiel. "The missionaries really wanted me to invite my family to the baptismal service, but I thought it best not to."

Karen clenched her fists as her knuckles whitened. Why would her sister-in-law torture her like this? So cruel.

George walked to Karen and put his arm around her. To calm her. She didn't want to be coddled like a child. She jerked away from him and said in a tone more gruff than planned, "Stop worrying. I'm not having another panic attack."

"It was the topic of Mormons and your fear of them that triggered the last one," George whispered, his arms folded across his broad chest.

Karen pursed her thin lips.

"You're over-generalizing," George said.

"Stop playing like you're my shrink." Karen sighed. It wouldn't be so bad if Betsy weren't staying in the upstairs apartment, but since she was, Mormons were bound to end up crawling all over her house. She wished she could spray them like one did for cockroaches.

An uncomfortable gnawing overcame her, as though someone tried to read her mind. She glanced up and saw her husband's blue eyes; her daughter, Mikey, holding her breath; her son, Sam, rolling the soccer ball between his feet with his brown eyes fixed upon her; and Betsy flicking her purple nails.

"Stop staring like I'm going to freak out." She waved her hand in front of her face as if to wipe away their gazes. She could ignore all of them except Mikey and Sam. Her children's eyes radiated fear. Oh, what had she done? "I get depressed, not crazy."

Cold silence penetrated the room. Everyone gazed at the floor except Karen, who stared at the group. "It's Betsy's life." With that she hustled to the stove. The noodles threatened to boil over. After one stir, a couple of bubbles splashed over the pot, sizzling onto the burner, filling the room with a burnt odor and steam. Some of the tension seemed to evaporate with it. Funny, she hadn't noticed how stressed she'd been before. Shaking her head, she spoke before she realized. "Bizarre thing to do, but that's Betsy."

Betsy chuckled and batted her indigo eyelashes. Her make-up measured up to its daily dosage of weight — a pound. Being a Mormon didn't seem to change her make-up habits. "It's true. I've been bizarre, but now the bizarre happens to be the truth," Betsy said.

"They sucked you up in their vortex you've always warned me about." Mikey smiled, lurking behind her stringy tresses. Her young face showed a mixture of amusement and confusion, which faded with the sound of a deep, soft laugh. The noise grew louder until George had to pause to catch some air. He'd taken off his suit jacket, revealing a wrinkled white shirt and trim waist. His hair bounced as his laugh changed from a soft chuckle to a full-blast roar.

"What's so funny?" Karen pivoted around from the stove, placing her hands on her hips.

"Sorry. I can't help feeling bad for those poor Mormons." He laughed again. "Can you imagine their faces when they find out who they baptized? Aunt Betsy will take over the whole church and demand to be their next pastor."

Karen sighed, running her fingers through her short brown hair; he wasn't laughing at her.

"For your information, sweet brother," Betsy said, smiling a fake grin, "there are no pastors at this church, and I'll fit in quite nicely, thank you very much."

"Yeah, I bet. How caught up are they on their chakras?" George gave a broad smile, revealing his perfectly aligned teeth.

"Don't know," Betsy said, "but if they need lessons on how to get their systems aligned, I'll be glad to teach them — free of charge. They gave me the truth, and I'll give them some back."

"Sounds like you're planning some sort of stock exchange," George said.

"Kinda. I'll be as good for them as they are for me."

"Betsy can't be the pastor, or whatever they call it, because only men are in charge," Karen said. She hadn't meant to say anything, but the absurdity of this situation irritated her.

"Men and women have different responsibilities," Betsy said.

"Yeah, men have the power and women the babies," Karen said.

Betsy flashed her gaze on her sister-in-law. Karen shrunk in as though guarding herself against the coming attack. Betsy said, "I know you think that any organized religion is a cult, but Mormons aren't. They believe in thinking for themselves, and the best part is they found a system that helps them experience their higher selves through saying prayers and feeling the Spirit. They know how to radiate peace from their souls."

"Well, this radiating peace and touching ghosts isn't going to happen here," Karen said. She drained the noodles. "I won't have any of those devils under my roof. Don't you let one of their little toes into this house."

George grabbed the hot pot from Karen's small hands and placed it on the counter. He wrapped his strong arms around her. "There now, let me help you." He held her firm until she silenced.

"I'm going to my apartment to do some yoga. Karen, you look a little stressed. Wanna join me?" Betsy asked.

"No, thanks," she said. "We're going to eat. Want some?"

"I already ate," Betsy said. She swept out of the room with a mysterious smile.

A thick fog seemed to creep into the room, wrapping around everything in its path. Karen flinched in an effort to shake off the ugly mood. Were the others thinking she'd been too hard on Betsy? What was her problem? Betsy had only joined a church. Karen rubbed her wet palm on her apron. "Why would she deliberately pour acid on my open wound? Doesn't she care?"

"Karen!" George pinched his long nose between his eyes. Until he talked, Karen hadn't realized she had spoken the words aloud.

Oh, boy. The social acceptability police had arrived. No one spoke. Karen cleared her throat. "The only thing I don't like about this is the thought of Mormons in my house. I won't allow it. Did I make that clear?" She set the noodles on the counter and began opening the spaghetti sauce jar.

"I'm sure Betsy heard you like the rest of us," George said as he set the table.

Karen's face crinkled into a frown. "Will she take it as a dare? You know how she handles challenges."

"Yeah, she thrives," George said and smiled.

Karen groaned. Had she set up a ricochet that wouldn't stop until Betsy proved to her Mormons weren't devils? A tear fell to the counter. She peered up at George's speckled gray hair and the strength of his jaw line; then she embraced him. He had forks and knives in his hand, but this didn't stop her from absorbing his strength and love. She wanted all the energy and courage she could muster to fight this war. Backing away from his embrace, she noticed her children staring at her so she smiled to reassure them. "Why don't you guys do your homework while you wait for dinner?"

"We already did," Sam said, spinning his soccer ball.

"You heard your mother. Go," George demanded.

"But I want to play soccer," Sam said.

"I don't care what you do. Just leave. Be back in fifteen minutes on the dot," George said.

Sam ran for the front door, and Mikey stormed up the stairs, a bomb exploding with each step. The pounding turned into a muffled sound of the television.

Karen gazed tearfully into George's eyes, then embraced him again. "Please, make it so she can't have them in our house. Please."

"She's our guest."

"No, she's not. She's been sucking off our charity, living in our apartment free of rent. She's wealthy from her divorces and doesn't have to work. The least she could do is pay rent."

"Come on, Karen," George said, releasing her from his hug. "You know she's been a godsend. What would we have done without her for the past couple of months?" George's finger wiped at Karen's tears.

"I don't know anything about God. Neither does Betsy. First, she believes in some universal organization and now some kind of God that lets spirits touch you. This is getting too strange even for her, and I can't believe you're going to make me tolerate it. This shouldn't be allowed in our home."

"Has she helped you?"

"What do you mean?"

"Could you explain how we could have made it through the past several months without Betsy?"

"That's not important." Karen walked toward the door only to be caught by George's powerful hand.

He flipped Karen back so he could see her pale face. "Sure it's important. Now answer."

"I don't see why — "

"Yes or no. Would we have made it without Betsy's help?"

Karen listened to the silence. A pout spread across her face to chase away her husband's insistence.

"I'm waiting. Yes or no?"

"No," Karen whispered.

"I can't hear you."

"George, you're being obnoxious again. I answered and I'm not going to repeat myself," Karen said. She searched the cupboard for a frying pan to heat the sauce, pretending not to see his satisfied smile.

A lone seagull squawked, and the rush of waves broke against the sand; more birds sang. Karen soaked up these familiar sounds as she sat on her bed surrounded by darkness. Dinner was long over, and she had retreated to her room alone to enjoy her icecream and to listen to the recent tape Betsy had bought her. Nature's music was supposed to help relieve stress, and Karen decided to put the claim to the test. So far, her mind dwelled on Betsy becoming a Mormon. She could see it now. She had driven by their churches on Sunday and seen the lawn totally covered with tons of women dressed in those floral waistless jumpers with a white shirt underneath. The women would stroll up her sidewalk with wooden grins nailed to their faces, sending the subliminal message that Mormons were happy. Tucked under their arms were blue book, which they'd pester her to read. That was what they'd tried with Mikey, only to capture Betsy. The muscles around Karen's lips tightened; she wouldn't allow a parade in her house. Betsy's friends or not! Betsy always became so involved in her new beliefs — for a season.

Before they moved, Betsy changed cars like Elizabeth Taylor changed husbands. The shades of the cars weren't normal, Pepto Bismol pink and deep Barney purple. She'd explained that the color helped her focus on the different chakra points. Her daughter had called them "eye sores," and Karen couldn't help but agree.

Now Betsy committed herself to a church that wouldn't let her drink or smoke or even watch certain movies. It sounded so restrictive. The whole thing made Karen's muscles tense to the point of cramping.

Her only real experience with Mormons came from her daughter's friendship with the girl up the street. Karen had tried to stop it, but, ironically, it had bloomed when she'd gone to the hospital with one of her "episodes." The girl's mother had to drive her to the hospital because Mikey had wrecked the car. What Karen gleaned from the situation was that Mormons like having children and believing in angels.

Karen dug her spoon into the chocolate chip icecream as she sat on her bed. Two scoops to go before she finished the whole quart. Drowning herself in icecream, she'd discovered, was a better way to deal with stress than sitting around, worrying. Icecream at least woke her senses with each bite. The sharp coldness was a constant reminder she was alive. Trying to relieve stress wasn't the only reason she pigged out on the ice fat. The other was to stuff her guilt for saying such harsh things toward Betsy, who, in all reality, had been an angel of mercy. After enough icecream, her thoughts wouldn't be on how mean, ungrateful, and self-interested she was, but on what a pig she was and how sick the icecream made her. Her reasons for the icecream binge made no sense, but she gave it a try.

The ocean roar and the chirping birds stopped. The tape needed to be flipped over, but Karen remained motionless, sitting against her metal bedpost. The motivation to move hadn't come, so she stared into the black abyss, letting the experience absorb her. She should walk on the treadmill and work off what she so easily had eaten on, but her energy had vanished. Her body, even though it weighed only a hundred and fifteen pounds, was a heavy lump and would be too much work to move. There was no reason for her to exert herself since she'd made dinner and done the laundry. Chores of a housewife were endless and tiring. Besides, tomorrow would be a big day finding a job. It was best to reserve her energy; she should take a nap.

She had slept for only ten minutes when a light darted across the room. Moaning, she peered toward the door to identify the intruder.

"It's so gloomy in here," George said, filling the door frame. "Are we thinking negative thoughts?"

"No." She flopped her pillow over her face. Why was he acting like her father? She wanted a husband. He loved her and that was great, but his constant bugging her about her depression made her want to rip out his voice box.

"What are you doing?"

"Trying to take a nap. You woke me." Karen rubbed her eyes.

"You've been tired a lot lately, haven't you?"

Running her fingers through her hair, she thought. She recognized this trap. If she said yes, he'd lecture her about positive thoughts and how she should learn from Betsy to be an eternal optimist. That speech would make her feel worse. But, on the other hand, if she said she hadn't been tired lately, he'd ask her what she was doing in bed at nine p.m. Time for a diversion. "I love you, dear. How was your day?"

"Love you, too, and you didn't answer my question."

Karen remained quiet. How was she going to get out of this one without the lecture? There had to be a way. Her mind raced over different approaches, and she decided to call him on his real motive. She hadn't tried this before, but it seemed like a good time. "Are you worried I'll sink into another depression because Betsy decided to become a Mormon?"

The mood grew more chilly. George blinked his eyes and his mouth hung open. Karen almost laughed. This was something she would try more often.

"Yes," he finally said.

Karen reached over and pulled him to the bed, wrapping her arms around him. "Thank you for caring. I appreciate it but I'm fine; really I am. I was listening to the ocean sounds for my relaxing exercise and fell asleep. I'm getting good at relaxing. My shrink would be proud."

"Are you sure Betsy's announcement doesn't bother you?" George asked.

"Nothing I can't handle."

"Positive?"
"One hundred percent."

Chapter 2

Once in her apartment after announcing her baptism, Betsy gravitated to the mirror to check how her make-up endured. Dark lines under her eyes and the few wrinkles she'd earned through having many failed relationships made deep crevices on her canvas. Fortunately, she only married twice, but had been engaged seven other times.

She needed another layer of foundation to perk up her tired plump face. At her vanity table, she pulled a bottle of ivory out of the drawer. The cold liquid oozed over her fingers as she worked it into her skin. She'd done well. Karen seemed to be handling her news much better than expected. Perhaps she could activate the second part of her plan sooner. First, she'd have to keep her sister-in-law busy with diversions; then she'd help her find the truth.

Betsy's hands fell to her lap. It felt so good to finally discover the answers she'd always searched for. She enjoyed the warmth the Spirit brought to her life. Karen would know this feeling too, even if it killed her. She would make sure her sister-in-law received this comfort because it offered a break from depression for Karen.

Betsy finished with the foundation and advanced to the powder. Since she'd arrived here, she'd had two goals in mind: one, to help Karen achieve emotional health and, two, to keep herself to stay away from men. Betsy had done a great job staying away from men. Every time she saw one she'd remind herself that they were the very symbol of hurt. But she did miss their friendship and the romance. Deep inside she knew her resolve couldn't last. Men just had something about them, something irresistible.

After the powder, she moved onto her rouge to enhance her chiseled cheek bones. A quick touch up on the blue eye shadow, a glide of red lipstick over her thick lips, and she'd be done. She batted her eyes and a trace of blue shadow fell down her cheek. Carefully, she wiped away the dust and applied mascara on her eyelashes. Finished.

What should she do? Her yoga exercises? No, she'd wait until dinner settled in her stomach, but she should do them tonight to help shed the last twenty pounds that needed to vanish. She glanced at her ceiling ascending in an upside-down V. Pine rafters crossed it, and various plants hung from the beams. Her spider plants and ferns thrived as they spread across the wood and shot for the floor. The herbs also flourished. None of them needed watering today.

Her gaze moved to the small kitchen that someone else had done in hospital white. The tile floors, refrigerator, oven, counter tops, and the walls were all plastered in the sterile hue. She shivered at the lack of color. It was so blah. She'd put in a rainbow of shades: orange, purple, red, blue, and green. That would be more homey then, but the creative mood hadn't struck.

Her eyes roamed to the nightstand by her bed. The blue Book of Mormon waited there, radiating positive vibes. She plopped on her bed and picked up the book. Odd, or maybe it was the way life worked, that the first time she saw it, a few months earlier, she had such a negative reaction. That experience flooded her mind as she laid down on her bed. Karen was sick upstairs, and she and Mikey were cooking in the family's kitchen. They mixed sprouts, seeds, and herbs in a special salad to rid Karen of the poisons in her body. Eating the right food was an important ingredient in allowing your spirit to soar in meditation.

The doorbell had rung that day, sounding like a jingling bell. Betsy wiped her hands on her apron, told Mikey she'd be right back, and headed to the front door to find Agatha, the Mormon girl who lived up the street and who had become friends with Mikey, despite her ugly name. Betsy had shuddered. The name gave off such a bad aura. Poor child.

Agatha was a plain girl, with long brown hair dangling around her thin face. A pale glow, which almost appeared ghostly, surrounded her. Betsy longed to add color to the child, but resisted the urge, not wanting to scare her away.

Agatha had walked into the kitchen like a trembling speaker about to address a thousand people. The girl's muck-colored eyes peeked from under her thick eyelashes. "Hi," she said to Mikey, stalling, her arms twitching at her side. After a painful delay, she said, "I have something for you." She held out a blue book.

Betsy, standing behind her niece, had read the title long before Mikey. She'd seen the book around. Those guys in the suits and bikes always carried at least one, and she didn't like what the blue suggested. Dark blue was the color of the fifth chakra, which signaled a communication problem. Chakras were points in the body that everyone had. If they're aligned properly, then a person has happiness and mental health. But if they aren't aligned correctly, a person needs color breathing to the problem areas.

The dark blue foretold of ill feelings and anger. A Freudian mistake. She had tapped into the souls of the founders of this strange religion.

On that summer day, Betsy believed that if these Mormons would listen to her and do color breathing, their inner turmoil and hatred would dissolve. If they could let go of the anger, they'd be washed in a wave of relief. Love would spill over them. But teaching Mormons how to find happiness didn't concern her most. Mikey, and her safety from a group who obviously had a lot of problems, did. Since Mikey's mother lie upstairs ill, she must be the protective mother figure. Nothing Karen wouldn't have done for her had the positions been reversed.

How to stop the attack? Betsy glanced around Karen's lime green kitchen, noticing a strainer, a fern plant, empty cups and bowls, and a spatula. What would signal to Mikey how dangerous this stuff was? Nothing registered until she spotted the knife she'd been chopping herbs with. She lifted the butcher knife high and waved it as she stood behind Agatha. Betsy pursed her red lips in a whispered "no."

Agatha continued her spiel. "I-I, well, since you were asking questions about the Mormons, I thought you'd want to have a book that tells about us — if you're interested."

Betsy grabbed an imaginary book in the air and stabbed it as she mouthed, "Danger."

Despite all this, Mikey accepted the book, though she looked a little worried.

Now, Betsy was glad her niece had taken the present, but at the time she had been disappointed and worried Mikey would become snatched up in a cult while under her care. Telling Karen that the Mormons, who had stressed and worried her so, had persuaded her precious daughter to join their ranks would've been the worst.

Betsy chuckled, remembering this. No, Mikey hadn't been sucked away by the Mormons; it had been her. And the evil book she'd thought represented their inadequacy was actually filled with ways to learn to communicate with people better, along with useful tools to learn forgiveness. She'd forgotten that surrounding herself with blue brought serenity and helped reduce irritability. The book had done this for Betsy in a powerful way. It taught her of Christ and His ultimate example of sacrifice. If He, innocent of wrong doing, could forgive in the midst of severe pain, then everyone could learn to forgive.

Betsy had experienced a whirlwind conversion. It happened

faster than her first rushed marriage. She smiled. Winds blew in and out of her life, a constant flow of change, keeping life fresh and exciting. The conversion began with a simple thought, a question, which led to her whole life evolving. If she had anything to do with it, everyone who knew her would progress, too.

That day Agatha brought over the Book of Mormon, Mikey had taken it and agreed to go to the movies a few days later. The girls nominated Betsy as chauffeur when several days had passed by, and on that day Betsy's fatal thought that started her whole interest in the Mormons entered her mind.

The beginning of the thought came as she drove her purple sputtering Cadillac. The car crawled up Thomsons' steep driveway. "Those bleeps hadn't fixed my car," she said to Mikey. It meant she'd have to take it back again. And this was a brand new vehicle!

Betsy drummed her plastic nails on the steering wheel, mad she'd given in, and thought pessimistically. This would project negativity out in the universe and return tenfold. She gave herself mental slaps and focused on Agatha, who now had appeared, dressed in jeans and a plain navy T-shirt.

Betsy chuckled. Mikey wore jean shorts and a blue T-shirt. Teenagers wanted space to discover themselves, yet they dressed like clones.

Mikey tugged the hem of her shorts.

Come to think of it, Betsy hadn't ever seen Agatha in those "leg revealers." Did Mormons have a dress code like the Amish?

Agatha sluggishly followed Mikey down the cemented sidewalk. Betsy studied the young girl's face. What did that young thing believe? A worried glance crossed over Agatha as she stared at Mikey. Her face underwent several rounds of blushes. This shyness Agatha had initiated Betsy to think the fatal question. Why would a child who felt so uncomfortable with sharing beliefs do so?

Betsy pulled up to the curb of the Scera movie theater and slowed to a stop. "Thank you," Agatha said, struggling out of the back seat. Hearing Agatha's voice reminded Betsy how Agatha sounded when she'd given the book to Mikey. The child's voice had intense emotion in it when explaining why she loved the book. The tone was a mixture of feelings, the obvious one, embarrassment. But she heard something more, perhaps confidence in its message. Betsy, being a truth seeker, wanted to know if the book's pages had anything to offer her. Pushing the thought away, she waved good-bye. Silly. Hadn't she found happiness in her own beliefs and achieved complete mental oneness?

Maybe there was more? Had she missed something? She'd always been open to new ideas. Why should things be different?

She knew why. Through questioning the Mormons at the grocery stores and restaurants, she discovered the men were in charge. This was something she couldn't accept. And this thing with having lots of kids...well there was only one way to explain it...weird.

She had tossed out the idea of investigating more about the religion until a week after Agatha gave her gift. Betsy was putting away Mikey's clean clothes when she spotted the book turned over opened as if to save a place. Mikey had been reading it. What pollutants zipped around in Mikey's mind? She stared at the book. Karen would be devastated if Mikey turned a Mormon, and Betsy couldn't allow that. It had to be stopped, but she didn't know what she fought against, so she had no choice but to steal the work to see what lie inside. She planned to browse its pages that evening, returning it the next day. Knowledge seemed the best way to handle the situation.

That night she found her interest aroused when she learned the Mormons claimed the book contained the history of the American Indian people. What guts!

After she'd read parts of the Book of Mormon, sleep overcame her. As she slept, she saw two boys dressed in black suits with their hair cut very short. They shook as she drilled them with questions about the inequality of their church. She enjoyed questioning those boys so much in the dream; she decided to have a little chat in reality with those fellows.

Betsy squirmed in the Lotus position as if to fade the memory. Enough of the past. She needed to refocus her thoughts to her sister-in-law. If caution wasn't used, Karen would sink into depression and grow ill again. That must be stopped. Yoga would be the trick.

Nine-forty-five at night and she found her sister-in-law rummaging through the refrigerator and cupboards. "Looking for something to eat?" Betsy asked.

Karen sighed and closed the cupboard. "There isn't anything. I ate all the icecream."

"I'll go to the grocery store tomorrow."

Karen smiled. "Thanks. That'll be great since I'm going to be looking for work."

"What about signing up for nursing school?"

"I'm going to hold off on that. Right now we need extra cash to pay the bills." She pulled out a chair from the dining room table and slumped onto it, rubbing her lower back.

"Got a backache?"

"A little."

Betsy scooted her chair from the table. "I've got an answer for that."

"No, that's okay, really," Karen said, as Betsy walked over and seized her arm.

"Up and at'em. Let's go."

"I'm tired. It's getting late."

"You'll sleep better. Tomorrow you'll feel like dynamite. Trust me — if you want to do a good job with the interviews, you do yoga now." Betsy marched out of the room, pulling her sister-in-law up the stairs. Once in the living room, Betsy seated Karen on the floor, then plopped down by her side. "Let's work on the tension in your back. First, we'll do stretching. The ones specifically designed for back tension are the alternate leg pull, the cobra, and the twist. We'll do the fish after because it works good to relieve stress through the entire body."

"I'm too old to be sitting on the floor like this."

"Nonsense," Betsy said, bouncing her legs against the carpet.

"No, seriously, I'm going to rip something." Karen struggled to rise.

Betsy pushed her to the floor. "Don't worry. We'll go easy. For the alternative pull sit with your legs straight ahead of you."

Moaning, Karen moved her legs in front of her about a foot from each other, knees up.

"Now, straighten your legs."

Karen inched one knee down, complaining, "I'm too old. I don't have the flexibility I once had."

"Didn't you used to run every day?" Betsy asked. "Try to get your legs closer together."

"Yeah, I ran, when I was a young."

"Baloney, we'll restore your youth."

Karen laughed. "Doubt that."

"I'll get you running again."

Color drained from Karen's face. She looked at the floor and whispered, "I'll never run again."

"Why?" Betsy asked.

"Too many memories."

"Does this have something to do with your murdered friend?"

"I don't want to talk about it." Karen's thin lips pressed firmly together. "So what's the next thing I need to do for this pull-my-leg thing?"

Betsy noted an almost gray cast spread through her sister-in-law's face. Her eyes narrowed, acquiring a far-off gaze as the wrinkles around the corners of her brown eyes deepened. Deciding it would be best to get Karen's mind off her memories, she said, "Have your foot touch the inner thigh of your leg. Then see how close you can bring your foot to you."

Scowling, Karen worked herself through the exercises, giving a complaint or two every few minutes.

"Okay, now we're going to do the last stretch," Betsy said, secretly relieved she'd processed Karen through the whole ritual. This was bound to loosen her sister-in-law's tension. "The Fish. We'll try the modified posture until you become more advanced. This stretch is in the traditional Japanese sitting position. Tuck your feet underneath your bottom like I'm doing. It's almost as if you're praying."

"This one doesn't seem so bad," Karen said, kneeling.

"Now, put your hands behind your feet and lean backwards."

"I take it back." She wiped at the bangs touching her eyebrows and groaned as she leaned.

"Allow your head to fall back and shoot your stomach toward the sky. Hold for ten. One…two…three."

"You got to be kidding."

"Hold it or you'll have to do it again."

Karen held it, blood flowing to her face. Once finished, she collapsed onto the floor and groaned. "I'll never feel the same."

"That's the spirit," Betsy said. "Like to do a couple more for health's sake?"

Karen rose and swiped at her bangs, revealing her creamy white forehead underneath. "That's quite all right. I need to pick an outfit for my job search."

Betsy smiled as she went to her apartment. She'd stopped her sister-in-law from falling back into bed and eating herself into a depression. Tonight had been successful. Maybe it wasn't going to be so hard to convince the Ashforth family the Mormons weren't bad. Who knew? Maybe she could baptize them all!

Inside her apartment, Betsy walked over to the middle of her room about a foot in front of her purple-and-pink-striped bedspread and sat in the lotus position as the Buddhist monks did. She'd found this position created the fewest pressure points on her body. It was time for her to do her meditation. Now that she had the Holy Spirit with her, she felt sure her spirit would soar and her mind could travel through the universe. She had tapped so strongly into the powers of the cosmos that she could do anything.

She wiggled her shoulders in preparation and saw the scriptures that she had carefully posted at eye level when sitting. A reminder she wanted to read before her meditation sessions. It was the first scripture the sister missionaries had read to her. The scripture said:

> And ye can do good and be restored unto that which is good, or have that which is good restored unto you; or ye can do evil, and have that which is evil restored unto you (Helaman 14:31).

Those missionaries had been wise. They asked her what kind of system she believed governed the universe and she had said, "Karma."

Sister Richards' green eyes twinkled as she said, "The idea of there being some organization to the universe and that our lives can affect others is a very interesting principle I also believe." She pulled the blue book out of her briefcase and asked, "Have you seen this before?"

The Richards girl flipped through the pages until she found that passage Betsy now had posted on her wall.

Betsy had responded by saying, "You Mormons can't be so bad if you believe in karma."

Miss Richard's partner stared, mouth opened wide, revealing a steel mill on her teeth. A typical closed-minded snob, Betsy thought, but, oh well, she liked this Richards girl and would listen to her. "Please tell me more," she had said. "I like adding insight to my own beliefs."

That was how her contact with the missionaries started. Betsy sighed and took a deep breath in preparation to do her open eye meditation. Somehow, informing her brother and his family about her conversion had misaligned the harmony inside herself. An investigation was needed to discover where she was out of alignment.

A trance spread quickly through her, opening her senses. The outer world faded as the colorful inner world grew brighter. Her breathing increased to a deep, harsh sound. When she had first heard the noise, she thought Darth Vader had come to visit, or someone with a serious sinus problem, but now the sound had a soothing effect. It promised great peace. She'd begun another journey into her soul. A self-evaluation started. Focused, she searched her chakra points to see if they were aligned. The first point went smoothly, but the second needed fine tuning. She sensed something in her would keep her away from God. When she worked on the second chakra, she was supposed to visualize and breathe orange. She let the color fill her mind, picturing a soft, warm orange like the setting sun. This chakra point represented harmony in relationships.

What was her trouble? Her mind drifted from one loved one to the next, looking for rough spots. She envisioned Sam. He had a soccer ball in hand and wore a smile. Go, she thought to him, play soccer and continue to be happy. He waved good-bye as he vanished.

Mikey, the actress. She had questions in her eyes. She didn't understand. Betsy needed to do a lot of explaining. "I will, child. I will." This seemed to satisfy her, and she left to wait for Betsy.

Then there was Karen, moaning on her bed. So sad. "I thought the yoga helped make you happy?" Betsy asked.

"Depression is swallowing me. I'll be devoured soon," Karen whispered.

Betsy grabbed her hand and brought it to her cheek. "It's okay. I'll save you."

Karen smiled and slipped into sleep.

George. He stood in the distance, back turned. Betsy didn't want to be near him. Why? She waited, wondering what to do until at last she extended her hand and called to him. He faced her, laughing, grabbing the sides of his stomach as though it hurt, and the laughter continued.

"Why?" Betsy asked. An ill feeling pinched a nerve in her mind, shooting a pain through her head.

George said, "I can't help but feel sorry for those poor Mormons. Can you imagine their faces when they find out who they baptized?" His face scrunched up again, and he wandered away, laughing.

Those were the exact words he said when she announced she'd joined the Mormon church. Anger spewed through her stomach. How dare he laugh at her? The juices that brewed now boiled. This relationship was out of whack.

Why would he feel sorry for the Mormons? She stewed on this for a while and decided to ask. "George," she said to the figure in the distance.

"Yes." He wiped at his eyes.

"Why do you feel sorry for the Mormons?"

"Because you're a spiritualist. You'll push your energy rock philosophies and cold symbolism ideas on everyone. I don't think they'll appreciate it."

"Of course they will," Betsy said in a huff. She felt her wrinkles sag.

"Face it, Betsy. You're different. You've always been different. Don't fool yourself that some conservative organization is going to accept you lickety split."

He must be wrong. Surely Mormons were open to new ideas. They kept adding new books to the group of scriptures. She had learned about the book called The Doctrine and Covenants and another named The Pearl of Great Price. She could write the next one. She wasn't much of a writer, but they could find someone to smooth out her rough edges.

She couldn't become the pastor. The church hadn't progressed to that yet, but the position of Relief Society president was obtainable. She'd hold monthly lessons on the proper way to do inner transformation. The missionaries had informed her they didn't teach that kind of stuff at church, but it was time for a change.

She paused, refocusing on her breathing, taking deep, long breaths. Was this why her brother had laughed? Did he believe Mormons were a lot like other people who feared change or something new? What if her brother was right? She breathed heavily again in an effort to refocus. Now she discovered the problem — she feared not being accepted by this group. She could forgive her brother. He had merely pointed out her fear, nothing more. She needed to realign her thoughts to positive ones. In her mind, she pictured the congregation dressed in their Sunday best. Their arms extended, open, loving, accepting her. She felt the warmth of their love and wanted to return it. Peace hummed in her soul. There was nothing to worry about because the Mormons wouldn't find her strange. Besides, they were Christians, and the missionaries said it was their practice to love everyone, wanting no lost sheep. Her fear was in vain.

She pictured George again. "I know you didn't mean to hurt me," she said. "You were trying to be silly. I forgive you for the pain you caused and for thinking I'd have a problem fitting in with the Mormons. They're Christian people, and one of their gospel principles is to love everyone. I'm not a hard person to love. I have a lot to offer." She saw George, smiling, a bit startled. So she continued, "You'll see."

He answered, "I guess I will."

Betsy gave another deep breath, slowly exhaling. She'd prove George's prediction wrong. She could forgive him if he didn't mean what he said. Normally she didn't let other people's opinions bother her, but this was her brother, and he knew of her virtues better than anyone. Somehow it ruffled her beautiful, harmonious colored feathers to let him get away with thinking of her as strange, someone people would have a hard time accepting. She was resolved. Not only would she prove to her dear wonderful brother the Mormons would accept her with open arms, but she'd do one better — she'd get him to join the Mormon church. That would show him. But how? Now that would take a plan.

Chapter 3

The next day in the late afternoon, Betsy thought of Pierre, her second husband. He'd call her periodically, but hadn't recently. She wondered how he was and secretively longed to hear his deep hypnotic voice. She needed to resist him. He spelled danger. All she needed to do was remember their past and know that was the total truth.

She peered through her white apartment kitchen window overlooking the hourglass-shaped pool. Mikey laid out in a green and white polka dot swimming suit. A chilly breeze must've blown across her because the branches on the trees bent northward, and Mikey had sat up to wrap her jacket over her narrow shoulders. Late September in Utah. Back home would still be hot, and her niece must be missing the warmth of the California sun; Betsy knew she was.

She laughed as she noted the dark hippie sunglasses Mikey wore and her permanently pointed toes. Mikey was such a dreamy child, her thoughts soaring in the clouds, visions of fame and stardom surrounding her. It was common for girls to dream such dreams, but Mikey took hers to a new height. Perhaps since she was always acting the part, she would one day become the next superstar. One never knew.

A knock sounded against Betsy's apartment door. "Yes?"

Sam poked his head in. The sunlight highlighted the red tones in his dark brown hair. "Hi. What ya doing?"

"Finishing up the dishes, then going to go on errands. Want to come?"

He shook his head. The sun had kissed his face over the summer, causing freckles to break out on the tip of his nose. "Naw, I just wanted to ask you something."

"Shoot," Betsy said as she walked over to the couch and plunked herself onto its welcoming cushions.

He stood as a bronze statue, staring.

"Come on in. Sit down. I don't bite."

He remained unmovable.

"Come on." Betsy slapped the cushion next to her.

Finally he forced one foot to follow the next, but with heavy hesitation, making Betsy think of a robot instead of a human.

Once he made it to the chair across from her couch, Betsy asked, "So what is it?"

His face pinked as his brown eyes stared into hers. "Why are you doing this silly religious thing?"

"What do you mean?"

"It's stupid. It's something you've found to pass the time. Why don't you give it up so Mom can have some peace?"

Betsy's mouth opened slightly. "My religion is not some silly pastime."

"Get real. You always have some new thing you talk about. All I'm asking is you bypass this one. It's too painful for Mom."

"This isn't a fad." Betsy's voice rose.

"Whatever. Just don't freak-out Mom." He stood to leave.

"I'll think about what you said. The universe knows that I don't want to hurt her."

He shrugged and touched the doorknob.

Betsy said, "By the way, would you please ask your sister if she wants to run errands with me?"

"Fine," he said, leaving.

The door closed firmly behind the man-sized frame. Sam was growing up, becoming more and more like his father. Those two men lacked respect for others' beliefs, and neither of them knew how to treat her. They thought by insulting her, it would somehow solve the problem. It was as if they blamed her for Karen's depression. She shook her head in irritation and gathered her purse and car keys. She needed to go do the dishes downstairs also to help Karen out, then to the bank and the mall to pickup a package of stress-reducer bubble baths and a bottle of fruity-smelling lotion. She liked the pear fragrance.

She made it downstairs, pausing to change a load of laundry when Sam returned to report Mikey didn't want to go.

"What took you so long?" Betsy asked.

He laughed. "Sorry. It was just that Mikey was talking to herself again."

"You didn't spy on your sister?"

"Couldn't help it. I swear I've got the weirdest one alive."

"How? What did she do?"

"She was talking to her stuffed bear."

"In front of you?"

"No, I hid behind a tree. A fifteen year old talking to a bear?" He shook his head.

Betsy had seen Mikey talking to the mammel too, but she didn't think it so odd. A lot of teenagers possessed strange attachments to stuffed animals. Mikey was too old for talking to them, but that was probably habit. Black Bear and she had a long history. "What else did she say?"

"You don't want to hear." He flashed a big cheesy grin.

"I think I do."

"You don't. It was about you."

"Tell me."

"She asked her bear, 'How could Aunt Betsy become a Mormon?...It makes no sense she'd join a group of sexist pigs.'"

He stopped talking so he could more closely watch Betsy's reaction. He'd enjoy it if she showed pain, but too bad for him, this news didn't surprise her. Her meditation session had been right on about Mikey. She was confused, and Betsy needed to clarify things.

Another grin spread across his face as he tried again. "She said, 'Maybe she should ask you about it, but she wouldn't understand your answer.' Then she said, 'Maybe Aunt Betsy was in a stage and it wouldn't last.'" Sam smiled in satisfaction. "See, I'm not the only one who thinks that you're in the Twilight Zone.

"Was there anything else you heard?" Betsy asked, feeling sleepy. She immediately began to do the dishes in the Ashforth's sink.

"She mumbled something about a title. I heard the words 'Mormons,' 'destroy,' and 'Aunt Betsy.' I guess she's making up another one of those dumb movies." He shook his head with overemphasis. "Get this. She even said out loud the movie directions she was shooting in her head. Wait 'til my friends hear this."

"Sam!"

"She said something like, 'And action. Wide shot of the top of the trees, catching a glimpse of the mountain and valley,'" Sam said in fake excitement. "Like the top of trees would make a good opening." Sam laughed. "Stupid."

"Sam."

"We're getting to the good part. She got this dumb look plastered on over her face and said, 'Hi, I'm Mikey Ashforth,'" he continued in a high-pitch tone. "'I live in Provo, Utah...something, something, something.'" He fluffed his pretend hair by his ears and puckered out his lips. Then he leaned in with his hand over his mouth and said in a softer voice but with the same high-pitch tone. "'Mormons are everywhere. It wouldn't be so bad if they didn't constantly try to make you one of them.'

"She's as freaked as Mom. She's really losing it." He walked to the cupboard and pulled out his supplies for icecream. Betsy sighed and washed a couple more pans.

"She then told the camera or the air or wind or whatever she was talking to that her problems began when her aunt became one of them. Since that only happened yesterday, I don't know how many problems she could have. I asked her right after if she wanted to go. She said no and she would be in soon cause she was freezing. Imagine being cold when you sit outside in a bathing suit when it's thirty degrees. My sister has a definite hole in her head."

Mikey entered the kitchen through the side door.

"What are you doing?" Betsy asked, smiling.

"I'm a human icicle, and I've come in to defrost."

"That'll teach ya to lay out in the cold," Sam said through a huge bite of icecream.

Mikey rolled her eyes and left the room.

Sam ate another big bite then asked, "Aunt Betsy, what made you take the plunge into Mormondom?"

Betsy moved from the window to face Sam. Mikey must have heard the question and wanted to know the answer, too, because she popped back into the kitchen. Sam winked at his sister.

Betsy continued to wash the dishes, her face turned to the window. The wind had worked up another gust, and rusty leaves danced over the backyard. "It was right. I can't logically explain. It just felt right."

"Oh," Sam said. He returned to devouring his icecream.

Betsy glanced at Mikey in time to see her grin. "What's the smile for?" she asked.

"Sorry. You just said that perfect for the movies. You did a marvelous job in putting conviction behind your voice. Your facial expressions were true. You'd be great in a film. Ever thought about trying out?"

Betsy laughed. That girl was always in dreamland. "Sounds like you got an idea for a movie going on in your head."

Mikey smiled shyly. "I do."

"Want to tell me about it?" Betsy asked, scrubbing the frying pan from last night's spaghetti.

"You might get mad."

"Promise, I won't."

"I was thinking about doing something with you joining the Mormons."

"Sounds interesting. You did a splendid job picking out the main character."

Sam made a gagging noise that both Mikey and Betsy ignored.

"So what about me and the Mormons?" Betsy asked.

"This is the part you won't like."

"Humor me."

"Well you said you couldn't explain logically why you were in the Mormon church, so all I have to do is come up with information to prove the Mormon beliefs are wrong. After that you won't feel good about your choice and will quit the group."

Betsy laughed. "Sounds reasonable. Good luck trying. I bet it'll be dramatic watching you attempt it."

"I thought it'd make a good story," Mikey said, looking all business.

"To help you out let me give you a hint."

"What?"

"Why don't you join forces with your brother? He doesn't think my conversion is strong and would love to see me not be a Mormon any longer."

Mikey raised her narrow eyebrows at Sam, who nodded.

"But I also have a pin to burst your bubble," Betsy said.

"What's that?"

"I believe in this church. You'll have to work hard to prove it's wrong. If you do convince me, I'll quit. But I have to be a hundred percent sure."

"Want to team up?" Mikey asked her brother.

He circled his spoon around the now empty bowl, searching for a couple more drops of ice sugar. "I guess. What's your plan?"

"I'm gonna ask Agatha over and pick her brain until I have a ton of things that make no sense about her religion. When I point these things out to Aunt Betsy, her conscience won't let her be in a group she knows is wrong. She'll have to break lose from their clutches."

Betsy laughed as she slipped the dishes in the dishwasher.

Mikey hurried to the snack cupboard to find some munches. It was then Betsy decided to make her move. "Mikey, how's your sense of oneness?"

"Fine," she answered. She grabbed the Fruit Loops from the cupboard.

"You aren't out of alignment because I became Mormon, are you?"

"Look," Mikey said, waving her spoon. "I don't understand it, but then I don't understand most of the things you do."

"Are you angry with me?"

"No, I think it's weird, but as long as you don't pick me up at school in that purple Cadillac of yours with your huge glasses and scarf, I'll be doing great." Mikey headed to the fridge for the milk. "It's embarrassing."

"The church has been the most beneficial thing I could do for my relationship with the universe. They have some stimulating concepts. One I like is — "

"I don't want to hear about it. Besides, I've got to call Agatha." With that she left of the kitchen with her bowl of Fruit Loops in hand. As she left, she said, "The Mormons aren't going to get me even with my aunt helping."

Sam laughed. "Here, here."

Ten minutes later Betsy was in her purple car fastening her seatbelt when she saw Mikey slipping out the side door. She honked and waved for her niece to come over.

Mikey rolled her eyes. "What?" she asked after Betsy's window wound down.

"Where you going?"

"Agatha's."

"I thought she was coming over here?"

"She wants to sew." Mikey rolled her eyes. "The price I'm paying to produce a good film is high. Sewing's such an old lady thing to do."

Betsy laughed. "Have fun. Don't be too late. I don't want your mom to worry."

"Okay, Mom," she said and started the hike to her friend's house, but stopped and turned back.

Betsy rolled the window down. "What is it?"

"Do you think Mom's okay?"

"Why do you ask?"

"This morning she seemed kind of out of it. She complained about not being able to find her keys and black shoe. She walked around muttering and twisting her fingers. You know she does that every time she's nervous…You don't think she's having a relapse?"

"Oh, sweet child, no. Those are normal things to do when one's looking for a job. It's nerves."

Betsy's words seemed to thaw Mikey's panic. She saw relief wash over the child's face as though the wash cycle had been switched on.

"I'm glad I'll have my jobs come to me. Everyone will beg me to act in their movies, and they'll never grow tired of the great job I do," Mikey said.

Betsy laughed. "Yep, you're lucky. Very lucky."

❧

Late that afternoon, Karen walked to the front office door and paused, staring into the beveled glass. Her stomach churned like it was making taffy from her insides. Maybe she should go home, but no, she decided to try one more job lead. She lifted her right foot from her black shoe and wiggled her toes. It had been stupid to think her feet wouldn't blow up like balloons wearing those feet crunchers all day. She shoved her fat foot back into the narrow stylish shoe not wanting to make another trip here tomorrow. She had been rejected four times in this complex alone; she wouldn't take the risk of running into one of these people who had rejected her.

The receptionist sat behind the wooden counter with his head bent over the computer. He had some kind of nervous movement that caused his beard to twitch to the left as he typed.

Karen rocked on the points of her heels as she waited for him to acknowledge her existence.

"Yeah," he muttered, without looking.

"Job Service says you're hiring."

The man glanced up, green eyes seeing through her.

Karen struggled to keep from blushing, but felt heat floating off her face.

"You got a degree?"

Her lungs immediately squeezed shut. She doubted she could swallow air if she wanted. This was the same dumb question everyone asked.

"No," she whispered.

"Oh," the man said, peering at his work. "How're your computer skills?"

The anger that pulled taffy in the bottom of her tummy all of a sudden changed, causing the candy to harden and shatter. "Why does everyone keep asking those questions? I wanted to apply for file clerk. What does a degree have to do with that?"

The man typed a few notes.

She slapped her hands on the counter. "Why is it so hard to get a job in this town?"

The man remained silent but stopped typing.

Karen continued to stare, demanding an answer.

Finally he spoke, with his beard twitching to the left. "It's a university town. Lots of graduates like it here so much they stay. There's tons of over-qualified people fighting for jobs."

Karen sighed, withdrawing her hands from the marble counter. "That explains it."

The man's eyes softened. "Provo's a great place if you're well-versed in computers," he said in an encouraging tone. "There's normally lots of job offers with that kind of skill. If one company fades out, another is on the rise. Are you computer literate?"

Karen shoved her hands in her jacket pockets. "I could learn."

"Oh." The man reclined in his chair. "You might as well not even apply here. They won't look at you. Sorry."

"What do computers have to do with being a file clerk?" Karen asked.

"You'd be amazed."

A Mormon town full of graduates? Strange. If the women were educated, than they should know better then to be dominated.

She shivered as she jogged to the car. The weather grew colder, and she hadn't been prepared for its bite. She dug her nose inside her jacket. The wind howled and she quickly slipped into her car. She drove silently home until she spotted Mikey pacing up the mountain, head hunched against the cold air. Karen honked the horn.

Startled, Mikey jumped, then slipped on some rocks causing her to fall onto the road. Karen rolled down the car window, laughing.

"It's not funny," Mikey said, glaring.

The smile faded. "Sorry, I didn't mean to scare you."

"Sure," Mikey said.

Karen yawned.

"Tired?" Mikey asked. Karen saw worry in that question.

"Been a long day."

"Have any luck?"

"We'll see. Whatcha up to?"

"Agatha wants me to come over and sew."

Karen's eyes narrowed. "We don't have any fabric."

"She says she has plenty to share. With the amount her mom buys, they could clothe the whole world. It's no big deal if I use some."

"Sure?"

"Yeah."

"I don't want them talking to you about funny stuff."

"What?"

"If they talk religion, come home. It's bad enough Betsy's one of them. I won't have you doing it, too."

"Like I want to." Mikey rolled her eyes.

"I know, dear. I trust you. It's just that these people are tricky. They captured your aunt. There's no expense that cults won't go to lure people into their trap."

"Don't worry. They won't get me."

Karen sighed. Teenagers always thought that nothing bad could happen to them. They were too strong and wise. Charissa had been that way.

"Besides, they can't watch R-rated movies, and I won't give those up," Mikey said.

"Since when have you been watching them?"

Looking trapped, Mikey said, "I haven't. But when I become a famous movie star, I'm sure I'll have to play in a few of them to make ends meet."

Karen yawned. "I'm exhausted. We'll talk about that later. Have fun and be home by seven."

"All right."

"No talking religion."

Mikey nodded.

Karen shifted the car to drive; Mikey put her hand on the windowsill. Lifting her eyebrows, her mom looked at Mikey.

"Don't worry about Aunt Betsy," Mikey said. "You know how she goes in and out of phases. This is another one."

"I hope you're right," Karen muttered, noticing her daughter's worried eyes. She drove away, waving in the rearview mirror. Her daughter's shoulders slouched.

Karen drove to her house. Mikey was at Agatha's (grr), and Betsy's purple eyesore car wasn't parked in front. Karen smiled; she might steal some quiet time for a recharge.

She parked her car in the garage, then closed her eyes in an effort to get a handle on the mounting pressure. She wanted to be in control before going into the house. Sam might be there waiting, and he always grew upset if he sensed her worried. When she'd been taken to the hospital, he had run away. Karen didn't want a reoccurrence.

Her mind raced over the failures of the day. It was only this morning she thought she had something to offer and could perhaps get a better job than before — a grocery clerk. But now she doubted she was even qualified for that.

Tears rose in lumps, which she pushed down. She'd spent the whole day as a panhandler, begging the mercies of the bosses. They simply kept on with their work, not noticing her.

She dragged herself from the car and headed for the house, flipping through her mail. Her eyes drooped shut, more tired then she'd realized. At least with her eyes closed, she wouldn't see what kind of state the house was in. She had a feeling she wouldn't like it. She stumbled through the kitchen making crunchy sounds with every step, except for a few silent sticky pauses. Dinner needed to be created. She moaned. But on the bright side, Sam mustn't be home yet because the food wasn't being attacked — except by her shoes. She continued into the living room, where her achy body found the couch.

She kicked off the feet-killers, lie down, then sorted through the mail. This was when she spotted the electric bill, yelling for attention. Heaven knew what bad news lurked underneath the seal. Why didn't she worry about the increase in their bills before they bought the house? Perhaps she should shove the bad news next to the other ones she hadn't dared open. Hopefully George wouldn't find them before she dealt with them. He'd think she was so irresponsible.

If she felt more energetic, she'd have laughed. Her house seemed to hover over her in a grandiose manner. Room after room spread out like melted butter, needing cleaning and sucking-up power. Oh, she didn't want to open that bill. Tossing it on the coffee table, she noticed the view out of her colossal array of bay windows overlooking Provo. Her vision filled with dark green trimmings of vegetation, intermixed with a grayish blue meandering Utah lake in the distance and a circle of rugged protective mountains. An icy blue sky settled on top with a few lounging cream clouds. She adored this view.

Goose bumps ran across her skin as her stomach flopped. This was too much. She shouldn't be living in a mansion on a mountainside. She'd spent her whole life in a beat-up beachfront house that had been in the family for years. That old rotting abode offered more peace than any mansion ever could. If she lived there now, she wouldn't be under the stress of keeping up a mausoleum.

She and George shouldn't have let Betsy bulldoze over them and force them into such a big decision within an hour of seeing the house. They had been so excited that it was close to the same price as the house in California that they'd just sold. She hadn't realized the amount of responsibility a mansion would be. Cleaning alone was a killer. She did have Betsy and Mikey to help, and rarely Sam and George, but even with all that, it demanded more attention and work, like a spoiled child.

Peering at the coffee table, she spotted the electric bill. Karen sighed. It wasn't right for her to live in one of the richest parts of Provo and be searching for a low-income job because she was unqualified. Those two things didn't add up. It was like putting a lady decked out in a million-dollar coat in an old VW wagon. She fluffed the couch cushion, rested her head on it and allowed these thoughts to drift away as sleep guided her eyes shut.

⁂

The sound of clinking keys jolted Karen out of her dreams. A door closed. Karen shuffled toward the kitchen, preparing for the questions about her job hunt. She'd pretend it went well. But if they saw her lying down, they'd think she was slipping back into depression. She wasn't.

Karen made it halfway to the cookbook cupboard when Betsy barged in through the side door.

"Hello," Betsy said, causing her foundation to come apart a little. Ever since Mikey pointed out that Betsy wore so much make-up that it cracked and pieces fell off, Karen couldn't help but notice.

Betsy smiled. "How's it going?"

She's trying to hide the fact she's putting me under the microscope, Karen thought. Take a deep breath and play it cool. "Can't complain."

"Good." Betsy's small blue eyes checked Karen out.

Karen felt as though she was a vegetable at the grocery store, being studied with careful consideration for a dinner planned for an important person. Betsy searched for emotional bruises. More taffy started pulling in Karen's stomach; she didn't need another mother.

"Stop staring," Karen said.

"Sorry." Betsy batted her eyes. She leaned back a little, but continued to watch.

Great. Now she'd created more suspicion. Was there any way she could throw herself a life-preserver?

"Have you gone to that new church of yours?" Karen asked.

Betsy's gaze relaxed. "I've visited a ward once to see what it was like, but I haven't gone to my new congregation, if that's what you're asking. The missionaries told me the groups are supposed to be the same all over the world."

"All over the world. So there really are Mormons everywhere?" Karen used extra effort to keep out the hint of panic.

"Yep. Those scouts of theirs are busy. They go everywhere when the countries will allow them."

"You sound like you're some authority on world religions or something," Karen said. She shouldn't have brought this subject up. Her heart beat faster than she liked.

Getting a glass of water, Betsy said, "I'm an authority. You know that."

Karen's mouth fell open.

"I've been studying different beliefs my whole life, so it shouldn't shock you that when I was finally presented the truth, I listened."

"The truth, huh?" Karen slumped onto a dirty wooden chair and watched Betsy hunt through the junk pile for a clean pot.

"Where's the rice?" Betsy asked.

"White?" Karen hoped.

"Brown, of course."

"Don't know." If healthy food was on the menu, she'd be giving no help.

Betsy searched through the cupboard.

"What makes this church different?"

"Karen, why are you so afraid of Mormons?"

Karen's taffy-pulling stomach worked hard. Why was she so afraid of them?

"You should give them a chance. It would bring you happiness. They have the truth. This time I guarantee it."

The taffy shattered again. "I've had it with your preaching. I'm not your child. I don't need you to waltz into my life every time you think I'm doing something wrong."

Betsy looked Karen straight in the eye and said, "Prove it." Dropping the rice on the counter, she left.

Karen sighed, then glanced to the stove. Black stains shot up in jagged flames around the edge of the empty pot as it waited on top of the stove to be filled. Brown rice spilled out from the mouth of the bag from where Betsy had dropped it.

Karen shrank from exhaustion. Betsy would have made dinner if she had kept her mouth shut. Her head throbbed as she shuffled through the freezer's frosty packages of corn and peas. After unloading a whole shelf of vegetables and fruit, she found one lost bag of French fries. Tonight's meal. If people didn't like it, then more for her. She didn't want to share anyway.

She flipped on her kitchen TV to entertain her while she labored over dinner. News time. The camera flipped around, settling on a man dressed in a blue ski parka. The gushing sound of wind blew in on the mike. The newscaster had a few strands of hair that floated upward as the wind tossed it in ill-shaped circles. He waited silently until he was cued. "Not only is there a storm brewing, but our local bank has reported one of the workers, Marcia Gonzales, has held up the people in the building at gun point. Shooting has taken place. There have been reports that Gonzales has become increasingly stressed and often complained about work."

Karen's hand shook as she snapped off the set.

Sounds of screams and sirens filled her head. They were her screams. She heard mumbled deep voices directed at her, but she couldn't make out the words. Her cries faded out the others' commands. She took a deep breath to chase the noise out. The connection between religious cult extremists and whacked employees didn't seem far apart.

Those extremists were bad. Just plain awful, and she wouldn't allow her family to be vacuumed up by them. George would say she acted like an over protective mother bear, but God gave this protective trait to mothers to preserve their young. That was, of course, if there was a God.

She ripped the French fry bag open. The hungry mob would be home soon. As she slid the cookie tray into the oven, her thoughts wandered to Mikey. Her stomach throbbed. How she wished Mikey was back home under her protective roof. Why did children have to grow? It was so much easier when Mikey was an infant and she had control of where she was.

Her baby could be getting brainwashed right now. Depressing. She'd have to stop these negative thoughts, or she'd be a nervous wreck. Her heart already beat a rapid pace. She took a deep breath and closed the oven door with her hip.

Maybe a quick walk in the rain through her backyard would lift her spirit as she waited for seven to arrive.

Chapter 4

Betsy stormed up the stairs to her room. Once inside she looked around her colorful abode, wondering if she was right in walking out on Karen. It wasn't nice, but it wasn't her Karen was mad at. Karen was frustrated with other things, and Betsy suspected it had to do with her sister-in-law's past. Pacing the room, Betsy felt reckless. She hadn't done her yoga yet, but wasn't in the mood, and reading wouldn't do. Extra energy from the fight pumped through her blood. She should go on a stroll. But where?

Agatha's house. Mikey hadn't come home yet, and having her over at a Mormon's house had to be eating at Karen. She'd bring Mikey home; that would help her sister-in-law relax. Throwing on a jacket, she braved the cold to Agatha's house. One of the young children answered the door, opened it wide, looked over Betsy, then dashed off, yelling, "Mama!"

Betsy sauntered in and closed the door, noting the window drapes accented the cheer of the room with pastel blue backgrounds and a foreground of yellow and white flowers. White frilly lace trimmed the edges to set off the atmosphere. Karen would like those curtains.

As she walked around the entryway studying the different craft displays, the aroma of baking cookies filled her nose. It smelled like chocolate. Betsy's tongue stole over her lips.

The decorating matched the autumn weather. Rusty, golden leaves twisted into crafts that sat, stood, or hung in every available spot. Betsy fingered a little bunny resting on a hutch in the entry. His cotton tail snuggled close to the leaf-covered ground.

Agatha's mom finally whisked into the entrance. Betsy smiled and extended her hand. "Hi, Mrs. Thomson. I'm here to get Mikey. I'm her aunt. Remember me?"

Mrs. Thomson's large brown eyes grew slightly bigger and she swallowed before she said, "Yes, of course. You were the one asking me if ducks had anything to do with our religious beliefs." She wiped her dough-covered hand on the dirty apron tied around her protruding waist. They shook hands.

Betsy laughed. "You don't have to worry about me asking you strange questions about your beliefs. I'm one of you now."

"You are?"

"Yep. Got baptized yesterday."

"Well, congratulations." Mrs. Thomson smiled weakly.

"You don't need to be surprised to learn I'm a truth seeker, and when I find it, I latch on. You Mormons couldn't keep the gospel from me too long."

Picking up a blonde child who had been tugging on her leg, Mrs. Thomson said, "Mikey and Agatha are downstairs. They're starting a sewing project. You can go get them, if you want. I have another batch of cookies to pull out of the oven before they burn. Wait a minute, and I'll send some with you."

"Great. Smells divine. My mouth has watered since the moment I walked in."

Mrs. Thomson smiled. "In a minute you can taste them if you want."

Junk food, but it smelled worth it, Betsy thought.

"Oh, by the way, Mikey says her mom's doing better. Is that true?"

"I hope so. I truly do. It's kind of early to tell."

"Oh, dear. Is there anything I can do to help?" Mrs. Thomson asked.

"Not at the moment, but I'll let you know if there is."

"Please do," Mrs. Thomson said. "Go straight. The stairs are on the right. They're in the first room." She hurried to save her cookies.

Betsy sniffed the melted chocolate that continued to tease her taste buds. Her stomach growled as she suppressed her craving. Through the dimly lit hallway, she crept toward the basement. The door howled like the wind when she opened it. Once in the rectangular room, she spotted Mikey and Agatha in front of a huge mirror that covered the wall. Agatha had a partially sewed blouse thrown over her shoulder.

Neither girl noticed Betsy slip in. The radio's volume blasted as they yelled at each other.

Agatha asked, "What do you think?" as she twisted, showing different angles of the blouse in the mirror.

"Awesome," Mikey said. "You can wear it when we go to the Scera."

Betsy yelled, hands around her mouth, "Time to go." Both girls looked up, startled.

Mikey groaned. "What time is it?"

Betsy peered at her watch. "Ten to seven."

"Ahhh. I'm late. See you later," she called to Agatha and ran up the stairs.

Once Betsy made it up in the narrow hall, Mrs. Thomson greeted her with a paper plateful of cookies with melted chocolate oozing.

Betsy and Mikey said their thanks to the Thomsons and headed home in the rain. Neither of them could wait for the cookies. They devoured them as they marched up the hill. "These are good," Mikey said.

"They are."

"Yeah, why are you eating them?" Mikey asked. "It's junk food. Health nuts aren't allowed treats." Extending her hand, she said, "Give me the plate. I must keep this evil temptation away from you."

Betsy brought the plate close to her body. "Oh no you don't. Everyone's allowed one vice, and mine's chocolate, so I'm enjoying."

"Don't eat 'em all," Mikey said. After taking a couple of steps, she added, "Are you sure you only have one vice?"

Betsy ignored her and focused on eating the cookies before Mikey woofed them all down.

"Did you see the different crafts the Thomsons' had?" Mikey asked. "They're cool. I wish Mom knew how to make things like that."

"You'd be surprised."

Mikey shoved the last bit of cookie in her mouth and said in-between chews, "I've got to hurry. I promised I'd be home by seven. I don't want her freaking out."

They continued their journey, the wind howling in their ears, rain splashing across their bodies. Betsy laughed when she saw Mikey's face as they passed under a night light. Her niece's thick lashes blinked away the raindrops. Her nose and cheeks had turned pinkish-red, but her jaw was set firm, creating a determined air of the hardy adventurer. She must be acting again, Betsy thought with a smile.

"What's going through your head?" Betsy asked.

"That Mom's waiting by the clock for me."

"Not a nice thought."

"Nope," Mikey agreed, stepping faster. Her pace lessened. "Unless Dad has already come home…with roses, a bit of wine, has begged Mom to waltz the evening away. Mom wouldn't be thinking of anything but how perfect her Romeo is and wondering how she'd ever managed to catch him." She puffed great gasps and continued her determined march, but with less of an attitude of panic. Her dream had convinced her that her father would take care of things.

Betsy couldn't help but be humored by the scene. Oh, to be young and innocent, dreaming romance would solve every problem. She'd once thought that way, but life had a way of teaching crueler lessons. There was no mistaking the painful slaps it gave. Love equaled pain and frustration. It wasn't worth filling the empty void with a romantic relationship.

She swiped at the rain on her face. The slimy substance of her make-up covered on her hand. She paused to wipe the goop on the grass. The wet seeped into her clothes, bringing a chill.

"Isn't this great?" Mikey said in a happier mood.

"Why?"

"The rain is so…so…dramatic. It makes scenes so much more — intense. I got the perfect scene in mind for this very spot."

"Dare I ask?" Betsy said.

"Of course, you'll love it Aunt Betsy. It's about you. You star as yourself and have just joined the Mormon church."

"Has a familiar ring."

Mikey smiled. "Aunt Betsy stop it. You already told me I could take anything from your life if I'm inspired."

"I did?"

"Yes, you did because you know I will be a mega star, and you want to help me out as much as possible along the way."

"I do?" Betsy gave her niece a surprised expression.

"Aunt Betsy, would you quit it," Mikey said as she gave her a slight shove on the shoulder. "I'll never get to the plot if you keep this up."

Sighing, Betsy said, "Sorry. I'll behave."

"Anyway," Mikey said sternly as she walked up the hill. "This Aunt Betsy character knows the Mormons are bad, but for some reason has to do this charade thing and be involved with them. I haven't decided why yet, but when she realizes her adorable niece has stayed at a Mormon's house too long, the aunt scampers over to see if her favorite teenager in the whole world is okay."

"You think so?" Betsy asked.

"Wait there's more. The audience knows that this adorable niece is fighting a ferocious battle inside, so they are on the very edge of their seats to see what is going to happen."

"Why the internal battle?"

"Because of her mom."

Betsy waited for Mikey to continue. When Mikey didn't, Betsy still remained quiet in hopes the discomfort of silence would loosen her niece's tongue. The patience paid off.

Mikey broke the quiet by saying with a slight wailing tone, "My mom's going to use her piercing brown eyes against me as a weapon, and I always melt under it and tell the truth."

"Did you discuss religion with Agatha?" Betsy asked.

"Of course. I have to prove they're evil to you. My movie wouldn't be a movie if I didn't."

"Oh."

"Don't tell Mom. Please."

"You know your secrets are safe with me. You need to have someone you can talk with."

"What should I do?"

"What do you want to do?"

"Lie. Mom will sink into a depression if I don't."

Betsy was quiet. Best not to talk at these times. Let her niece's conscience do the work.

"But lying is wrong," Mikey said.

They stopped at the back door. Mikey kicked some orange and yellow leaves off her shoe. One leaf remained stuck to her sole so she flicked it off. She inched herself into the mud room.

Dishes clanged. Karen must be cooking. Remembering the earlier fight, Betsy judged it was best if she left Mikey to sort her own problems. Oh, the joys of growing pains.

Karen sniffed, loving the smell of apples mixed with cinnamon. She inhaled again, drifting away, intoxicated with its pleasing aroma. She was glad she'd taken a brief stroll in her backyard and discovered the apples. The former owners had taken great care of the trees. Not one worm hole in any of the fruit. She inhaled another whiff as she hovered over the boiling pot. The sweet scent of cinnamon always reminded her of the fall. When she was a child, her mother would cook a million different things with apples as sort of a cerebration of autumn. It was a strange tradition since California had no real fall.

"Smells good." Mikey approached behind her.

Karen flipped around to see her daughter take off her coat. She watched the rain drip from the jacket onto the floor. "Thanks," she said. "Put your jacket in the laundry room. Tomorrow I want you and Sam to pick the apples in the backyard before you play."

"Play?"

"Sorry, goof around with friends."

"But Mom — "

"They're too beautiful to waste."

"But — "

She shot the evil-eye glare at her daughter and watched Mikey's protest crumble. Her daughter, with defeated form, headed toward the laundry room. Karen recognized her ploy to escape in case work was ahead. "Just a minute. I want to talk to you."

"What?" Mikey rubbed her shoe across the linoleum floor.

"How's Agatha?"

"Fine."

Mikey said that too quickly. Something wasn't right. She rolled her hand in a circle to encourage her daughter to talk. "And…?"

"We're making me a shirt." Mikey pulled off the lime green and white check fabric she had wrapped around her shoulders and held it up to the light for inspection.

"Is that all you did?"

"Basically."

Karen stepped closer. "Did she try to talk to you about Mormon stuff?"

Mikey stumbled backward, panic washing over her face. Her gaze darted across the room, and she refused to look into her mother's penetrating eyes.

"Well, did she?"

Mikey watched the floor. Her light pink complexion had paled. "Yes."

"Oh," Karen said. "What did she tell you?"

"That families are forever."

"What?"

"That when we die we go to heaven and live with our families, if we do good things on earth."

"That's crazy. For one, when we die, we die. That's it. Hasta la vista, baby. Kaput. Gone. No more. Zero. Nada."

Her daughter's head lowered.

"It's a fairy tale people made up to make losing loved ones easier. Nothing more." Karen frowned at her daughter's sunken posture.

"That's so sad," Mikey said.

"What?"

Her daughter glanced up. Her hands tighten into small fists.

The blood in Karen's head pounded in huge waves, crashing against each other, spewing anger. Why did her daughter have to appear so helpless when she spoke such damning ideas? "They're getting you. They've got their claws dug in deep. I can tell. I won't have you become a Mormon. If you do, you're out of the house. I might not be able to kick your Aunt Betsy out, but I can you. I don't like how those Mormon people think they have a right to push their ideas on everyone. They should show respect for others' beliefs."

Tears brimmed in Mikey's chocolate-colored eyes, then the tears escaped, drifting in a shaky snake shape. Karen sighed, finally registering Mikey's anguish. Karen spoke more softly, "Maybe there shouldn't be any more dealings with Mormons. Obviously even their children are well-trained in manipulating." She banged the dinner plate on the table. The noise startled her because she didn't realize the force she'd used. Maybe having this cult thing right in her own neighborhood bothered her more than she admitted. It was one thing for her to grow up with evil in her life, but completely another for her daughter to have to be confronted with it. She was going to protect her offspring no matter what. "I knew there was something going on. I knew it."

"What's the noise about?"

Both Mikey and Karen turned to see George standing, with his long coat draped over his suit and the newspaper dangling by his side.

Karen saw a hopeful glance come from Mikey. She counted on her daddy to come to the rescue. "Mikey's just been talking to those Mormons about their religion again," Karen said as she hugged him. "Sometimes..." He stiffened under her embrace. She looked up at his pointed chin.

He asked, "So?" then glanced toward Mikey, whose tears had magically reappeared.

Karen stepped away from her husband. "So...I can't have that." She slipped her lower lip under her front teeth.

"Why?" George asked.

"Why?" Karen shouted. "Don't you know?" She grasped her hands into a fist, then said in a slow strained voice, "Because they're evil. They're going to destroy this family if we let them."

"Stop overreacting. The ones I work with are nice."

"Oooh, you don't understand." She punched his chest, crying. "So now you're going to become one of them?"

He pulled her close. After Karen's crying stopped, George led her to a chair and sit her down. "Okay, what seems to be the problem?"

"Those Mormons are tricky. They're so good they caught Betsy."

"Hold it a minute," George said. "No one catches Betsy. Whatever she does is her own free will and choice. She's gotten herself into some strange stuff, but never dangerous. I talked to her this morning about her joining that church, and what I learned was their beliefs make her happy. I don't see what's so wrong in letting her be in an organization that does that. Do you?"

Karen shrugged.
"Do you?"
"I don't know."
"Now what have they done with Mikey?"
"They're forcing their beliefs on her. They're manipulating her mind."
"Mikey, is this true?"
She blushed as she looked into her mom's eyes, then she glanced at her father. His expression said, "Out with it."
"They didn't force it on me," Mikey whispered. "Agatha isn't like what Mom thinks."
"What? You said they did," Karen yelled, feeling her eyebrows squinting.
George put his hand on his wife's shoulder. "Calm down. Let the child talk." Motioning to Mikey, he continued, "You're frightening her."
Mikey studied her fingers.
"Sweetie," George said, "It's okay. You didn't do anything wrong. I want to learn what happened. Did you talk about the Mormon religion with your friend?"
Mikey nodded without peering up.
"See." Karen pointed her finger at her daughter.
Mikey gazed at the table.
"Shh, Karen, please," George said.
She glanced, annoyed at her husband, then asked, "Did she bring it up?"
Her daughter shook her head.
"I see," George said.
Karen mumbled. "Would you care to tell us why?"
"I-I wanted to find out more because — " Mikey paused. "Because I wanted to discover something stupid they believed in so I could tell Aunt Betsy how dumb their religion is so she'd quit and be saved from their evil snares. I don't want Aunt Betsy to die." Tears flowed again.
Karen ran to her daughter and embraced her. "There now, baby. It's okay." Mikey rested her head on her mother's chest and continued to sob.
"Are you going to kick me out of the house?"
A knife lunged into Karen's heart. How could she have been so thoughtless? She had overacted. "Of course not," she whispered. "I'm sorry I said those things. I didn't mean them. You know that, don't you?" She tipped her daughter's wet chin up. Mikey shrugged.
"I was just overreacting. I love you. I always want you with me."

Mikey let her mom embrace her. Then she asked, "Do you really believe it's the end of us when we die?"

Karen sighed. "Not really. I wish I did, but it doesn't feel right. I can't imagine there being no more of me because my heart stopped beating." She gripped her daughter's shirt.

"There must be something more because scientists have figured out that our bodies completely renew themselves about every seven years. So how do our minds continue with memories, learn motor skills, etc., if our brain cells die and are replaced? There has to be a part of us, invisible, not recordable, that scientists cannot measure. If that's the case, there could easily be so much of us that scientists don't know about like 'souls.'"

Straightening the fabric that she had grabbed on her daughter's blouse, she said, "Maybe you were right in thinking there was more. I don't know."

Mikey tucked her head against her mom's cheek. "Is Aunt Betsy in real trouble with those Mormons?"

This time George answered, "Doubt it. So what was this evil thing Agatha told you?"

"That families can be forever," Mikey choked.

George burst into laughter. "Some people are getting slightly sensitive."

Karen clenched her teeth.

George looked at her and his sky-blue eyes widened.

"Oops, did I say the wrong thing?"

She nodded. "It's okay," Karen said. "Go ahead and think I over-react and my feelings aren't real. It doesn't matter."

"I'm sorry," George choked.

Karen would be talking to him later about the burst of laughter. Sometimes his actions made her feel more lonely than if she hadn't talked to anyone at all.

Chapter 5

Utah weather offered hosts of surprises. One day cold storms brewed, and the next morning warm heat radiated in a vibrant array of colors, ranging from rusty reds and forest and leaf greens to honey yellows and burnt Roman ocher orange. Betsy absorbed nature's painting as she floated through the house, humming, dusting, and picking up things out of place. The glowing sunlight lit its magic throughout the house, giving a sense of aliveness. Once a good majority of the miscellaneous stuff was put away, she couldn't resist the call of being outdoors any longer so she grabbed her Jewish novel, folding chair, and sunglasses to bathe in the outside glory.

Worry over Karen took its toll on Betsy, showing up when she sat down. Sleep overcame her until she heard the familiar laughter of her niece and nephew. She must have slept for quite a while because their appearance meant school was out and it was late afternoon. She saw them gather around an apple tree, plastic mixing bowls in hand. They glanced into the branches sagging with ripe fruit.

"Think there's enough of them?" Mikey asked, her face, scrunching up like a sour grape.

"Did Mom say to pick them all?" Sam asked.

"Yeah."

"She's crazy," Sam concluded. "It'll take us years. What's she gonna to do with them?"

"Probably make applesauce," Mikey said. "No, correction, make us make applesauce."

Sam groaned. "I ain't no cook."

"I bet I can fill my bowl faster than you," Mikey said, tugging an apple from the branch.

"We'll see about that," Sam said, joining the race. The two worked fast with their gazes locked on each other. Betsy smiled to herself. Children had a way of turning work into games.

Once they'd picked several bowls full of fruit and each declared themselves the winner, they collapsed onto the grass to absorb the beauty of the sky.

"Did you learn anything interesting at Agatha's yesterday?" Sam asked.

"She said families are forever, which I find weird because people die. I asked her about that, and she said they believe in life after death, and God wants families to be together again. But in order to be with their families again, people must do good things on the earth; otherwise they won't live with God."

"Where do people go who don't do good things?" Sam asked.

"Hell, of course."

"Sounds mythological," Sam said.

"What?"

"You know, some humans favored by God, others not. The favored get to go to Field of Ellisyum in the underworld, the others go deeper into Tartarus."

"How do you know all that?"

"We're studying Greek stuff at school."

"Oh."

"Might as well point out Mormonism sounds as primitive as the Greeks."

"Oooh, big word."

Betsy saw Sam smile a huge cocky grin.

"You think this is enough to convince Betsy she's in a whacked society?" Mikey asked.

"No," Betsy said.

Both children jerked their heads up startled.

"Sorry kids, but life continues and everyone either earns rewards and suffers consequences agrees with my sense of rightness." Betsy sat straight in her chair.

Mikey picked up a bruised apple off the ground. "The earth is always replenishing itself. Why wouldn't it do that with people?"

Betsy couldn't help her half-grin. When was it? Last year, or maybe just a couple of months ago, she'd taught Mikey about reincarnation. The child had listened. "You do listen to my lectures."

Her niece glanced sideways at her. "I try not to."

Betsy laughed. Scooting to the edge of the lawn chair, she said, "I don't believe in reincarnation any more. The idea is too exhausting. Living this life once is enough. Besides, reincarnation would perfect people because they'd live so many times. I've never known any perfect people. Have you?" She paused then asked, "Are you two still planning to convince me Mormons are evil?"

Mikey nodded and Sam shrugged.

"If so, let me give you a bit of advice."

"What?" Mikey asked, her thick eyebrows raised, the whites of her eyes showing. She held her wonder expression for twenty seconds, making sure all the invisible cameras comprehended her emotion.

"The best way to change someone else's mind is through repetition. You don't bombard them with tons of information at once. They won't accept your ideas 'cause they're too new. What you do is present the idea and let them think for awhile, then tell them a little more. It's a great system. Benjamin Franklin came up with it in the Revolution. He first wrote about his ideas in the newspaper and waited a couple of years, until people believed the ideas were their own, before he grouped them together and added a conclusion of actions. That's how he won the American people's support in the fight against English."

"Enough of the history lesson," Sam said.

The conversation quieted as gigantic white clouds crawled across the horizon. The sun had dipped away, taking the heat with it.

"Do you think Mom's mad at me about last night?" Mikey asked.

"What did you do?" Sam rose.

"Nothing. Mom just found out about me talking about religion with Agatha."

"What?" Panic swept across Sam's face.

"Calm down. She just started overgeneralizing, that's all," Betsy said.

"Is that bad?" Mikey asked.

"I used to do it. It's where you see something as negative and think this bad thing will never end. Your mom also likes to jump to conclusions, especially when it comes to Mormons. She thinks because her friend died in a religious group that everyone who belongs to one will be murdered too."

"We know all this," Sam said. "I'm tired of talking about it. If she becomes upset with anything to do with Mormons, then you shouldn't be one."

Mikey nodded.

"Sorry guys, but I can't have my happiness determined by what your mother's willing to accept and what she isn't."

"How can we help Mom if you're not going to quit?" Mikey asked. Her shoulders slouched.

"I'll help your mom recognize her negative thoughts are getting out of control," Betsy said.

"It would be best if Sam and I convince you Mormons are phony," Mikey said.

Sam agreed. "I'll talk to my soccer buds tomorrow and see if they have any insight." He stood up. The rest of the group followed his lead, wandering in the house.

❧

In the early evening Betsy finally made it to reading her Jewish novel, but the phone interrupted the story. "Oh, Philippe, I'm so glad you called." Betsy perched on her striped bedspread in the early evening.

"You've missed my romantic voice?" rushed a thick French accent.

"Desperately. What would my past fifteen years have been like without your sporadic calls?"

"Devastating."

Betsy laughed. "You know it's so much easier talking to you than husband number one."

"That's cause I'm so much better, n'est pas?"

"Oui."

"So how's life in Mormon land?" Philippe asked.

"Interesting." Betsy scooted under the covers even though it was only six o'clock. Philippe's chats were notoriously long.

"Have they — "

"I'm one of them now." Betsy grinned. Oh, if only she could see his face. That would be the cherry on top of this delicious sundae.

"Have you gone, what they say, gone cuckoo?"

"I got baptized a couple of days ago."

"Betsy, my sweet cakes, I should have guessed this one. Why didn't I see?" He paused. "Have you told Karen?"

"Yes." The lines on Betsy's forehead sank into a crevice.

"How'd she take it?"

"Not good, I'm afraid. Her negative fears are controlling her." Betsy leaned her head against the bedpost and sighed. "Oh, I'm worried."

"Hang in there, mon cherie. She will pull through."

Betsy smiled, remembering why she liked talking to him so much. If only he'd remained as faithful as he was encouraging, they could have enjoyed a beautiful oneness forever.

"You are quiet." Philippe broke into her thoughts. "Are you worried she'll have another meltdown?"

Betsy twisted her fingers around the corner of her blanket. "This time it would be my fault."

"Oh, mon amie, don't be so hard on yourself."

"I could have waited to tell them until Karen found a job. I didn't need to add to her stress."

"But you were so excited about this new truth you couldn't keep it in. It seeped out of your seams, n'est pas?"

Betsy laughed. He always had great clothing metaphors. She guessed it was because he designed them for a living. "You're right. I can't hold water when I find something I know will help others. Do you want to know about Mormons?"

He chuckled. "Non."

"Their real name is The Church of Jesus Christ of Latter-day Saints. Mormon is a nickname after one of their prophets."

"Jesu Christus?"

"Yeah."

"Mon amie, you have changed. Do you believe Jesu was the Savior, a Dieu, or something?"

"You'll laugh, but yes. I more than believe it. I know it."

Philippe laughed lightly. "Comment?"

"By the incredible feeling I get when I hear or pray about their principles."

"How many times have I heard you say you couldn't believe in a person being part-Dieu part-man?"

"Countless."

"Americans. Wasn't it too supernatural for you? Unrealistic?"

"Okay, I deserve this. I did say all that."

"And now you believe?"

"Yes."

"Incredible. There must be something in their water to get you to switch over."

"Maybe. But if only you knew what they believe, you'd believe it to."

"Let me guess. You think it would aid Karen?"

"Yes."

He didn't say anything. She knew what he thought. She wouldn't be helping Karen any by forcing new stuff on her. But he had never felt the Spirit so he couldn't understand.

"The Mormons have some wonderful ideas I'm sure you'd enjoy hearing — "

"How about next time, ma belle. I got to work on the spring line."

"All right." Betsy sighed. "Till next time."

"Au revoir, ma cherie."

Betsy pressed the receiver, then brought the phone to her chest. He, like Karen, needed to feel the Spirit. It was so much like her own need had been.

It happened during the missionaries' first discussion. The two girls and she had met in the deli at Barnes and Noble. The girls had wanted to meet at Betsy's apartment, but Betsy thought it best to keep them away from the house.

Sister Richards, the sister who did most the talking, had flowing brown hair that bounced down her back and had worn a khaki skirt and blouse with a wide brown belt, emphasizing the narrowness of her waist. She had puppy brown eyes and an angelic smile.

Her partner, Sister Stewart, was a contrast. Her hair was blonde and short, and she wore a floral pink dress without a waist. The fabric spread in all directions. Her eyes had no distinct color.

"Hello," Sister Richards said, extending her hand as they surrounded a table. "We're glad to meet with you again."

They talked a little about their homes, explaining how they'd worked for years to earn the money to go on missions.

Betsy was impressed. These *young* kids saved their money to talk to people about religion. If they were that committed to this church, they probably had something to offer.

They asked a few questions about her past, which she dodged. It didn't do any good to dwell in history. After that they dove into their lesson. Sister Richards leaned forward, causing long strands of hair to fall in front of her. "Do you believe there's a Supreme Being?"

"Yes," Betsy said.

"Why?"

"Our souls are just too great to stop existing after we die."

"That's a good point."

"So what do you believe this Supreme Being is like?"

"Well. Hum. That's a hard one." Betsy tapped a nail against her lip. "I don't know."

"Do you think this Supreme Being has form?"

"I don't know if I believe in a specific thing being a God. Maybe I believe in a universal form of organization that has rules the whole Universe follows."

"That's a good point. I also believe there must be an organization of uniform rules we must live by. I want to tell you I also know there's a God. We are His children. And He — "

"His children! Are you crazy? Why would you think we are the product of God?"

"To explain that, would you mind reading a scripture from the Bible?" Sister Richards asked, stroking the leather binding of her

Bible that she had set on the wooden table.

"Have no Bible," Betsy said. "Never had a need for one."

"Don't you believe in it?" Sister Stewart folded her hands in her lap.

"Every Bible says different things. Don't like that."

Sister Richards explained how the Bible had been changed after the Savior's death. Then she read several scriptures stating that people were the spiritual children of God.

Betsy remembered dragging her violet fingernail down the page, searching for the verses the missionaries wanted her to read. She had taken a deep breath, making the connection with her purple polish, hoping it would help her obtain the feeling of integration with God. Could the message these sisters were giving be the missing key? The answer she'd been searching and meditating for all her life? A strange calm spilled over her. Other times when she thought she was close to obtaining the answer, she'd been elated, but this instance a comfortable peace wrapped around her. She read the scriptures.

After pondering the passages the missionaries suggested, Betsy was convinced the Bible did support the concept of people being God's children. But, she told the missionaries, she couldn't accept something just because a group of people joined together and decided to call it scripture.

"We don't expect you to either," Sister Richards responded.

Betsy stared. "Then why are you here?"

"Because there's a way you can learn if these things are true for yourself."

"How's that?"

"By praying."

"How am I supposed to know if my prayers are being answered?"

Sister Richards explained how the comfortable feeling she had earlier was the spirit, and would answer her prayers if she asked. Then the sister had challenged her to pray about the existence of God and share her experience at the next visit.

"Sure. I'll give anything a shot once."

Betsy stood, sighed, enjoying the memory of the first time she felt the Spirit. Simple, yet right. Now she must get Karen to feel the same thing. It would make her life a whole lot easier and then Karen wouldn't have to suffer as much. But first things first. Karen was very uptight in the kitchen today, heading for a break down. Betsy would try to make her relax, whether she wanted to or not.

Grabbing her seashore music, she tiptoed across the upstairs level into Karen and George's room. There she slipped the CD into the machine and adjusted it so it would blast the relaxing sound throughout the house.

She smiled at her good fortune when she saw the intercom near the music player. She switched it and whispered smoothly, "Relax. Take deep breaths. Let all the tension in your body release from your pores. Feel the stress escape your body. Let it go. Don't fight it. It's useless to struggle. Breathe deeply. Focus on the tension in your feet. Let it float away."

And on Betsy continued, until she heard a male voice boom. "What do you think you're doing?"

Startled, she yelled over the intercom before seeing George glaring at her. "What?" she asked.

"That's what I'm asking you. Why are you blaring noise all over my house and talking nonsense into the intercom when we're trying to have a nice family dinner?"

Just then Sam, Mikey, and Karen thundered into the bedroom.

"Is everything all right?" Karen asked.

"Yes," George snapped. "Why wouldn't it be?"

"We heard screams like someone was dying." Mikey watched her with large eyes.

"Your father scared me," Betsy said.

"Well what do you think would happen if a seagull sneaked up behind you and started squawking?" Karen asked.

"Sorry," Betsy said. "I wanted your dinner to be more enjoyable."

"By having us do relaxation techniques at the table?" George asked. "How could we relax with your hoarse voice cracking the paint?"

"Yeah, she wants us to choke on the noodles. I'm sure that would make our lives better," Sam said. He stood with his shoulders spread wide, his chest risen to make himself look strong. It worked too. The long hours he spent lifting weights inbetween soccer practice paid off.

"Okay everybody, back to dinner." George clapped his hands.

Betsy's shoulders sank. She walked halfway to the door before George put his arm in front of her like a bar. "Just a minute. I'd like to have a talk with you."

"Would you stop treating me like a child? I'm your older sister. Let me remind you — older."

"Just a minute," George said, then he kissed Karen tenderly and whispered he'd soon join her. The kids left without a sound. George peered into Betsy's eyes. "What's going on?"

"Karen's getting a little tense. I wanted to help her." Betsy's chin tipped upward.

"Why not do yoga like you did last night?"

Betsy pressed her lips together, then said, "Cause we got in a fight and aren't talking."

"I don't even want to get into this one. In the future," George held up his finger at her, "will you please resist disturbing our dinner?"

"You're acting like you don't even care about your wife." She planted both hands firmly on her hips.

George's shoulder lifted slightly. "Why do you say that?"

"Cause you make it seem like your wife's problem's are irritations that you shouldn't have to deal with."

His eyes widen. "Look, I do care about my wife, and it's none of your business."

"You don't have to get so uptight. I care about you. I care about Karen. I want to help you, and I sense things are a little tense around here."

"I don't have time for this," George said, stepping toward the doorway.

"That's a cover up." She seized a hold of his sleeve. "You need to talk. It's not good to keep it bottled in. Now out with it."

George remained silent as Betsy peered into his square face that sported a dark shadow of beard stubble.

He huffed. "Fine, you want to know the truth. I'll tell you. I'm sick of the whole thing. If I'm too nice to Karen, the shrink said she might get excessive with her concerns and worries. I have to set the proper behavioral boundaries." He bit his tongue, then said, "If I set them rigid and don't listen to her worries, then she might go off into the deep end as well. I can't win. Either way it's my fault."

Tapping her finger against her lip, Betsy said, "Sounds like you're walking on egg shells."

"I am."

"That's tough." The palm of her tapping finger had become purple from the lipstick smearing onto it. "What do you think the true source of the problem is?"

George's shoulders raised again. "I'm a good husband."

"I never said you weren't. I can't help suspecting her strange behavior has something to do with her friend. You know, the one who died in a cult."

"I don't doubt it, but the past is past, and we can't blame our behavior on history," George said.

"Yeah, if she still has vivid memories of the incident and can't shake it, the memories could prove to be extremely dangerous to her mental heath. And if she's dealing with unresolved pain from that situation, it would explain some of her bizarre behavior."

"Perhaps you're right," George said. "But how does that explain you?"

"What do you mean?" Betsy asked.

"You're always behaving crazy, and you didn't have a weird past. I know because I lived it with you."

Betsy pushed George's chest. "Come on," she said, trying to hide her grin.

"I need to get back to dinner," George said.

"Are you going to be okay?" Betsy glanced into his pale blue eyes, which immediately looked to the top of her head.

"Yeah, fine." He left.

Betsy gathered her CDs. Another failed attempt. Oh, well, "the Greats" were never understood. She definitely wasn't understood in this house. She'd have to keep doing different approaches until she found one that worked for this crazy family.

Chapter 6

"We need to have a talk," Karen said to George, clenching her jaw. She'd been reading a psychology book on the bed, which rambled on about the evils of storing up frustrations until a person exploded or had a break down. Might as well relieve her aggravation.

Her husband scanned the newspaper as he lounged in his swivel chair by the fire. The newspaper made a crinkling noise when he flipped the page. "Why?"

"Cause we do. When would be a good time?"

"After I finish the newspaper." He flipped over another page.

Karen's lower lip sunk under her front teeth, and she tapped her nails against her book. George shot an irritated glance from the corner of his eye at her bouncing fingers.

She continued to tap. "How long is that going to take?" she asked, closing her book against her finger to mark her spot.

"A couple minutes."

"Fine," she said, flopping her head onto her pillow. The bed springs groaned. Sure she'd wait like always. Why was he putting her off? He could glance at the newspaper later. She needed to talk now. She grunted and turned her back to him.

She felt his gaze on her for a long second, and then he said, "Since you're so impatient, talk. The newspaper's not that important."

"I can wait," she said as she watched him approach her.

"What's the problem?" George sat on the white sheet on his side of the bed.

Would the world end? He had set down his paper. Perhaps she did come slightly above his nightly read.

"I'm sorry. I'm upset about what went on before dinner," Karen said.

"With Mikey?"

"Yeah. It's not fair for you to undermine me in front of the kids. They'll see you do it; then they won't respect me."

"How did I do that?"

"You disagreed with me with Mikey in the room."

"I'm not allowed to have an opinion?"

"Don't undermine me."

"I can't express my views? That hardly seems fair."

Karen sighed, setting her book on the nightstand. Her husband could make things so difficult. How was she ever going to convince his logical mind that when he spotlighted her faults, it made her long to dry up like a fall leaf until she crumbled into extinction? All she had tried to do was to save *their* daughter from a dangerous extremist group. It was totally unreasonable for him to minimize her efforts by making her seem hypersensitive.

"You made it appear like it was perfectly fine for Mikey to talk with the Mormons about their religion!" she blurted out.

"What's the problem?"

"She already believes some of their philosophies!"

"That there's life after death?"

"Yes."

"So?

"Do you want our child to believe in polygamy and become a wife of a hundred-year-old man at the age of fifteen?"

"Calm down." He put his hand on her shoulder.

She rotated her shoulder in a circle to knock it off. The warm hand remained, pressing. "No, I won't! This is our daughter. Not some girl down the street. Our daughter. I'm sorry, but I love her too much to watch her waste her life because you want to be open to somebody's ideologies."

George rolled her toward him on the bed, then wrapped his arms around her. He gently pushed her head against his chest. She listened to his strong powerful heartbeat. "Shh," he whispered as she went to talk.

She couldn't move her lips. He was controlling her as he would a child.

"Calm, sweetheart. I'm sorry I upset you. We should talk about this after you get some rest."

Pulling herself a little loose from his grasp, she said, "I'm not tired. Don't you dare blame this on sleep."

"Okay, hormones," George said with a smile.

Her hand swung to whack him, but he caught it in mid-air. He laughed.

"I hate it when you say sexist jokes," Karen said.

"Sorry, dear." He still smiled. "Let's talk about this over lunch tomorrow. I'll take you out to a nice restaurant, and we can enjoy a meal together. It'll bring us closer."

"Of the wackiest things to say. Arguing over how to raise our children is going bring us closer?"

"Sure. Why not? Delicious food. Mmm."

"Let's talk — "

"Fine dining. The kind you're always bugging me to take you to."

"But — "

"It'll be a nice break during your job hunt."

He didn't have to say more. They'd talk at lunch over a delicious hot plate of food that she didn't have to cook.

A loud crash boomed from the adjoined room next door. Karen and George looked at each other. George was the first one off the bed. Karen followed behind, admiring her husband's broad shoulders and narrow waist. He'd managed to keep his shape. Age had been good to him. She, though, was a different story — her muscles had turned to flab from lack of exercise.

George pushed open the wooden door to discover Mikey's pink face. "What?" he asked her.

Mikey smiled, her dimples indenting both cheeks. "Hi," she said.

"What's going on?" George asked.

Karen scooted farther into the small square room. She liked the feel of it and planned to make it her office — maybe transform it into a craft room. It had been so long since she'd been creative; she'd been itching to make something. The room reeked with inspiration. Wild golden flowers raced up the walls. Outside, Indian yellow maple leaves framed the otherwise bare windows. Beautiful. Just seeing it inspired her to create, but her supplies hadn't even made it up from the basement. She'd been too tired.

"This room is great," Mikey said. "Can I have it?"

"Sorry," Karen said, "I'm going to use it."

"For what?"

"A craft room."

"Crafts? You don't do them."

"Used to a long time ago. I wanted to start them up again. That's why I packed my craft supplies. Where were you when we spent hours packing them?"

"I don't remember seeing anything like that. But it sounds cool. Can I make some things with you?"

"When I get the room put together."

George unfolded his crossed arms. "Now that's settled, can someone please tell me what that loud noise was?"

Mikey batted her long eyelashes as she peered up at her father. "I was looking around and sort of tripped."

"Why were you here?'

"'Cause I thought it would make a great sitting room and wanted to make plans."

"Mom?" Sam's voice floated from the parents' bedroom. His voice was crystal clear. The walls were paper thin!

"You were eavesdropping," Karen said, raising her eyebrows at Mikey.

"You mean, ears-dropping?" Mikey swiped at her bangs.

George smiled.

"Don't try to be cute to get out of trouble," Karen waved a warning finger.

By then Sam had joined them. "What's up?" he asked, glancing around.

"Nothing," Karen said. "What do you want?"

"To talk to ya."

"Can we later?"

"Sure," Sam said. "I'll be in my room." He left, but first looked at everyone questionably.

Karen turned back to Mikey. "Okay, out with it. Why were you spying on us?"

"I wouldn't call it spying," Mikey said.

"Whatever," Karen said, running her hand through her short hair. "I wanted to know what you were doing."

"I was ears-dropping for more reasons than being nosy. I was on a mission. I want to know how you're really doing. Not the act you put on in front of me and Sam."

"What do you mean?" Karen asked, her voice weakening.

"I wanted to know if you're getting sick again and are on the verge of having another one of those breakdowns. I know you like to talk about what's bothering you to Dad. And you do this when he's trying to read the newspaper."

George laughed. "That's the truth."

"I do not," Karen said. "I normally hold things in."

"Like a strainer with water," George said.

Karen rolled her eyes. "Go on with your story, Mikey."

"I was just going to hang out long enough to learn if the Agatha-religion-thing had upset you. That's all. I'm not a complete snoop." A strand of hair had slipped loose from her pony tail, and she tucked it behind her ear.

Karen looked out the window, watching the yellow leaves on the maple tree flutter. White clouds smothered the grayish sky. She didn't know how to respond. What could she say? She walked into the hall, leaving George and Mikey to talk.

"If you're so worried about your mother maybe you should help her more," George said.

Mikey's head lowered. "I picked apples for her like she asked."

"You need to learn to help without being asked."

"But..." Mikey groaned, then nodded her head, her chin coming close to her chest. "I've really blown it. I've done such a bad job in helping Mom that I'm pressing my ear on the wall to see how much damage my lie about promising not to talk to Agatha about her church and doing it had done. I should have at least done the dishes before I went to Agatha's. I'll do better, Dad. Promise."

"It's all right. If you're worried about Mom, why don't you focus on the things you can do instead of wasting your time spying?"

"I'll make applesauce out of all the apples."

"That'll be great," George said. "I'm sure your mom will appreciate it."

Hearing the two moving toward the hall, Karen hurried into her bedroom.

George called, "Mikey, wait."

"What?" Karen heard her say.

"You know I love you, don't you?"

There was a big pause. Then her daughter choked out softly, "Why do Mormons bother her so much?"

Karen couldn't hear the response and didn't care. Misery swept through her. She shouldn't be causing this kind of pain to her children. She was a failure as a mother. A complete failure.

After not succeeding with her last attempt in helping Karen and George, Betsy decided to bury herself in studying. Nothing took the worries of the day away like learning. She engrossed herself in a pile of books as she sat in the middle of her apartment. A small tap sounded on the door.

"Come in," sang Betsy.

The door creaked when Mikey pressed it open. Her niece looked around carefully as if afraid someone would see her.

"Have my positive mental waves drawn you in here?" Betsy asked.

"No. I want to talk."

"Your aura says it's serious. Grab a chair or scoop up the floor."

Mikey opted to scoop up the floor. She slipped over to her aunt's bed and sat in front of its pink striped comforter. Betsy smiled. The pink went well with Mikey's green shirt. She went back to flipping through her books, left eyebrow raised. It would take Mikey some warmup time to gather her courage to tell why she had come. Learning time was rare so she mustn't waste it while waiting.

"There's too many colors in this room," Mikey said.

"What do you mean?" Betsy questioned still reading.

"There's pinks, purples, blues, greens, yellows, oranges, and reds splashed everywhere."

"I love the sense of vitality." Betsy flipped the page of her book.

"The kitchen is great. It's all white."

"I've been meaning to get to that," Betsy said. She read a passage in her book and said, "Hun."

The silence quickly faded when Mikey said, "So your religion doesn't have all the answers after all."

Betsy peered up and saw a smug look cross Mikey's face as her niece raised her eyebrows. What was the child talking about?

"Have you decided not to be a Mormon anymore?"

Understanding seeped into Betsy. The child thought since she was so absorbed in her books that she was on another quest for knowledge. What the Mormons had to offer simply wasn't satisfactory. "Nice try. I'm studying my religion more in depth." She put the books on her lap down to her side. "What's bothering you?"

"I don't know. Everything seems to be weird."

"What do you mean?"

"I hate Provo. It's dumb. It's filled with those dumb Mormons and all they do is make my dumb life miserable. I want to move back to the beach."

"You're having internal trauma because your surroundings are so different from your old ones."

"What? Why can't you speak English?"

"That was."

"So I can understand."

"Let's put it another way."

"Please."

"You seem upset about the move. Is that better?"

"Much."

"Things have been hard on you."

Mikey nodded. "Why did you have to make it harder by becoming a Mormon? You knew it would upset Mom."

"I didn't have a choice."

"They forced you like Mom is always saying they'd do?"

"No. They taught me the truth, and I wouldn't have been honest to my being if I didn't embrace full-heartedly its light."

"How did you know?" Mikey rubbed her tennis shoes against each other.

"From a feeling."

"That's not knowing."

"But, Mikey, it is. That's what the missionaries taught me. They pointed out the feeling inside is how God communicates to us."

"Great. Now you believe some God-like creature comes floating out of the sky and talks to your insides. That's stupid."

Betsy sighed. "No. How can I explain this?" She tapped her finger against her chin.

Mikey stared at Betsy's fingers.

"I've got it," Betsy said, moving her right hand under her left. "Have you ever felt sick inside like you're going to throwup because you knew what you were doing was wrong?"

Mikey shook her head.

"Like maybe when you wanted to cheat on a test you hadn't studied for."

"A throwup feeling?"

"It doesn't have to be that exactly, but a real uneasy feeling where maybe your heart beats fast and your palms sweat."

"Perspire. Girls perspire."

"You know what I mean."

"I had the heart beating and the clammy palms when I was going to lie about Agatha to Mom."

"Well?" Betsy lifted an eyebrow.

"I know what you're talking about."

"How did you feel?"

"Icky."

"Okay, some people would call that your conscience. They'd say your conscience told you when things you're doing were wrong. Now think back to a time where you knew what you were doing was right."

Mikey tapped her foot as she thought. "Once I collected and dried a bunch of flowers for Mom that grew by the beach. Mom always loves that kind of stuff."

"How did you feel when you gave her the collection?"

"Good."

"At peace or comfortable perhaps with what you were going to do?"

"Maybe."

"Some would say your conscience was telling you were doing the right thing. We all have these built in mechanisms that put some kind of moral value on our actions. This conscience the Mormons believe in is the Holy Ghost or a special helper sent from God, letting us know when we're doing good and when we're doing bad. That's how God talks to you."

"If these feelings happen to everyone, then why would you want to become a Mormon?"

"Mikey, believe me, I'd never hurt your mother on purpose. But there's more to it than feelings. When I read the book Agatha gave you, I had an overwhelming amount of those good feelings. They were so strong it almost hurt. It was unlike anything I had ever known. The missionaries explained that was the Holy Ghost and that I could have Him with me all the time if I got baptized. Mikey, I needed that."

"But you said it was the Holy Ghost that makes us feel good and bad. You're confused. Either everyone has it or they don't."

"I did say that. Hmm. I wonder how that works? It seems like you have a good point. I'm going to have to find out. Cause it's strange that everyone has the Holy Ghost and then you have to get baptized to have Him with you."

Mikey smiled.

Betsy knew the child considered this a success in proving the Mormons weren't a good group. "You seemed worried about your mother?" Betsy said, leaning over her books to tip her niece's chin up with her big nails.

"I kind of am."

"So am I."

Mikey peered at her with wonder. "You are?"

"Yeah. I thought she was well enough to handle my becoming Mormon. Oh, I knew she'd get upset for a while and sulk around the house. I just hoped she was well enough that she'd get through it without major complications."

Mikey stared at her aunt. "You knew it would hurt Mom and you did it anyway? How could you be so cruel? Is this what your new religion teaches? If it is, then it's evil like Mom says." With that, she raced from the room.

The door slammed, echoing. Betsy had blown it with Mikey. Now the poor girl thought she'd tried to hurt her mother. It wasn't true, but how would she make Mikey understand?

This problem needed to be discussed out loud. It would help her reach a solution faster. Philippe was the person for this task. Yes, she had just talked with him last night, but he was so good at comforting her, and he had great insight when it came to family problems.

Philippe always had the answers for her, even when they had been newlyweds, and Betsy was confronted with long-distance parent challenges. She and Philippe lived in Paris at the time. The trouble began when both of them worked in their small but cozy apartment. Philippe was cutting away in a frenzy on his new design fashion for an upcoming show. Catching his wave of creative energy, she was painting a colorfield of impressions throughout their apartment.

The phone rang. George on the other line. Betsy remembered saying, "Slow down, mon frere, you're talking too fast." Philippe continued to snip the fabric, his long curly hair bouncing gently as he worked.

"Mom won't stop screaming and yelling," George said.

"What are you talking about?" Betsy asked.

"Mom. About an hour ago she threw her food across the kitchen and hasn't stopped yelling. She says there's miniature mice in it eating her tongue."

"What?"

"Then she started yelling and saying I'm going to scream until I've killed every single mouse. Once I stopped her yelling, or she took a break, I don't know which. I got the food and said, Look, no mice."

"She said they were invisible and only she could sense them."

"Ohhh!" Betsy said.

"Quoi?" Philippe asked, his scissors had stopped snipping.

"What should we do?" Betsy bit one of her nails.

"Quoi?" Philippe asked, nearing her.

"I don't know," George said sadly.

"Quoi?" Philippe asked again.

Betsy tipped the speaker part of the phone away from her mouth. "My mom's freaking out, and George doesn't know what to do."

Philippe brushed a strain of Betsy's hair onto her back and asked, "What's she doing?"

Betsy gave him the phone and after saying a couple of "uh's" and "ah's", he asked, "Have you checked with all her doctors to see what kind of medicine she's on? She might have overdosed." He was right. After that Philippe had continued to correspond with each of her doctors until she passed away.

He had the right answer then. Surely he'd have the right answer now. Betsy did need to guide Karen on the road to recovery quickly. There was no other reason for the call, Betsy determined. Why was she justifying the call to herself? They had a great friendship. What was she worried about? That she'd fall for his sexy French accent a second time? Naw, he had roaming eyes. She remembered that and his charming spell vanished with that knowledge. She dialed his number.

A muffled sound answered.

"Are you answering the phone with pins in your mouth again?" Betsy asked.

After a delay, a voice clearly said, "Ma cherie, what do I owe this privilege?"

"Out-loud problem-solving."

"Ah, more difficulty in Mormonland. Are you sure you want to live there?"

"Do you want to join me?"

"Non d' Utah. Une moment, let me put you on the speaker. Got a new design I have to finish pinning."

Betsy waited, her nails tapping against the phone.

"All right. Problem solve away, mon amie."

"It's Mikey. I'm worried about...she's so jumpy. It seems impossible for her to hold still. She constantly bangs her knees against each other or taps her fingers. Watching her makes me nauseous."

"Taps her fingers, n'est pas?" Phillipe asked.

Betsy looked at her fingers banging against the phone and stopped them. "I'm not obnoxious like she is. It's her nerves."

"Pourquoi?"

"Her mother. She's so fearful if she breathes wrong her mother will have another panic attack."

"Personalization distortion."

"Exactly."

"She needs to recognize illogical thoughts."

"She's still a child."

"No matter."

"You're right, but she's not speaking to me. She wouldn't listen to my lecture on illogical thoughts."

"Wouldn't focusing on thoughts fix the problem?"

"Exactly."

"Is there anything you can do?"

"Her mother is the answer. Get her healthy, then the daughter will follow. I tried pumping meditation suggestions through the intercom, but George put an end to that."

Phillipe laughed.

"What?" Betsy asked.

"No blaming you for not trying."

"I want that on my tombstone. Last night I tried yoga with Karen."

"Was bien?"

"Well, I thought, but this morning she moaned about how sore she was and how she'll never do that again."

"No shape. More, do better."

"She won't." A frown spread down Betsy's face. This problem seemed to have no bottom. "Food won't work. She doesn't care about health. She says she has fat and so does her food…so aggravating."

"Exercise and food are patch-ups. No root of the problem," Phillipe said.

Silence filled the phone waves. "What's the root?" Betsy asked.

"Ma cherie, simple. She needs to face fears — her bad memories."

Betsy gasped. "You're right. I'm going to introduce Karen slowly into the Mormon world. It'll be so subtle she won't know what hit her. Thank you. That's perfect."

"Non, I didn't say convert…"

"I'll teach her their principles and she'll believe without know — "

"Possible traditions that — "

"This'll be wonderful. Thank you, Phillipe."

"Anything, for ma belle."

They made kissing smacking noises and hung up. Betsy sighed, Philippe was so wonderful to talk to.

Chapter 7

Betsy pulled her car a few feet in front of the mailbox and strolled to the house. Today had been enjoyable, and now it was time for her to check on the kids. They should have come home from school about an hour ago. Shildren shouldn't go too long unsupervised.

She entered in the kitchen from the side door. Mikey stood in front of the sink peeling an apple. "I'm glad somebody's not letting those wonderful apples go to waste."

"I have to make applesauce."

"Sounds like fun."

"Get real," Mikey said, her big eyes pleading her aunt for help. "I have homework too. How am I ever going to finish all this?" Her hand waved over the piles of fruit that filled the sink and most of the counter.

"I'll help you," Betsy said, going to the apron drawer. "I wouldn't want to see you fail to do your homework."

The two fell into a system. Mikey washed, destemmed, and deleafed while Betsy peeled. Then Mikey would chop, boil, and dash the sugar and spices in the mix.

"Did your mom ask you about Agatha yesterday?" Betsy asked as she flipped the peelings onto the table.

"Yeah, she and Dad were both there."

"What did they say about it?"

"Dad said that I need to help Mom out more. So I volunteered to do all the apples."

"So that's how you got stuck doing this?"

"I would've anyway."

"That's probably true. Doesn't it feel good to be honest with your parents?"

"No."

"You're building character. I'm proud of you."

"I wish I could build my character without putting up apples," Mikey said.

Betsy laughed. "It's a good skill to learn."

"Why?"

"The Mormons believe in being prepared in case of an emergency and to have a two-year supply of food."

Running water into the pot so she could start another batch boiling, Mikey said, "Mormons again. It seems that's all you ever talk about."

"Sorry. I'm so excited about the organization I can't help myself."

They drifted to silent work again until Sam barged through the door. "Hi, guys. Looks like you're busy making applesauce." He set his soccer ball on the counter and headed to the cupboard for a bowl. "I'll have to try it out. Hopefully I won't die."

"It hasn't killed you yet," Betsy said.

"Why don't you help us?" Mikey asked.

"Let me eat and I'll think about it," Sam said. He dished up his bowl to the top and shoved in the hot sauce. "Pretty good. Could use more cinnamon."

Betsy walked to him and dumped two shakes of cinnamon on top of his head.

"Hey," he said, with his hand guarding his head.

"Sweet enough now?" Betsy asked, the bottle of spice held high.

"Yes, yes. Thank you. It's perfect."

Betsy smiled and returned to peeling.

With his mouth half-empty, Sam said, "I talked to some guys on the team about Mormons today."

"Oh, yeah?" Betsy said.

"Find out anything else bad about them?" Mikey asked, pouring chopped apples into the boiling water.

"Not really. Most of the guys were LDS. They said they're not a cult but a mainstream religion like Catholics."

Mikey seemed disappointed as she stirred the boiling apples.

Poor Mikey. But the new information didn't surprise Betsy. "Maybe some day you two will believe me when I tell you Mormons aren't a bad group of people."

Sam took another bite of applesauce. "Do you think I should tell Mom about it? Maybe if she knew they were just another mainstream religion she wouldn't be so upset."

Betsy's forehead wrinkled. "I doubt it would do any good. Your mom believes any group with a set of beliefs is a cult. It isn't, but that doesn't matter. What matters is how she sees it that way, and telling her about what you learned might do more harm. She gets real upset when she discovers her kids have talked to Mormons about their religion. Doesn't she, Mikey?"

"She does."

"I guess I won't say anything, but there must be some way to help her," Sam said.

"Believe me, honey," Betsy said. "We're all working for it."

"We got to try to be extra helpful, then maybe she won't be so frustrated," Mikey said.

All nodded in agreement.

❧

The next day passed in a busy blur of job interviews and application forms. Before Karen realized, it was early Friday morning. She wandered around in a sleepy daze, trying to prepare herself for another day of job hunting. Feeling like a zombie, she stumbled downstairs to eat Rice Chex cereal for breakfast. When she walked into the kitchen, she was caught off guard. The kitchen sparkled. The apples and their remains had been put away. Dishes had been done. The floor had been swept and most of the counter scrubbed. Mikey was busy working on the last dirty surface. "Mikey, this looks wonderful," Karen said. "You even mopped."

Mikey beamed, her cheeks dimpling.

"Having a sparkling clean kitchen, what a perfect way to start out a Friday!"

Mikey smiled and said, "I couldn't have written a better line."

Karen laughed then glanced at the clock. Nine o'clock. "Why aren't you in school?"

"We've got the day off, remember?"

"Oh, yeah." Karen grabbed the milk for her breakfast. "Thanks for spending your vacation helping me. I appreciate it. Now I get to eat breakfast on a clean table. I'm lucky."

"You're welcome. I'm going to help more often," Mikey said, wringing out her rag.

"You are?"

"Yep."

"May I ask why?"

"I want to."

Suddenly Karen froze. "You're not planning on becoming a Mormon, are you?"

"NO!"

Her mom chuckled. "Relax, I was kidding. If you want to be perfect, I'm not going to stop you. I'm going to love it. Absolutely love it."

Mikey beamed, then glanced through the window. Karen followed her gaze. The signs of the coming winter had vanished. Summer returned, or Indian summer as some insisted on calling it.

"Mom, I'm going out for a while."

Karen couldn't blame her. If she didn't have to find a job, she'd be outside too. "Where?"

"To ride my bike."

"Okay, but wear your helmet."

"It'll ruin my hair."

Karen gave her daughter a sympathetic smile.

"When I'm in the movies, I'll have a hair artist to fix it right after I take off the helmet, and everyone will wonder how my hair could remain perfect under the sweat, heat, and pressure of a helmet."

Karen smiled again.

As Mikey turned to leave, she ran into Betsy, wearing her purple and orange tie-dyed bathrobe. Her hair seemed to have been plugged into a light socket. "Mikey, there you are."

She didn't say a word but set her jaw firmly, causing the tip of her chin to stick out. She looked at her aunt's toenails. They were painted in a rainbow. The big nail was purple, the next pink, then bright yellow. The color scheme started all over again. Was Mikey mentally shooting those nails for her film? The child's silly dream seemed so real to her that she wondered if Mikey differentiated reality and fantasy.

"It took me a while to find it, but I did, right in front of my senses," Betsy said, not noticing Mikey trying to inch around her. "I can't believe I didn't see the answer."

"What?" Karen asked.

"Mikey asked me last night that if I felt the Holy Ghost, why did I need to get baptized."

Karen's eyes widened as she stared at her daughter. No wonder Mikey was helping around the house. She was buttering up her mother so she could go around doing whatever she wanted. It didn't matter that she was messing with dangerous, life-threatening things.

"The answer was so simple. I must have forgotten," Betsy rambled on, "but it says here in *Gospel Principles* on page 138: 'A person may be temporarily guided by the Holy Ghost without receiving the gift of the Holy Ghost. However, this guidance will not be continuous unless he receives baptism and the laying on of the hands for the gift of the Holy Ghost.'"

Karen kept her focus on Mikey, who studied the floor, and frowned, giving her aunt several irritated glances.

"This excites my soul," Betsy said, slamming her book shut. "The fact

I can find answers to my questions convinces me the Church is true."

"This is depressing. I need a bike ride," Mikey said, slipping out the side door.

Karen sighed and took another bite of her cereal. "Sometimes I wonder about that child."

Betsy smiled.

"What are you smiling about? Are you trying to make my kids Mormon?" Karen slammed her spoon against the bowl.

"I-I-I," Betsy said.

"Pretty sneaky if you ask me." Karen stood up.

"Just a minute, Karen."

She turned with her hands on her tan suit jacket and glared at Betsy. "What?"

"I'm not trying to make your children Mormons. Honestly I'm not."

"Sure," Karen said, heading from the room.

❦

"Get the spinach saga. It'll awaken your senses." George said at lunch.

"Spinach?" Karen questioned, but was too full with awe to use much emphasize. Had she stepped out of Provo to the other side of the world?

The dimly lit restaurant was filled with exotically dressed people, dancing through the shadows. The servers' dark skin intrigued her. Their coloring was blacker than she'd ever seen. It held a radiant beauty within its richness.

The waiters wore expensive robes, draped toward the floor. Their shirts fell to their calves, and pants sunk down beyond — figure flattering and comfortable. Where could she get some?

George crossed his arms onto his chest with a bit of a twinkle in his eye.

Once Karen watched him, he said, "Wait 'til you taste the curry. Much better than ours."

"When did you eat here?"

"Last week for a business meeting. They do everything family style, so we'll share our dishes."

"How can this exist in Provo?"

"There's a lot about Utah that will surprise you. It's not as bad as you'd guessed."

"The server arrived to take their order. He spoke with a heavy accent, and after he left, Karen leaned onto the table and asked,

"What did he say?"

Her husband shrugged.

They chatted lightly about George's work through the fine dining of spinach, rice, and garlic pita bread. George had been right, it was good and different from anything she'd eaten. Hot and spicy.

"There must be fat hidden somewhere in here," Karen said. "It tastes too good."

"I bet they use olive oil."

"Good. I was getting worried I was liking something that didn't have fat grams."

"Karen."

She looked up.

"I'm sorry you feel I'm undermining you with Mikey."

"I am too."

"I'll try not to do it again."

Relief spread through Karen. That had been so easy. George was finally coming to his senses.

"But I, on the other hand, don't feel it's right to scare our children half to death over something we know nothing about," George said.

"We do too. They're evil — "

"Please let me finish."

The water boy arrived and tipped his pitcher to the side, filling the glass cups to the top.

"I've known my sister a long time. And yes, she's unusual, but she's not dumb, and she doesn't get involved in stuff that's dangerous. My sister has a practical sense about her that you might not suspect. He paused for a bite of food, then continued. "If she thinks there's value in the Mormon church, I'll trust her judgment."

"That doesn't sound good — "

"I'm not finished."

"But — "

"When I was in high school some of my friends brought home Dungeons and Dragons, a fantasy participation game — it has Satanic tendency to it. They said that it was a real kick, and I'd love playing it. My sister was as curious as I. They told her about it too, but she said we shouldn't play it. It was evil, and if we got caught up in that kind of stuff, we'd regret it. I, of course, wasn't going to listen. My sister grabbed my shoulders, glared at me, and said, 'That game will suck you up into devil worship. Stay away.' I asked her how she knew, if she'd seen it before. She said, 'No, I sense it.' I laughed at her, but she made me promise I wouldn't play."

Karen stared at her husband's pained face. His blue eyes seemed to have changed into a grayish blue, reflecting a stormy sky. "Were those the ones you've talked about before who made a suicide pack and killed themselves?"

"Yeah. Two years later the game progressed into satanic rituals and other things. This had such a strong hold on them… My sister knew. We all have special talents. My sister's is to detect good."

"That story is awful. I know it was hard on you."

"Not so bad," George said, avoiding eye contact.

"Come on. I can see it affected you terribly."

"I'm healed. The only reason I bring it up is to show that my sister has good sense and you should trust her."

Karen ate a slice of garlic bread in silence. He wanted her to accept the Mormons because his sister sensed good. Nonsense. She also had a right to be angry at Mikey because she had lied, and that wasn't acceptable. But Karen wasn't going to mention that. It would ruin lunch, and she wanted seconds.

George finished eating the last of the pita bread, which Karen looked at longingly until the last crumb disappeared in his mouth. Then he said, "I don't see how you can call Mormons a cult anyway. Aren't they like Baptists and Protestants, just another branch of Christianity?"

"The definition of a cult, according to my Webster Dictionary at home, is a religion regarded as unorthodox or spurious. The Mormon church fits this definition because they're illegitimate. They don't claim to be a break-off from the Christians churches like the Protestants and Lutherans. Their church didn't begin until the 1800s with Joe Smith."

"That's not a cult. A cult is where some whacked leader brainwashes their followers and has them do crazy stuff, like Waco and the Hale-Bopp groups. Those I'd be wary of, but Mormons don't shave their heads, collect a bunch of weapons, or live in a compound where outsiders aren't allowed."

"You never know. Maybe they're even more dangerous than the others because they appear harmless," Karen said. "The group my friend's mom belonged to didn't appear harmful either until we found Charissa dead."

George scooped on another serving of sage and rice from the center of the table. "Tell me about what happened."

Her body stiffened. "I don't remember."

"Come on, Karen, something that traumatic? Surely you can recall a detail or two."

"I remember going into the house looking for Charissa, feeling scared and like evil pressed on me from all sides. Her room was empty. It felt snoopy going into her mom's bedroom, but the answer waited there. That's it. The same thing I always tell you."

"Before, then. Can you remember anything that happened before that? Do you recall anything unusual? Did her mom meet with this group? Did they wear the same clothes?"

Karen shook her head. "Nothing." But the word "meeting" triggered something in her mind — a familiarity. A scene flooded back where she had questioned the organization and wanted to learn more about their meetings. She could hear herself asking Charissa questions from a long time ago. "Why are there always so many people at your house?"

"They come for meetings. They call them the Magdalene Management Meeting."

"It seems like they're always here," Karen had whispered as one of them walked passed the girls. The women were dressed in a long brown robes with other clothes underneath, which gave a layered look —

"They are," Charissa said, pointing to them entering her back door then slip silently downstairs. "I wish they wouldn't come. They give me the creeps."

"Have you told your mom?" Karen had asked.

"No, she wouldn't understand. She'd make me be with them more so I'd learn how great they were. No thanks. I'd rather spend my time with my best friend. Doesn't that sound like a good plan?"

"Sure does."

Karen hadn't blamed her friend for not wanting to hang out with the group. They were strange. The memory faded as she heard her husband's insistent voice. His voice registered in her mind. "Nothing, nothing at all?"

"No, nothing. My mind's blank," Karen said. She'd lost her appetite and longed to be at home sleeping.

❧

It was Saturday night and uneasiness drew Karen from her sleep. She struggled for more rest, but something hovered over her, casting a shadow against the spilling morning light. She slowly opened one eye, then the other, and came face to face with Sam. "What?" she grumbled, closing her eyes.

"Can we talk?"

"What?" she muttered, bending her arm over her eyes.

"Why are you avoiding me?"

"What are you talking about?" Her arm slid up just above her eyebrow.

"The other day you said you'd talk to me after you finished with Mikey. You never came."

"What?"

"The day when everyone talked in the room next to this one."

Karen wished morning had never arrived. "Sorry, I forgot. What did you want?"

"To see how you're doing and tell you I made the soccer team." He plopped on the mattress next to her.

"Congratulations. That's great." She touched the sleeve of his shirt. "I'm so lucky to have a son like you. Most parents gripe up the wall about how terrible their teenagers are, but you're not like that. You're not self-centered like the magazine articles say you should be. I'm grateful."

Sam continued to stare. "Most moms don't end up in the hospital because they had a panic attack over a religious group, either."

Where did that come from? Words refused to form in her mouth. He was being nice and then suddenly shot her with a zinger. What could she say?

"Mom." Impatience spread across his face.

"Yes."

"I don't get why you're so freaked about Mormons. I heard they're like other mainstream Christian churches."

Karen sat up in her bed. "Have you been talking to your father?"

"No, why?" The sunlight highlighted the auburn in his hair.

"You sound like him. That's all. Listen," Karen said, placing her hand on his knee. "I appreciate your concern for me. Really, I do. I'm fine. Don't worry. Okay? I'm a big girl and can handle myself."

"But Mom, if you'd listen to me then you wouldn't worry about Mormons anymore. They're not as bad as you think."

"Look," she took her hand off his knee. "I'm fine and I don't want to talk about it. So how's your grades?"

"All right," he said, searching her face. He must have decided she meant business because he gave up the effort to talk to her and left, mumbling about kicking a ball around.

Chapter 8

Sunday. The birds chirped, welcoming the day. The sun spread over the red maple trees and the pea green cedar. The light cast a golden glow. Betsy turned from her window, filled with nature's glory. Time to prepare so her new ward could meet her at her best. What dress would truly represent her? She flipped through a rainbow of choices — alabaster, ash, acorn or amber, auburn, crimson, flamingo, apricot, dandelion, lilac — until her hand surged with electricity at the touch of her deep royal purple dress trimmed with lavender. It had golden sparkles spread throughout the silky fabric. Perfect. Purple revealed her heritage, and gold represented the value she'd be to the congregation. She added long earrings and two-inch purple heal shoes to the ensemble. Smiling, she felt satisfied she'd be noticed.

A fleeting thought of Philippe raced through her mind. She wished he could see her decked out in her best decor... Why was she thinking these thoughts? She needed to take a broom and sweep away such ideas. They were crossing over the lines of friendship, and she definitely didn't want anything more. Hadn't she learned her lesson? But, she had to admit it was lonely being alone.

⁂

The time had come for her to enter the Seventy-ish looking church building and make her mark. She watched the others heading for the front door. A few people dashed by her, giving her a quick smile before being swallowed up in the chapel. She joined the gravitation and was greeted by a wrinkled man, who nodded and handed her a paper.

"What's this for?" she asked.

"Program."

"I thought I was coming to a church service not a program. Is there a charge for this production, and what are they putting on?"

The man cleared his throat and stared at her with wide eyes. "Um, it's an outline of the service. There's no productions in the chapel."

"Why didn't you say so?" Betsy walked on. She spotted two

elderly ladies, leaning toward each other, chatting. They sat in the middle of the bench, and the rest of the space was empty. One of the ladies leaned in even closer listening, her hair twisted in a bun the color of a grayish-blue sky.

The other lady, the talker, had deep brown hair with tight frizzing curls swirling outward, aging her more than her years. Typical elderly.

Betsy neared them. Might as well give them a go. "Hello," she said loudly.

They gazed up in surprise. "Hi," one muttered.

"Nice day for a church service, isn't it?" Betsy asked.

"Yes," Blue-Bun lady said. "It is." She studied Betsy's outfit. Her nose slightly turned. "I don't believe I've met you."

Betsy smiled. "You haven't. I got baptized last week, and this is my first time here officially."

The second lady leaned forward to see around the first. "Really?"

"Yep. I'm sinless. Perfect. I bet you two wish you were just baptized."

The ladies smiled weakly.

"So are you in our ward?" asked Frizzy-Brown-haired lady.

"Sure am. I live in an upstairs apartment in my brother's home. He and his wife bought the Melvilles' old house."

"You don't say?"

The place impressed the two. "Yeah, I'm the first in the household to be buried in the water, but I'm working to get the rest to take the plunge. How about you two sisters helping me?"

"Us?" they asked, staring.

"Yep. You two would be perfect." Betsy turned to Blue-Hair and said, "I like your aura."

"Are what?" Frizz-Hair asked.

"Aura."

"Oh," they whispered.

"Well, will you do it?"

"Do what?" Blue-Hair asked.

"Help me baptize my brother and his family."

Silent shock crossed their faces. Blue-Hair's mouth dropped slightly open; then she said, "Wh-what do you mean? What do you want us to do?"

"You see, my sister-in-law has depression and some other problems, and she thinks you Mormons are evil and is afraid of you. If you come over and show her we're not that bad, then she won't be afraid. Maybe she can learn about the Spirit like I did and have comfort. It's important for her. She's so sad and thinks you're devils who are going to destroy her family so — "

A bald man in his late fifties drifted to the pulpit. "I'd like to welcome you all out to church this morning. It's so nice to see your happy, smiling faces."

Betsy glanced at the two elderly ladies. They had many expressions, but not a smile. What was the problem?

"How about it, girls?" she whispered.

"Well, hmm — "

"It'll make such a difference in her life. I'm excited thinking about what the church will do for her."

"We'll do it," Blue-Haired lady said.

Brown-Frizz planted her elbow in Blue-Hair's side. Why wouldn't they jump at any opportunity to share the gospel with someone, especially someone who needed it as badly as Karen?

The meeting continued. Betsy's thoughts drifted, especially when a heavy guy got up and rambled on in a monotone. Betsy smiled when she saw the skinny bald guy who sat on the stage nodding off to sleep.

A lot of the meeting she spent observing, familiarizing herself with the people who'd become a part of her life. Most reflected good auras, but some caught her attention because of their unique vibes. If her paths crossed with theirs, it would be interesting.

The one that drew her senses most was a young boy with brown hair long on top and butched on the nape. He snapped his gum in a continual round, sounding like a machine gun going off. He'd look at the speaker, roll his eyes, and pop his gum. Once he caught one of Agatha's sisters watching him, with her curly blond hair draping into her big eyes. He sneered at the child, then blew another bubble in her direction. He sucked the bubble back in his mouth, as though he wanted to devour her. The little girl grabbed Agatha's arm in terror. Agatha wrapped her arm around her protectively.

That boy needed straightening up. Betsy bet he'd gotten his way because people felt sorry for him being perched in that metal wheelchair. She didn't. She could whip him into shape in no time.

After the closing prayer, Betsy turned and asked Blue-Hair, "What's your name?"

"Sister Stanfield."

"And your friend?"

"Sister Dahl."

"Nice to met you Mrs. Stanfield and Mrs. Dahl. I'm sure you'll do a great job teaching my sister-in-law that you aren't suppressed by men. You two fine ladies would never put up with that kind of abuse."

"Humph," Brown-Frizz said.

Mrs. Stanfield rubbed her hands and cleared her throat. "You said you're a new convert, didn't you?"

"Did." Betsy batted her eyes.

"Then you've met the Bishop and know what class you're suppose to go to?"

"Haven't."

"The missionaries didn't even introduce you to the Bishop?"

"Nope. The top guys demanded they go somewhere else, so they up and left in a hurry."

"You mean they got transferred?" Mrs. Dahl asked.

"Just don't live here any more. The guys in charge figured they'd done enough damage in one location. They did baptize me."

The two ladies laughed weakly.

"Well," said Mrs. Stanfield, "let's go meet the Bishop."

"Point the way," Betsy said. "Or better yet, I bet I can pick which one it is from his vibrations. Oh, this is going to be fun to try." The two ladies raised eyebrows as they looked at each other, while Betsy barged ahead of them.

"Let's see. I bet he's one of those people who sat behind the speakers."

"That's right," Mrs. Stanfield said.

"Hmm, he probably wasn't the snoring one because that wouldn't be a good leader quality. Maybe he was the one with the thick glasses that kept sliding down his nose?"

"Why don't we go toward them as you try to guess?" Mrs. Dahl asked.

"What a great idea," Betsy said. "I'll get a better sense of their vibrations."

They headed toward the guy with the thick glasses. Betsy closed her eyes and stopped walking. She put her arms out and hummed. She opened her eyes again and said, "It's not him. I don't sense any power within. He's being dominated."

Mrs. Dahl said, "That's my husband you're talking about. There's no way he's dominated."

Mrs. Stanfield struggled to keep from laughing, but failed.

"He's not," Mrs. Dahl said.

"Okay." Mrs. Stanfield smiled. She turned to Betsy and put her hand on Betsy's arm. "You're right about at least one thing. He's not the Bishop."

Mrs. Dahl said, "Well, got to go." She marched over to her husband. Betsy and Mrs. Stanfield watched her go, pull him away from the person he talked to and pointed at them.

"Not dominated at all," Mrs. Stanfield said.

They next came to the second man on the stage. He had graying hair, a bit of a pot gut, and thin glasses. He walked up to them with an air of strong confidence. Betsy immediately liked the way he carried himself — with an elegance most men lacked. There was a sense of power yet kindness in this man.

Betsy couldn't help but smile. Strong confident men were so attractive. "Hold it right there," Betsy said, putting her arm out and touching his designer suit. His tie weaved shapes with shocking and shell pink, dabs of grass green, and alizarin crimson. A man with taste.

Betsy closed her eyes, sad at having to look away from such a work of art in his tie. She hummed.

"What?" the man asked in a deep baritone voice.

"She's tapping into your soul," Mrs. Stanfield said.

"What?" His voice had an absorbing quality.

"Shhh. She needs quiet to concentrate."

Betsy hummed for a couple more seconds, feeling the power within this man, then opened her eyes. "You're not, but I sense you will be soon. There's greatness within you."

"What are you talking about?"

"She's trying to guess who the Bishop is."

The man's deep brown eyes grew big. "You think I'll be the Bishop soon?"

Betsy nodded.

The man laughed. "Yeah, right."

"I'm not kidding," Betsy said, placing her hand firmly on her hips. "You doubt my powers of intuition?" She raised her eyebrows.

The man smiled, revealing perfect pearly whites. Another plus. What could be the chances of him being single? Slim to none, Betsy decided. Gold were always taken. She'd have to admire from afar.

"I can't be a Bishop."

"Why's that?" Betsy asked with a flirtatious smile. What was she doing?

He smiled back, causing her to melt more. No, she wasn't going to be another Elizabeth Taylor. She refused to have such a weakness. Refused. Betsy-old-gal, remember men are charming, but they cheat. Dang them.

"I'm widowed. They normally like their leaders married. You know leadership can be lonely." His bronze eyes consumed her.

"I imagine," she said. She'd been single for three years. She liked it that way. She was going to keep it that way, bronze eyes or not. "How long since you lost your…your wife?"

"A year." He lowered his eyes. Flashes of pain darted across his face.

"I'm sorry. She must have been some lady for you to choose her."

Still avoiding eye contact, he said, "She was. She was. One heck of a lady. She had cherry-red hair and was a pit-bull of a woman to deal with. Life's been real dull since she…" His voice faded.

"I'm so sorry. You must be a strong man," Betsy said, putting her hand on his shoulder tenderly.

He looked down into her eyes and smiled. "I'll survive. It's my son I'm worried about. He hasn't been the same since the wreck."

"How old?"

"Eleven."

"If he's anything like his father, he'll come out of this with flying colors."

He smiled sadly, and Betsy wished she could wrap her arms around him to comfort his troubled soul.

A bald man with a strip of hair around the crown of his head came up to them gasping, "Brother Chadwick, there you are. We've been searching everywhere for you. You've got to come now."

He turned sadly toward Betsy, "I forgot. Sorry, I got to go. It was nice meeting you."

"You too," Betsy said. "And don't worry, you'll make a great preacher." She smiled.

"Preacher?" the man asked as he walked away. He glanced back at her twice, running into a bench the second time.

Chuckling, Betsy turned to Mrs. Stanfield. "What is his first name?"

Jeff.

Jeff Chadwick. There was a nice subtle sound behind the letters. She ran her hands through her hair and said, "That means the sleeping guy was the Bishop."

"You got it. Let's go introduce you."

Betsy marched up the stairs and hustled to the man who wiped his eyes; his thick mounds of gray-ringlet hair bounced with his movement. She said, "Glad to see you've woken up." He gave her a faint smile, revealing signs of his age by causing depth to his wrinkles, probably in his late fifties.

Mrs. Stanfield jogged up to him and said, "Bishop, I'd like to introduce you to the newest member of our ward. Mrs.…I'm embarrassed. I never got your name."

"Miss Betsy Ashforth. Only been married twice, and both experiences were lethal. If I did it again, I think I'd shoot myself."

"Sorry. Nice to meet you."

"And you're the preacher," Betsy said, extending her hand out.

"A Bishop actually."

"Oh, yeah, that's right. I haven't got the terms straightened out."

"So are you a new convert?" the Bishop asked.

"Sure am."

"She was baptized last week, and the missionaries who baptized her have already been transferred," Mrs. Stanfield said.

"So they left you on your own, did they?" The Bishop smiled. "Well, since you're new, we have a special class for you that'll help you learn the basic principles of the gospel. I got the class going again last week. They'll love to have you. Why don't I take you?"

"So the other adults who know more go to a different class than the new members?" Betsy asked, flicking her nails against each other.

"Just until you've got a good grip on the basics. I don't want you to be lost."

"I'll go to that newcomers' class today, but I don't like the idea of going to a class different from all the other baptized members."

"It's only so that you can get a basic understanding of our beliefs," the Bishop said, with a faint pink color crawling up his face.

"What do I need to do to prove to you I have this understanding?" Betsy asked.

"Go through the course," the Bishop said.

"What if I don't want to waste time? I don't like waiting to learn 'til Sunday."

"Tell you what, if I give you a quiz and you can answer every question correctly, then I'll give an early promotion, but until then I'd really like you to go to that class. Is that a deal?"

"It's a deal," Betsy said, extending her hand.

The Bishop ushered Betsy into a small classroom. Two people sat in folding chairs, watching as a young man wrote on the board. The seated couple sent Betsy a weak smile as she joined them. They were young and glowed so much that they still must be newly married. Betsy knew too well the happy shine would fade. It was only a matter of time. The man was young and probably an underfed student by the looks of his skinny frame. The girl had pretty big speckled eyes and long permed brown hair. The couple was cute, but young enough to be mistaken for high school sweethearts.

"Here's the newest member of our ward, Sister Ashforth," the Bishop said.

"Welcome," said the young man teacher. He was probably one of those business want-to-bes, judging from his nice suit, but not quite the genuine thing. He also carried around a fake leather briefcase, which was opened, revealing neatly place papers, pencils, and pens, each in their assigned spot. He had the Ken doll haircut and ambition in his eye. "We're glad to have another person."

"Thanks," Betsy said, wiggling around in her chair. It excited her to be taught again even though it was a beginner's course. She enjoyed those warm feelings inside when the sisters had taught.

The Bishop exited, and the man cleared his throat and straightened his jacket. "Let me introduce myself. I'm Jack Kirby and this is Dan and Vickie Robinson. I was just asking them what feelings they have when they think of the word 'force.' Do you have any ideas?"

"Men," Betsy said.

Brother Kirby cleared his throat again while Sister Robinson laughed. Brother Robinson gave Betsy a few looks as though he wondered what she meant. The silence signaled to Betsy that further explanation was needed, though the word "men" explained it. "They've been in control since the beginning of time, trying to force women and children to be their slaves. They even tried to get the environment and animals to obey their commands."

"That's an interesting thought," Brother Kirby said. "Does anyone else have something to add?"

"My dad was always forcing me to do everything around the house," Sister Robinson said.

"Really?" Betsy asked. "How did he control you?"

"His belt. It did the trick nicely. All he had to do was touch it, and I'd run to do anything he'd ask."

"I hate the way men dominate with strength," Betsy said.

"Here. Here," Sister Robinson said.

"I don't control you," Brother Robinson said in a loud voice. He bit his tongue. "I don't. How do I control you?" The honeymoon was coming to a screeching halt.

"It seems we've strayed a little off the subject," Brother Kirby said, his right eye twitching. "Is it safe say to that when we think of force we don't have very good ideas come to mind?"

"You can say that again," Betsy said.

Brother Kirby sighed. "What comes to mind with the word 'choice?'"

"What the women's' movement has done for the whole female sex," Betsy said.

"Uh," Brother Kirby mumbled, barely audible. "Anything else?"

Did Brother Kirby not like her answers? No matter, he was male. The sister missionaries had warned her before coming to church that the gospel was truth, but the people were human as everyone else. They had good and bad, but this didn't mean the gospel wasn't true.

"Decisions," Sister Robinson said.

"Very good," Brother Kirby said. "Having decision or agency in our lives is a necessary part of our salvation. It's what this earth life is all about. But with choosing or making choices comes responsibility. Brother Robinson, would you please read to us from Helaman 14: 30-31?"

"Sure. '*And now remember, remember, my brethren...do good and be restored unto that which is good...or ye can do evil, and have that which is evil restored unto you.*'"

"Thank you. Can anyone tell me what that scripture means?"

"Oh, oh, I can," Betsy said, waving her arm in the air. "This was the scripture I heard when I first felt the Spirit. I was so impressed with the fact that the Mormons accepted free thinking philosophies. Most Christians aren't as accepting as to put this kind of philosophy into their doctrines."

Brother Kirby wrinkled his chubby nose. "What exactly are you talking about?"

"The philosophy of karma; what you do will be returned to you."

Brother Kirby picked up his scriptures and peered into them. "I guess you could get that. But let's look at it again from the perspective of choice and force."

"But karma philosophy is all about choice. If you choose to burn bridges with people and to be dishonest, eventually it'll catch up to you, and if you choose to be kind and work hard, that'll catch up too," Betsy said.

"I like that," Sister Robinson said. "That's what God's plan is about."

"How's that?" Brother Kirby asked.

"From what you said earlier about the council in heaven, we decided whether we wanted to follow Christ and have choices or follow Lucifer and be forced into being saved."

"Yes, and what did we choose?"

"Agency," Sister Robinson said.

Brother Robinson raised his hand.

"Yes, Brother Robinson?"

"This applies to the way we live our lives. We shouldn't force others to do what we want them to do even if it's the best thing. That would be following Satan's."

"Exactly," Brother Kirby said. "I'm excited how well you learned these principles. This is great."

Betsy raised her hand.

"Yes, Sister Ashforth?"

"Do you really think we're following Satan when we try to get others to do things?"

"That's a difficult question. And I don't think there's any clear cut answer. But in answer to your question, it's a danger. We have to be careful. Kind of like those evil men we talked about earlier. Why are their actions so wrong?"

"Cause they weren't allowing women to think and be themselves," Betsy said.

"Exactly. Whenever we inflict our will on others, we need to be careful."

"That's interesting," Betsy said. Was she guilty of this? She glanced at Brother Kirby. "But what if the other person is going to be a danger to themselves and perhaps even their existence?"

Brother Kirby's right eye twitched again, repeatedly. "That's why I said it's tricky. What would Jesus do?" The room was silent. "He'd try to save us, don't you think?" Brother Kirby asked.

Betsy agreed. He'd already saved them by dying for them, and He'd do all He could to keep us on the ascension to heaven.

After the class ended, Betsy thanked Brother Kirby.

"You're welcome. Glad to have you in our class."

"Thanks. I, mmm, I, kinda want to ask you something, but I don't want to be rude."

"What's that?"

"It makes me feel uncomfortable to belong to an organization and not know everything about it."

"Uh-huh?"

"And I like your class, but I don't like being on the beginner level. So how I can learn all this stuff by next week?"

"Next week?"

"Yeah."

"Well, I'm really busy at work. I've got a demanding job and a wife and kids — "

"Oh, no, don't get me wrong. I want to learn on my own. Is there a book that outlines your lessons?"

"You should try Deseret Book. They'd have a lot of books that could be helpful, and they'd have the manual I use."

"Thanks. What's the name?"

"Gospel Principles."

"Oh, I already have that."

"It should be a good resource."

Betsy found Sister Robinson waiting in the hall. "Hi," she said. "I liked your comments today."

"Thanks."

"Want to go to Relief Society?" Sister Robinson asked.

"Sure."

"Brother Kirby sure seems like a vacuum sweeper, doesn't he?" Betsy asked.

"How's that?" Sister Robinson asked.

"He's full of dust and hot air."

Sister Robinson smiled as they entered the Relief Society room. She saw empty chairs on the back row and pointed. "Want to sit there?"

Betsy shook her head. "There's a bunch of chairs on the front row." She marched up and sat in front of the pulpit. She turned around and watched Sister Robinson inching behind her.

A short round lady with gray hair pulled in a bun waddled over to them. "Hello, hello." Her voice sang a C note.

"Howdy," Betsy said loudly.

The lady's grin faded as she studied Betsy; then she asked, "You all new?"

"Yep, just baptized last week," Betsy said.

Sister Robinson said weakly, "I've been coming for about a month."

"You have?" the lady asked, taken by surprise.

"Yes, Sister Coons. You ask me if I'm new every week."

"I do?"

"For three weeks."

"How embarrassing. I can't seem to remember a thing." She laughed heartily.

"You need to work on your creative visualization and your positive scenario placement; then you wouldn't have that problem," Betsy said.

The lady's gray eyes widened. "What?"

"You need to work on your meditation powers."

"Oh."

"I can help if you don't know how. Do you?"

"Yes…I mean no."

"The first thing you need to do is release your limitations. In this instance it's your limitation in memorizing." Betsy looked up as the lady stared down at her. "This is going to be awhile. Why don't you sit?" Betsy patted the chair next to her.

"I've got to get this meeting started. Maybe some other time. I promise I won't forget who you are."

Mrs. Robinson laughed. "I bet she won't either."

The meeting passed quickly, and Betsy filled the time raising her hand with lots of questions and comments. She was glad she had chosen to sit in front, or otherwise, the teacher might never have seen her hand waving. The teacher did seem to have a vision problem when it came to noticing her hand.

Chapter 9

Sunday morning, Karen lie on her bed, eyes shut, not tired enough to sleep, but too exhausted to move. Last night she'd dreamed of Charissa, her thick straw-yellow hair, natural waves contouring her oval face. Glistening baby-blue eyes accented the perfectly matched blouses or dresses. She'd been a beautiful girl. In her dream they ran along the golden beach, Charissa ahead, laughing, tossing her head. Her hair bounced. Running faster, Karen struggled to catch up, but stumbled over a rock and fell. After she wiped the dirt and gravel off her hands, she yelled, "Charissa wait!" Her friend didn't hear. Charissa laughed. The sky grew gray, and the cold wind started to blow, making Karen's heart beat faster. She stopped running. The shadow of her friend had vanished. Something wasn't right. Charissa had been in front, but now she couldn't see a trace of her. The blackness swirled, wrapping around her like a big blanket. Her lungs squeezed with each piercing breath. When she inhaled, fire shot through her. She screamed and screamed until darkness consumed her.

The dream skipped to when she'd found Charissa — her creamy yellow hair smeared in dried blood. Karen's head spun. Blackness.

Why wouldn't these images leave? For years she could recall nothing and now they seem to consume her mind. Over and over since she woke, she saw her friend running — laughing — then bloodsmeared in her hair, lying in a pool of red. No!!!! Karen cried. It can't be. I can't...

She must stop thinking about it. Tomorrow she'd keep her appointment with the psychologist, and he'd get on her case about negative thinking. He didn't understand. She wasn't overgeneralizing; bad things were happening because Betsy had become a cult member. Circumstances struck her so similar to the Magdalene cult. The mention of Mormons drudged up her memory. Dang them. Dang Betsy. Karen didn't want to remember. She wished those remembrances remained asleep forever. It didn't warrant her time or attention. That cult had already taken the most important thing — her best friend. Those whacked people weren't going to get anything else. She squeezed her eyes shut and shook her head to cleanse her mind of the dark thoughts. No more. She needed to stop the source of the evil… her sister-in-law.

Betsy had brought evil into their house. Just yesterday Karen discovered Mikey wasn't talking to Betsy. Mikey refused to say why, but Betsy becoming a Mormon had to be the root. A cult's evil was infectious.

The distant grandfather clock struck twelve. Betsy would radiate poison in a few minutes when she returned from the meeting. Meeting…meeting…

"They're always meetings over here, more and more often," Charissa had said.

Toward the end, Karen had seen the cult members daily, dressed in robes with hoods pulled over their heads. They'd slip down Charissa's stairs and wouldn't acknowledge her. Once they had nodded, said hi, or smiled, but eventually they avoided her completely. When she snatched a glimpse of their faces, fear overwhelmed her. Each members eyes appeared glassy, as if drugged.

Shaking her head against her pillow, Karen groaned. Why were those memories coming back? She didn't want to remember. How could she stop them?…Stop Betsy from being a Mormon. How? Maybe Betsy could do that for herself on her first trip to their meeting. Maybe those Mormons wouldn't like Betsy and her bright purple hair, her inch thick make-up, or her overbearing personality.

How were the Mormons going to react when they discovered Betsy's plans to overtake the organization and become the new self-appointed leader, forcing everyone to perform yoga and breathing exercises? Their leader wouldn't tolerate such behavior and would cast her out of their church quicker than she'd chomp on her gum. The leader's only other option was to murder her.

Karen struggled to breathe. Danger. Cults were bad. Would it be possible to resist its evil power?

A high-pitched wobbly voice interrupted her thoughts. *"Put your shoul-der to the wheel; push a-long. Do you du-ty with a heart full of song. We all have work; let no one shirk. Put your shoul-der to the wheel."*

Betsy's voice grew closer. Karen twisted her blanket in her hand. She hadn't been cast out of church yet. Actually it sounded as if she had become entrenched with their witchery. Pulse racing, Karen waited for the purple concoction to enter her room.

"Good afternoon." Betsy poked her reddish-purple hair around Karen's bedroom door. She smiled.

"How's church?" Karen whispered.

"Marvelous. A little different, of course, and it's going to take getting used to. But I really like the way it calms me. An excellent experience."

"Enough of the sales pitch," Karen said. Betsy had been brainwashed.

"I'm going to warm up vegetable soup. Then we can go on a walk."

"But I don't — "

"It's such a beautiful day. You'll hate me if I don't get you out there to enjoy nature, especially since we live in the middle of it. Get dressed. Besides, you'll get blood poisoning if you sit all day. "

"I thought you were going to make me do all the cooking myself," Karen choked. The thought of a stroll with her sister-in-law was too much.

"You're doing a lousy job, so I'm helping. The soup should be ready in about twenty minutes."

Betsy left. Karen hated it when Betsy insisted she exercise, but protesting was useless. Like it or not, she would go on a walk with Betsy. Hopefully they wouldn't run into Mormons, and Betsy wouldn't try that brainwashing stuff.

❦

Betsy hummed as she floated down the hallway. The yellow daylight surrounded her. Church had gone well, and George's prediction that the people wouldn't accept her couldn't have been further from the truth if he'd said it rained every day in the desert. So much for his ESP. She'd fit nicely in this organization. She was the missing piece they'd been searching for.

When she had left this morning, Mikey was still in bed. Pretty normal, considering she was a typical teen who enjoyed mounds of sleep. Sam had risen earlier, of course, with a soccer ball bouncing off his forehead as he headed outside. She'd better check on her niece.

As Betsy neared Mikey's bedroom door, she heard New Age music. It wasn't the beach music or natural sounds Betsy liked. It sounded like elves dancing in circles with tiny bells sewn on their green pointed shoes.

Betsy banged on the door. The notes passed her; she pounded again, louder. Then again. Betsy called, "Mikey?" as she opened the door. The girl sat on the bed, fluffing her hair. Must be movie time in her head.

"Yes," Mikey said in a deep drawn-out voice. Maybe she was trying to imitate Marilyn Monroe. They'd watched one of the actress' classic movies together a little over a week ago.

Her face shriveled into a tight frown when she saw Betsy. "What do you want?"

Mikey looked like her mother, being in her bed, staring into space with a fixed expression. This wasn't good. She needed to help Mikey before the child sank deeper into depression. If there was one thing Betsy had learned through her own struggles with depression, was that friendship, activity, and positive thinking were key forces in beating the disease.

"Mikey?" Betsy said.

"What?"

"Come help me make lunch for your mom."

"I'm not talking to you." She lay down, turning away from Betsy.

"I don't care if you're talking or not. Get up. We're going to help your mom before this thing gets worse. Let's go. You're going on a walk with us after lunch."

"No — "

"Yes. Get."

Betsy saw another protest coming. "Now." She pulled the blankets off Mikey, who gave her an evil glare. Betsy ignored her and pulled Mikey's arm, leading her into the kitchen.

Mikey grumbled, "You don't care about Mom, so why are you putting up such a show?"

"You little brat," Betsy said, sharper than she intended.

Her niece lowered her head.

"Sorry. I don't want to hear 'I don't care about your mother' again. Will you please let me explain what I meant the other day?" Betsy asked.

"You can try," Mikey said, sliding out a kitchen chair.

"Sorry it'll be Mormon stuff, but it happens to be an important part of the story."

Mikey rolled her eyes and Betsy continued. "The only reason I spoke to the sister missionaries was because I heard the Mormons believed in spirits and conversing with God. Naturally, it got me wondering, and I wanted to learn more. I had no intention of joining. From experience I've found most organizations have some good stuff in them, but I don't agree with everything. So no use in joining and giving them money. Anyway, I thought the church would be helpful with my meditation. Give me a few points. That kind of thing."

Betsy paused as she washed the carrots. She slid the cutting board and a knife to Mikey. "Why don't you chop these carrot sticks to go with the soup while I talk?"

Mikey chopped without a word.

"The first time those ladies talked to me, they read a scripture explaining karma. A warmth spread inside me. It affected me more than meditation. I knew then there was something to these Mormons. The Sisters explained this warm feeling was God's spirit telling me the church was true. It gave me such comfort that I want your mom to feel it. Her getting the spirit is the only way to cure her. The rest of the stuff we do is helpful, but her soul won't be healed until she understands how God loves her."

Betsy finished putting the soup in the pot and grabbed Mikey's carrots. She kneeled and peered into her niece's eyes. "Do you understand?"

Mikey shrugged.

"Do you still think I purposely hurt your mother?"

"I guess not," Mikey whispered. Betsy barely heard. She tried to read her niece's face. Mikey looked away.

"Can't you see it might not have been the right thing to do, but I believed it was?" Betsy asked.

"Whatever," Mikey muttered.

That was the best she'd get. She might as well save her energy for the walk because then she'd have two depressed people deal with.

"Where's the food?" Sam said, sprinting into the kitchen, rubbing his hands together. "I'm starved."

"Good. You can help cook," Betsy said, searching for a spoon. "Find crackers, then stir this."

"Oh, man, that's woman's work," Sam said.

Betsy waved her long fingernail. "You better watch it, bud. Any more sexist expressions and you'll be doing the cooking and cleaning in this house."

In an overdramatic motion, he closed his mouth and swallowed.

Mikey chuckled. "Sam, she doesn't mean it. Say something sexist." She cut the cauliflower Betsy handed her.

"No way. I'm not crazy."

The group fell into silence as they worked. Betsy looked over Sam. He was shooting up like an ugly weed — too skinny, freckles, and pimples. His shoulders raised, then shrunk as though disappointed. "Whatcha thinking about, Sam?"

"I'm worried about Mom."

"Why?"

"She's pale and stays in bed a lot. We should — " he paused, glancing at the window then to the floor.

"What? Pray?" Mikey asked in a sarcastic tone.

"Why not?" Sam asked. "It might help."

"Yeah, just like it helps Aunt Betsy."

"What's that supposed to mean?" Betsy asked, putting her hands on her waist.

"She seems to think it works," Sam said, as if his aunt wasn't in the room.

"Let's don't talk about her." Mikey picked up the cutting board and carried it over to a plate, filling it with cut vegetables.

"Could you go easier on Mom?" Sam asked, as he looked out the window. "Maybe not hang out with that Agatha chick so much? You know how mad it makes Mom when she hears you've been with Mormons."

Mikey's mouth fell open. "Like you're not ever with the Mormons. Oh, mighty one, you can't tell me not one guy you play soccer with isn't one. Can you?"

"Playing soccer isn't hanging with them. There's a big difference."

"Like what?" Mikey shot a cold glare at Sam.

"Hey, I was trying to help Mom, not get you mad."

"That's enough, you two," Betsy said, feeling defeated.

❧

Karen dragged herself down the stairs, longed to stay in bed, but fighting Betsy would be hopeless. She'd eventually give in; Betsy was such a stubborn woman. Besides, she was hungry and didn't want to rock the boat when her sister-in-law had resumed helping with the cooking. Entering the kitchen, she smiled at her children. "Hi."

"Uh," they mumbled.

"How are we doing?"

No one answered. "Mikey?"

"Fine."

"Sam?"

"Okay."

"Betsy?"

"Wonderful. Church was great. I know you don't want to hear about its principles, so I'll tell ya there's a mighty fine man in that congregation." Betsy set bowls on the table and offered everyone a spoon.

"Betsy!" Karen said.

"I know. Stay away. But oh, you should hear his voice. It's deep and elegant, and his clothes… That man knows how to shop."

"I'm sure he's married." Karen sat.

"Widowed."

"He might appear to be a fine catch, but stay away. Some men cause pain for generations, remember? You used to say that countless times when you got divorced the second time. You told me not to let you forget that and not to ever let you have any kids."

"I thought you disagreed with me," Betsy said, also sitting.

"I do, but for you... Well, let's just say you pick 'em bad every time. No use challenging those odds. And, besides, you're in your fifties. That's no time to have a baby."

"I don't want kids, and Philippe wasn't so bad — " Betsy's voice took on a dreamy quality.

"Yes, he was," Karen said. "Have you forgotten he was unfaithful? That's the worst kind of creep there is."

"He was young then. Maybe he's mended his ways."

Karen slapped her hand on the table. "Have you been talking to him?"

"What if I have?" Betsy batted her eyes and couldn't resist a smile.

"My word. Some people never learn," Karen said. "All they are is talk. Men have been suppressing us from the beginning of time. It's time women changed. The next thing you know a man says a nice word and because they have a sexy voice you melt. Betsy Ashforth, you should be ashamed of yourself." Karen's voice had risen and so had she from her seat. She noticed everyone watching her and sat. "Sorry for getting worked up."

Betsy smiled. "That's okay. I deserved it. Yeah, I do always pick the wrong kind. My worst fault is my choice in men, but I get so lonely and they're so masculine..."

"Betsy!"

"All right, I'm stopping. Let's eat. I've got to show a better example for the younguns, anyway." She looked Mikey in the face and said, "The men I go for are no good."

"What's your type?" Mikey asked.

"The no-good type."

Everyone laughed, except Sam, who fidgeted in his chair. Poor guy, Karen thought. "There's many who aren't like that, though. Your brother is a wonderful example. He's a neat guy all the way around. It's just the type of men Betsy picks that are no good."

"How do you tell the difference?" Mikey asked.

"Yes, how do *you?*" asked Betsy with her eyebrow raised, revealing her misty blue eyes. She held her spoon in midair, waiting for

Karen's reply.

"By what they do. If they like to run all over the world exploring, its not a good sign. It means they get bored easily and aren't the kind to settle or make commitments. Even if they do make commitments, they go nuts until they're out traveling and having adventures without you. Because yes, they'd get bored with any one person.

"Another is their interests. If their friends are on top of the list, bad sign. A lady must insist on being on top, the very top." Karen stopped talking and began to eat.

"This perfect guy you're describing sounds *BORING,*" Betsy said.

"That's why you pick the wrong ones." Karen smiled sweetly.

Betsy grunted. Lunch passed quickly after that. Everyone ate in silence and in no time they left for their walk.

Karen noticed Mikey shooting her and Betsy lots of sneaky glances from under her gray sweatsuit hood. She seemed worried. Why did her daughter have to keep peering at her like that? Was she a science project?

Betsy's face proved as irritating as her daughter's. Her sister-in-law took one glance at Karen's black sweats, and her face scrunched-up like the pit of a date. Betsy believed black radiated negativity to the soul — the worst color a person could wear. Karen couldn't have cared less. Black felt right.

Soon Karen found herself breathing fast. The mountain shot straight up, causing her heart rate to shoot straight up too. "I'm out of breath." She struggled for air.

"Gee, Mom, you've got to exercise more. We've hardly started."

"We've gone at least two miles," Karen said, wiping her brow.

"More like two blocks," Betsy said with a smile. "But quite a challenging two blocks. Mostly up hill. We'll be heading down in a second."

"Great, then that'll mean we'll have to climb back up," Karen said. A sharp pain jabbed her right side.

"It feels great to be out, doesn't it?" Betsy asked. "Look at the view."

"Stop so I can," Karen said, gasping.

They stopped on the edge of the mountain. Gray fog settled in the valley, lapping over trees, bushes, and homes. A gust of wind blew against them, flipping their hair. Karen held her head high into the breeze and sucked its coolness. The wind made her feel more alive and tingling than she'd been all day. Betsy was right; a walk was good, but she'd never tell her. "Beautiful," Karen said, "but gray."

They continued to work their way down the valley. Betsy and Karen jabbered about the different houses, which ones they liked, and which were so ugly they couldn't believe anyone wasted their money on.

Karen was in mid-sentence about how the pillar look was classy, when Betsy called out, "You hoo, Sister Stanfield, Sister Stanfield..."

A middle-aged lady turned from her front door, glancing around. Betsy ran forward. "Hi."

"Oh, it's Sister Ashforth."

Karen's shoe rocked a dirt clod back and forth. Out of the corner of her eye she saw her daughter pose with an artful confusion. Mikey and those dumb movies, Karen thought. Never a break.

Karen walked backwards, slowly, one step at a time, trying to control her heavy breathing.

"It's okay, Mom. It looks like she's a friend of Aunt Betsy's. Nothing to worry about."

Karen smiled. "Worried? Who's worried?"

"I don't know. I thought you were."

"Nope," she whispered.

Betsy spoke animatedly with the lady wearing a green dress and high heels. Karen switched her weight from one foot to another, waiting for what might happen. Betsy pointed to them, talked a little more, then jogged up to meet them.

"Who's that?" Mikey asked.

"Sister Stanfield. She's sure a nice lady. You'd like her, Karen."

"Why's that?" she asked, staring straight ahead as she walked, her pace fast.

"She loves to do crafts like you do."

"Who says — "

"Come on, when you got married and had free time, you made crafts. I bet the only reason you don't now is because your stuff isn't out. If it were, you'd be busier than a beaver."

"Maybe," Karen said.

"Sister Stanfield told me about a night when she and a group of other ladies get together and work on some Halloween crafts. She's going to bring them over later to show me. Maybe you'll want to make them with us?"

"Doubt it." The rocks crunched under their shoes.

Karen felt her daughter's eyes on her. Why was she always watching? The child didn't understand. She probably thought crafts sounded fun. That was the problem. Cults were sneaky in their methods of luring people. They had to make the activities appealing or they wouldn't be able to brainwash people. "Is she Mormon?" Karen asked.

"That's not important — "

"Is she?" her voice sounded colder than the wind blowing around them.

"Yes."

"I told you no Mormons are allowed in my house."

"But I'm Mormon."

"I know."

Betsy stopped walking, staring at her. "Are you serious?"

"Dead serious. I don't know how to make myself clearer." What was she saying?

"I'll be gone within a week," Betsy said, turning around, heading home.

Karen stared ahead, sighed, then glanced at her glaring daughter.

"Mom, that wasn't nice."

"I know." They headed for the house too. She said, "I didn't mean she had to go, just that none of those people could visit."

"Dad's not going to be happy."

"I don't care," Karen nearly screamed.

Mikey shut her mouth and firmly crossed her arms over her chest.

"What's your problem?" Karen snapped.

"I hate the way you treat Aunt Betsy." Mikey took off running for the house. She paused for a brief moment to yell, "Why does our family have to be so messed up?"

Chapter 10

Betsy stormed in the house, up the stairs, and into her room. What was she supposed to do? Moving was a common enough thing for her, but her senses said, "Stay here." It was more than the swimming pool, the large house, or the incredible view. Here she had found deep fulfillment and had discovered intriguing people in her ward she'd like to know better. Thoughts of Jeff with his thick graying hair and fantastic smile raced through her mind. She should've at least had the chance to find out if they were…No, this was for the best. Karen had been right. She always did get into trouble when it came to men.

She tugged a large lavender, pink-flowered suitcase from under her bed. Light purple would remind her to work on her integration with God. She gave a half chuckle. This seemed an especially appropriate time to focus on that. She stuffed a week's worth of outfits in the case and a couple of her favorite books before she sat on the floor. Where would she go? In the past, her life directed her when it came to the point for her departure. She couldn't remember when she didn't know where to go. Karen wasn't reading the universe's signs.

Betsy's thoughts twisted into negative uselessness. If Karen was aligned with the universal flow or not, Betsy needed to chart a clear path. Maybe if she talked to someone, the confusion would dissolve. Who? Philippe. She'd call him so she could tap into his sense of direction.

She dialed his number; her heart thumping rapidly with each touch of the finger. The phone rang. She heard the throbbing beat of her heart in her ear. Again and again the phone rang until voice mail answered. At that moment, Betsy realized the time change. She guessed it was about six hours difference, making it close to midnight in Paris. Not too late.

After the phone message beeped, she said, "Philippe, my love, where are you? I've decided to take a vacation. Utah's seeping too much into my blood. I must emerge myself in the real world again. How about I visit France? Do you have a free day or two to show me around? I'd cook you a wonderful herb picnic, and we could lounge in the meadows and watch the flowers. What do you say? Give me a ring."

Sighing, she hung up. Why did she invite herself out there? She wanted to be with a friend for a few days to clear her head. That was it. Nothing more. She hoped she hadn't made a mistake. She also prayed Philippe wouldn't misunderstand her intentions or get mad he gave her so much money when they divorced. (She hated the idea of ever having to go to work. She wasn't that type.) He shouldn't get the wrong idea. They'd been friends for a long time.

❧

"You what?" George asked. "How dare you kick *my* sister out of our house? My family is always welcome no matter what they believe. How could you do such a thing?" He sank onto the couch and put his palm to his forehead.

Karen watched the storm rage through his body. She needed to calm him. How? "I'm sorry, dear. I didn't mean to. She misunderstood me."

"How did you not mean to throw her out of the house?" He clenched his fists tight.

"I just said no Mormons were allowed in my home. She assumed I meant her. I simply didn't want any of her friends coming over and having those meetings."

He paused. "What kind of meetings?" Some of his anger faded with the question.

"You know, cult meetings, where they program what you say and think."

His clenched fits relaxed. "I should have known." George gasped. "Come here. Sit by me." He patted the cushion.

Karen gazed shyly at him. He extended his arms and wiggled his fingers. Taking another short breath, she went to him. "What?"

His strong arms wrapped around her shoulders, and he whispered, "I'm sorry. I've should've known your cult problem was behind this."

"Cult problem?"

"Yeah. I'll talk to Betsy and explain everything. I'm sure she'll stay."

"But..."

"I'll make sure there are no 'meetings' in our house. All right?"

Karen watched her fingers.

"Sorry I got so mad," George said.

She nodded. "I don't have a cult problem."

George smiled. "Awe, my dear, you do."

"What is it then?"

"You know. You overgeneralize anything having the slightest relationship to cults because you never dealt with your fear of them since your friend..."

"That's not true."

"If you had dealt with it, you wouldn't be having problems now."

"Who made you so smart?"

"The shrink. Remember, I had an appointment today, and all we did was talk about you."

"Oh, great. Nothing like being the freak show."

George brushed his lips along the side of her forehead. "I only did it to get help in figuring you out. I want to be the best husband I can."

Karen smiled. "That's sweet."

He hugged her and whispered, "I love you."

Betsy was in the middle of her meditation when George popped in. "Sorry for interrupting, but can we talk for a moment?"

"Sure." Betsy stood, noticing his eyes straying to the waiting suitcase.

They both sat. "I'll get right to the point," George said, leaning forward. "Karen didn't mean what she said."

"Then why isn't she the one talking to me?" Betsy asked.

"You know how she overreacts. She's uptight about the cult stuff, and anything vaguely close to it sets her off. She doesn't know what she's doing; she's sorry and doesn't want you to leave."

"Look," Betsy said, "I'm fine with it. I can go. It doesn't hurt my feelings."

George grunted. "Truth is Karen needs you here. Please stay. You're good for her. She's actually dealing with past memories. She's never done that before, never allowed herself to remember. Now its gradually coming."

"If you think it's best, I'll stay. I didn't feel like going to France anyway."

"France?" George's eyes dilated. "You aren't seeing him again, are you?" Bitterness tainted his voice.

"We're just friends. Why?"

"You know better. Stay away from him. I can't tell you what to do, but stay away. He cheated on you, for heaven sakes."

"He's fun."

"Be careful." George said, then left.

❦

A black thickness hovered in the room when the phone rang. Still in a sleeping trance, Betsy hunted for the source of the buzzing. After what seemed the twentieth ring, she found the phone and flipped it on. "Hello?" she said yawning.

"Mon cherie, I thought you'd never answer."

Forcing her eyes open, she squinted at the clock. "It's three a.m.."

"Eight here, and I've waited hours for it to be this late."

"Why?" Betsy lay down on the pillow.

"Bien news, mon amie. I leave for the airport in half an hour. I have some business in Los Angles next week. You fly out and we'll spend as much time as possible together. It's not as pretty as Paris, but it'll do, n'est pas?"

"Sounds good," Betsy said. She hung up the phone and sank back into her trance. A startling thought awoke her. She ran to the mirror and gazed at her wrinkles, drooping. Blackness radiated around her aura. What had she done? Had she promised to spend a week alone with Philippe in California? Of all the dumb things! Her heart raced. She picked up the phone to book a flight.

The next morning she boarded SkyWest and tucked herself in a row of vinyl seats facing the back instead of the front. Being seated differently than the other passengers had a symbolic effect on her. It represented the whole trip. She was swimming against the tide of her family opinion. Granted, they cared and loved her and did have good reasons to be opposed to this trip. Philippe, after all, had once shattered her heart, not an experience she wanted to relive. But it would be good to take a short break from her brother's family. Let the situation cool.

The landing of the plane jolted her awake. She groaned along with the other passengers, then stood, allowing the people to pass. Philippe would be waiting for her in the terminal. She grasped the woven fabric of the seat in front of her. Was she ready for this?

She grabbed her Jewish novel, tucking it inside her purse. "Philippe, here I come." She exited the plane and walked down the ramp. She walked into the midst of the colorful California crowd and had passed the sitting area before she spotted her ex-husband.

Silver streaked his thick brown hair. "Mon cherie," he said soft, but deep. The curls still fell in twists to his shoulders. He moved gracefully to her until they were about a foot apart and smiled. "So good to see you." His face had maintained the perfect chisel with a long Roman nose and high cheek bones. An armful of roses appeared from behind his back. "Roses for the most beautiful rose of all."

Betsy smiled. "Oh, you're the romantic one."

He stared at her. "I've missed you."

Studying the depth of his baby blues for a few seconds, Betsy looked away. "Well, should we get my luggage? I'd hate for someone to steal it."

A small frown shot across his face. "Of course." He wrapped his arm around her shoulder and headed to the luggage pick-up area. They found the belt empty, with people staring at it as though they could will their suitcases to magically appear. Philippe's grasp on her arm tightened. Betsy stepped forward, breaking his grip. "I'm so glad I have a friend to enjoy my vacation with."

"Oh, mon cherie, we've never been just friends."

"What have the past ten years been?" Betsy batted her eyes.

"Moi, waiting for you to forgive. Since you've been calling and now invited me on this vacation, I know the time has finally come."

"Hold on a minute," Betsy said loudly. Several people glanced their way. "I invited you 'cause I thought you were my friend. I wanted someone to talk to. No more."

"Oh," Philippe said. "Then I guess my wait must continue."

The bell for the luggage sounded. Betsy inched closer to the conveyer belt to grab her lavender bag. Philippe's stare penetrated through her. She knew he watched, his eyes nearly digging a hole in her. So much passion resided in that man. She'd forgotten how the French were. She folded her hands across her chest with the roses resting on top of her arm. The red buds struggled to bloom. Her fingers trembled as she gently touched a petal. The sweet aroma filled her. Part of Philippe's charm had been his flowers. He flooded her with them. Every week of their courtship and every month of their marriage he'd given her some, but never in the same way. Once in the spring she'd arose from bed to visit the ladies' room. Upon returning, she found a bouquet of white lilies with yellow stripes flowing down the center of each leaf, lying on her pillow. Another time in winter, he sent her an array of potted bulbs: red tulips, white hyacinths, and blue irises. He said he'd forced the bulbs to generate beauty in the coolness of the season as she gifted him with her love. Such a romantic. The pleasing smell of roses filled her again, causing her to feel woozy. She'd gotten herself in deep this time.

❧

Karen made George his favorite dinner, roast, carrots, and potatoes. A way to make amends. He worried about his sister flying to

California into the arms of her ex-husband. She worried too. With men, Betsy had lousy judgment. The passion behind being in love had lured her into countless painful disappointments. Some women weren't lucky when it came to love.

She opened the oven and smelled the cooking roast, seasoning salt and onion blending into the scent. Rich brown liquid seeped around the meat. Almost done. She'd chosen well picking the meat, tender and juicy; George's mouth would water. The potatoes had also been cooked perfectly, fluffy and light — the kind that would melt with rich texture on your tongue. She looked out the window at the gray overcast sky and wondered if some kind of magical force was with her helping her prepare the food just right.

Dinner was almost ready. All she needed were George and the kids. The kids played upstairs on the computer. She hoped they completing homework tasks. And George she expected home any minute. She grabbed the newspaper and crawled on the living room couch to await his arrival. In the midst of reading an article on talking to your teenager, George came home. His normally pressed suit had withered into a pile of wrinkles, and his briefcase dangled in his hands.

"Hi, dear." Karen raced over to kiss his scruffy cheek. She had to stand on her tiptoe-toes to reach.

"Hi." His arms doubled around her back; then he let her go to set his briefcase on the floor.

"You look tired."

"It's been a long day. Work's crazy. Never thought starting up a new branch could be so exhausting." He laid his suit jacket and keys on the back of the couch.

"Come have dinner."

"You cooked?" The news seemed to cheer him.

"Your favorite." Karen smiled.

"Roast, potatoes, and homemade peach pie." George stepped toward the kitchen.

"You'll have to forget the peach pie, but the rest, yes."

"What, no pie?" He frowned.

"Sorry, didn't have enough time with job hunting and all."

"How's that coming?"

"I have a few good leads. Let's call the kids and eat. I'm starved."

The whole family seemed to be possessed with ravaging appetites. It was either that or the food actually tasted good. Karen concluded it was the latter. It was okay, though. When she did cook, her family didn't take it for granted, and they lathered her with compliments, which they did tonight from the moment they dished up their plates.

George assigned the kids dish-duty. Karen was grateful, being bone-tired. She laid on the couch. George followed after her, went to his briefcase, and shuffled through papers. "I was on the Internet today and found some stuff I thought you'd be interested in."

"What's that?" Karen bent her pillow, contouring it to the curve of her neck.

"I printed them off." He handed her a pile of ten pages or so and then grabbed the newspaper she'd left on the floor. He sat on the green leather chair, crossing his foot over his left knee. He swung his shoe.

Karen read the title of the page: *Determining Dangerous Cults*. She sighed. "Why did you give me this?"

"You need it," George said without looking from his newspaper.

"I do — "

"Yes, you do. You need to educate yourself and see what other people think makes up a cult."

"It says, 'Dangerous Cults.'"

"Isn't that the only type your worried about? You complain about Betsy racing into a relationship with her eyes closed, yet you haven't even learned what a cult is." He snapped his newspaper.

"That's not true. I looked up the definition in the dictionary."

"It's time to do more."

Karen rolled her eyes.

"Read them for me," George said. "See if you learn anything. It can't hurt, can it?"

"I guess not." She began reading. The piece started out by saying that anyone can accuse any other organization of being a cult under the grounds the organization sways people's minds, but to be a true cult, meaning a dangerous one, they needed to fit certain qualifications. She read on, her heart echoing, beating in her ears, and her body stiffened as her eyes flowed over the words. She came to the last sentence and leafed back through the pages.

"Did you read it all?" George asked, peering over his newspaper.

"Yes."

"What do you think?"

"About what?"

"Do you think Mormons fit the criteria for being a dangerous cult?"

Karen scanned the paper, swiping at her bangs that had fallen on her forehead. "I don't know. I guess I don't know enough about the Mormons to make a clear judgment. But I do know from one of the testimonies I read that if a group claims to have all the answers and they promise to make you happy, he suggests you be very cautious. From what Betsy has said, the Mormons do that, and I feel fine about being wary about them."

"That's smart. I for one am not trying to give the impression I'm a fan of the Mormons or want you to be one of them. But it's important for you to educate yourself about them."

Karen scooted up on the couch. "It couldn't hurt. Now I have a number of things to look for when Betsy talks about them. I can use the list against her and maybe help sway her away from their clutches."

"What's on the list?" George asked.

"Didn't you read it?"

"Yes, but I want to know what you got out of it."

"The charismatic leader — I need to discover if he is authoritarian — self-appointed — " Karen's voice drifted away. Memories intruded. She envisioned the leader of the Magdalene cult. The lady stood, uncomfortably rigid, as if in the army. Her hair, dark brown, greased back, was secured in a pony tail. No make-up. Her face wore a harsh pinkish tone, set off with small piercing hazel eyes. She stood very short. Almost the same size Karen had been at fifteen.

The leader of the Magdalene Members avoided the light. All lights must be turned off no matter the time of day when the leader entered the room. She only allowed one faint light in the distance. Charissa explained once that light would invite unchosen spirits.

"Karen?"

She blinked, focusing on her husband, who studied her.

"Sorry," she said. "Where was I?"

"The list you're going to use against Mormons. First you were going to check out their leader."

"And their lifestyle. How controlling is the group?"

"Judging that Betsy took off without a moment's thought, I think they're not that controlling. Some groups even control how much toothpaste and shampoo each member in the cult had, to how many seconds they could brush on each side of their mouths."

"True." Karen sighed. "But Betsy is educated and vulnerable like they search for."

"Good point," George said. "Her openness to things is a dangerous quality, but I don't see Mormonism as absorbing her whole world, becoming everything she lives for."

"I disagree. It's all she ever talks about."

"She's with Philippe right now, isn't she?" George asked.

"Probably to recruit him."

"Perhaps," George said.

Karen had been at Charissa's once when a new member had come who looked around the house with wide eyes. They weren't allowed to wear the tan robe until becoming an official member. "Where's the scriptures? Where's the scriptures?" she kept asking. Karen guessed it was some kind of lurement the group used to entice people into the group.

"We'll show them to you later," one of the group members said. "You must earn our trust. Come quickly downstairs." And they slipped into the basement.

Karen sighed. That had been so long ago, but it seemed like yesterday. What were the scriptures the lady wanted to see so badly? Karen tensed her muscles, her leg protesting with cramps. She pointed her toes. Did the lady stay with the group? So many secrets. Could she uncover them or would they forever remain a mystery?

Chapter 11

Betsy set the eye shadow brush on the marble cabinet, the masterpiece painted on her face completed. She turned her head left to examine her work, then right. Her fingers pinched a silver tube of shocking-pink lipstick. Another coat wouldn't hurt. Philippe could wait in the lobby a little longer. The pink glided over her lips; her fingers shook slightly. It had been a long time since she'd been on an official date, and she wasn't sure now if she wanted to join that world again. Taking a deep breath, she slipped out of the bathroom, over to her bed where her suitcase sat opened. The outfits slid easily onto hangers, which she then hung up. She continued to work until the bag was almost empty. All that remained was her copy of the scriptures. She set the book on the nightstand. Closing the lid to the suitcase, she carried it to the closet.

She did a dummy check on the room and spotted the Book of Mormon again. Sighing, she decided she needed its strength before she left. The chapter she chose absorbed her; nevertheless, she reached the end and closed the book, tucking it back on the nightstand. She gave the room another going over. Nothing else to do, but go downstairs. She grabbed her keys and headed out before remembering her personal prayers. She needed those too. Carefully she knelt at the foot of the bed.

After that she glanced at the clock. Philippe had been down there a long time. Would he give up on her? She took the elevator down ten stories, and at last the bell rung. She waltzed out with a smile. Philippe sat in a lounge chair, decked in an expensive suit. He leaned forward, tapping his fingers against each other. His blueberry eyes studied the pattern in the Indian rug.

"All ready," Betsy said with a smile as she twisted in one-sixty in front of him.

He smiled, boredom fading from his face. "This vision has been a worthy wait," he said. "The long wait."

Betsy beamed. Philippe had always appreciated her beauty. She'd missed those admiring comments.

Philippe offered his arm, and she settled her hand around his elbow. They were off. Betsy smiled at the double and triple glances people gave her and Philippe. They made a shocking couple even in L.A. But Betsy supposed heads always turned where Philippe was. He was striking.

Philippe escorted her to his luxurious rental sports car, and she slipped onto the leather. They took off sailing with angelic music consuming her. If only they could drive forever, but it ended when they pulled up to a steak house. "Up for steak?" Philippe asked.

"Yes," Betsy said, her mouth watering. Nowhere in Utah did they cook the way they did here. She was in for a fine treat.

They walked into the room, and Philippe spoke his name to the hostess. The lady behind the counter smiled and guided them to a table. "Here you go," she said, handing them the menus. "Your server will be right with you."

A small lit candle flickered in the center of the table, lightening the area. Soft violin music floated over them. Betsy picked up her butterfly-shaped napkin and spread it over her lap.

"Do you know what you're going to order?" Philippe asked.

"Steak and mashed potatoes," Betsy said.

"Sounds divine."

Betsy drank some of her water and waited. Philippe pushed his brown leather menu to the farthest corner of the table and smiled. Watching Philippe study her, Betsy suddenly felt like Mikey. A camera, Philippe, filmed her every move. Every action she did was being recorded. She smiled slightly and cleared her throat, using her napkin to cover her nose and mouth.

"It's so good to be with you," Philippe said, gazing into her eyes.

Betsy took another sip of water.

"This place has always been one of my favorites." He continued to stare with a dreamy expression.

"I love the atmosphere," Betsy said. "It forces you to relax."

"Ummm," Philippe said, still staring.

"How's your line-up for the spring show coming?" Betsy asked.

Philippe sat up straight. The dreamy expression disappeared. "Good. Good. I decided to take a couple more risks this year. I wanted to make a more impressionist effect with clothes. A blur of design and patterns, making a harmonious whole."

"Sounds intriguing. You'll have to show me when you get done."

"I will. It's been a challenge, but the result will be unique."

"I like the idea. The style has been too sharp and pointed as of late."

"To that I must agree," he said, and on their conversation wandered.

Betsy liked talking to Philippe. He was so knowledgeable and wise about many things, and he was a complete artist. He had graduated at the top of his art class from a French university; then he got scooped away in creating masterpieces in clothes. He influenced the world through style. Betsy couldn't think of a better way to make a difference.

Their salads came — art also, with the shiny greens twisted around the daub of purple cabbage and the sprinkles of brown pepper. Caesar salad had always been Betsy's favorite.

"I've missed talking to you," Philippe said.

"I have too," Betsy agreed, meaning her words.

"You're a rare treasure, mon petite choux. No other woman can fill your place. You're as beautiful as the rising sun. Intelligent. Full of mystery. I could never replace you."

Betsy blushed.

"I've changed, mon amour. I have. I no longer have wild oats, as you Americans say, to sew. I'm getting older and ready to settle. You can trust me."

Betsy looked away from his penetrating gaze and pointed at the waiter rounding the corner. "Our steaks are here."

His head lowered. "Think about it, mon amour."

"I will," Betsy whispered low. She doubted he even heard until she noticed the slight smile cross his face.

Philippe guided the conversation to the positive qualities of meditation, and why didn't more people try it? Betsy followed suit, and He made no more comments about them until their departure late that evening. He walked her into the lounge and took her hands gently into his. "Mon amie, I'm sorry if I scared you earlier with my affection. I couldn't help telling you how I feel."

Betsy started to talk, but he covered her lips with his finger. "Shh, say nothing. I'll give you time. Think about it. Think hard, mon cherie, and decide if we could make this work. I'll be good to you this time — very, very good. I've learned my lesson. My life has been empty without you."

With that, he left. Betsy watched him go. Though he seemed sad in his manner, he still displayed a confidence in the way he carried himself. Her head spun. She slumped to the couch.

❧

Late evening was Karen's favorite part of the day. She enjoyed snuggling with her husband as she chattered until they drifted to sleep. George's arm rested on her waist, protecting her from troubles. He leaned forward, his lips brushing her cheek. "I love you," he whispered, squeezing her tight.

Karen remained still, soaking in the moment. Feeling safe to expose her thoughts, she said, "I don't know whether to be grateful or irritated that you stopped Betsy from moving out."

"Why grateful?"

From George's tone, she could tell he was teasing. "Because this house would really become a landfill without her cleaning efforts. Haven't you noticed since she left?"

"Why irritated?"

"Cause I'll still have to put up with her goal to remake me."

George laughed. "Think you'll survive?"

"Have to. The only other choice is to sell my soul and become a Mormon."

"We wouldn't want that. Hang in there."

"Plan on it."

"How're the kids doing?" George asked.

"Sam's happy as ever. He got the highest score on his last test in AP chemistry and can't keep from bragging about it."

"That's, how would the kids say it…awesome."

"Mikey's doing better too. I've actually caught her a couple times cleaning."

"Really?" George asked. Karen didn't respond, so he asked the question Karen had been waiting for all day. "And your job hunt?"

"Oh, well," Karen whispered sadly.

"Hey, no worries. You'll find a great job soon. Any company would be lucky to have you. You've got to find one good enough for you."

Karen laughed. Her silly husband.

"That's it. Let's be happy."

"I got a better reason to be happy," Karen said.

"What's that?"

"I landed a job better than I ever dreamed."

"You did?"

"When?"

"Today."

"On Halloween? The job must be s-p-o-o-k-y."

"Enough jokes."

"Why? Are they s-c-a-r-i-n-g you?"

"I'm working for a software program company."

"You are?" George sounded impressed. "How did…"

"How did I manage to get a job like that not knowing computers?"

"Yeah."

"Because they recognized they'd be lucky to have me and thought perhaps, maybe, they were good enough for me."

George laughed. "Got me." He squeezed Karen tight and said, "Good for you." He paused, then asked hesitantly, "How's the pay?"

"Same as the grocery store, but there's opportunities to progress and good benefits."

"Sounds super."

"I'm scared."

"You can do it." George kissed her forehead; Karen responded by snuggling closer into his arms.

The next morning Karen woke to the smell of frying bacon. "I must be dreaming." She pulled the blanket around her shoulders, then reached for George. Gone. Could he be cooking breakfast? Too good to be true. She had to see.

She slipped on her bathrobe and headed downstairs. Before she reached the kitchen, her husband's deep voice sang, "She brings home the bacon, has her husband fry it up in the pan, 'cause she's the one who's in charge."

"I am?" Karen asked, stepping into the kitchen without anything crunch under her feet. The floor had been swept.

"Here's to the breadwinner."

George gave her a quick kiss.

Sam staggered in the room with a sleepy expression. "Mom, a breadwinner? You mean she won a contest or something?"

"Your mom got a job."

"You did?" Sam looked at his mother.

"Selling computer software."

"Mom?" Sam asked.

Dad laughed. "She's full of surprises, isn't she?"

Mikey entered. "What?"

"Mom's selling computer software?" Sam said.

"Door to door?" Mikey asked.

"No, at a business. I'm answering the phone," Karen said.

Mikey smiled. "All right, score! Way to climb the corporate ladder and show those men that women are worth something."

Karen smiled. She was setting a good example for her daughter. Maybe because of her influence, her daughter would get a head start on this business stuff and climb high and far — really being a success.

⁂

Betsy awoke in a ray of sun. Golden drops of light spread throughout her room. Philippe had been kind and romantic, yet uneasiness invaded the bottom of her stomach. Something wasn't right. Maybe it was the fact he moved fast and intensely. She hadn't expected this. Instead, she thought they'd continue on as friends. Perhaps his old girlfriend had recently dumped him. She'd have to ask. She closed her eyes, the sun warming her. She needed to get up. Philippe said he had another full day planned, but he wouldn't tell her what it was. A surprise. This made Betsy uneasy, but excited. Philippe was the most thrilling thing that had happened to her since the Mormons.

She got dressed, read her scriptures, then suddenly realized it was Sunday. She should go to church. She dashed downstairs for breakfast and found Philippe in the entrance of the restaurant. "Hi, mon amie." He smiled with natural ease.

"You're early. I haven't had breakfast yet," Betsy said.

"I thought I'd join you."

Betsy smiled. "That'll be nice." It turned out he had eaten an hour ago and waited all this time in the restaurant for her. He said he was perfectly delighted watching her eat. Betsy ordered a vegetable dish.

"I have a wonderful day planned for us," Philippe said, winking.

"Sounds great. Do you think you can squeeze church in? I almost forgot it's Sunday."

"You came here to get away from everything. Clear you head of the pollutants from Utah. We've got a busy schedule. First, the museums. They have wonderful new collections of the cubist, impressionists, and a few geometrical expressions. Then a picnic on the ocean. I've already packed the lunch. I've included fresh wheat rolls, smoked sausage, salad, and a variety of cheeses. Plus a chocolate surprise for dessert."

The day sounded intriguing. "You really don't think we could squeeze in an hour of church?" she asked.

"I only get you till tomorrow. I'm not sharing you with some church. I've traveled a long way and plan on making the most of my trip."

He had a good point, and Betsy dropped the subject and enjoyed the rest of her vacation. It was a day filled with wonder and many different types of art and expression. As they wandered through the mazes of art, Philippe softly imprinted his fingers on Betsy's forearm. "Mon amie, look at this painting of a little known impressionist."

A grayish-blue leaped from the canvases in small dots, forming a lake scene. The variety of purples made the vegetation along the shoreline. These plants reached for the distant lovers passing in a boat. The gentleman was on bent knee; the lady, clothed in white, gazed at the pending thunder cloud.

"Aren't the strokes magnificent?" Philippe asked.

"Masterful," Betsy answered, eyeing the approaching cloud once more.

Reluctantly, they bid farewell to the museums and hello to sand, sun, and laughter of the beach. It felt good to be with Philippe, and he didn't bring up "them" again. It wasn't until he drove her to the airport the next morning that he reapproached the subject.

He stood with her in the check-in line, waiting for the boarding to be called. When it was her turn, he said, "Mon cherie, I must talk to you." He grabbed her purse, put it on the ground, took her hands in his, and knelt. "My days have been so lonesome without you. You're the light of the sun. I've missed you and made a terrible mistake. I want you back for always." He pulled a small box out of his pocket. "Will you marry me?" He put the box in her hand, squeezed her palm against it, then stood, wrapped her in his arms, and kissed her long and deep. Betsy responded passionately. He released her. Betsy kept her eyes closed, relishing the moment. When she opened them, he was gone.

"Final call for flight eighteen-sixty-seven," came over the loudspeaker.

Her head floated. She picked up her purse in one hand, still clutching the box in another, and boarded the plane.

Chapter 12

The group with the tan hoods watched her from the shade. They stared and pointed. Karen couldn't make out their words, but heard, "Child...unbeliever...and bloodline." Straight ice rushed through her veins. She yelled in deathly fear.

"Wake up. Wake up." George shook her shoulders.

Karen gasped and stared at her husband in amazement. How did he get here? Slowly the time frame grew clearer. She'd been dreaming. Only a dream. But was it? Memories flooded in on her faster now, and this one happened a few days before Charissa died. Shaking from the cold, but wiping at her sweat, she whispered, "They were considering me for the sacrifice, but I didn't have the bloodline."

George didn't move.

"They pointed at me. I couldn't hear much, but one of them said angrily, "She doesn't have the bloodline. It must be pure."

Karen trembled, pulling the blanket close to her neck. Her eyes closed. "Charissa's blood must have been acceptable."

Tears welled in her eyes; she rested her forehead against George's firm chest. She sobbed as he wrapped his arms around her and caressed her hair. "There now."

Betsy's eyesight was still a little blurred; and she felt hot as she collapsed into the first available seat. A flight attendant passed her, and Betsy tugged on her shirt. "May I have a glass of water, please?"

The attendant paused to look at her. "Put your head between your knees. I'll be right back with the water."

Betsy followed the orders, and water appeared in her hand in no time. The heat dissipated. "Are you all right?" the flight attendant asked.

"Fine, now. Thank you." She smiled.

"Anything else I can get you?"

"No. I had a bit of a shock before I got on the plane. That's all." She still felt Philippe's firm, hungry lips on hers.

The flight attendant smiled sympathetically. "Sorry. Let me know if I can be of any more assistance."

Betsy nodded, twisting the black box in her hand.

"Does that little black box have anything to do with your dizzy spell?" A young woman seated next to her asked. Hundreds of tiny freckles spattered over her face and visible parts of her arm. She tried to cover them with a plentiful amount of make-up.

"Yeah," Betsy said.

"What does it look like?" The girl eyed the box with an eagerness sparked by her youth.

"I haven't opened it yet.

"What you waiting for, girl? Do it!"

Betsy sighed. Seeing the ring wasn't going to help figure out her situation. Her ex-husband had just proposed to her, for goodness sake.

"Come on," her companion urged.

Betsy took a deep breath and opened it. Inside lay a large marquee diamond, at least two carats, set in a thick gold band that wove up and down in a gentle wave.

The girl gasped. "Look at that rock." She extended her hand. "Do you mind if I hold it for a second?"

Betsy shrugged.

The girl slipped it on her finger. The ring was too big for her, but she held it out in front of her, waving her long fake nails. She tipped her hand so the gem faced her. "Mmmm, mmmm, mmmm, that's one mighty fine rock. Gorgeous. You're lucky."

Betsy swallowed a sip of water.

"Is the guy as good looking as the rock?" the girl asked, handing the ring back. She gave it another longing glance.

"Yes. He's French."

"French. Mmmm. I heard they're *soooo* romantic. Is that true?"

"Yes," Betsy answered. "Very."

"Sounds perfect. Why such a reaction?"

"He's my ex-husband," Betsy said, closing her eyes.

"Oh."

"Oh, exactly. What have I gotten myself into?"

"A big ring."

Betsy darted a glance at her and saw her smile. Yes, she had gotten herself a big ring. She sighed. Meditation was definitely needed.

⁂

Betsy had her suitcase halfway out of the car when Sam approached and asked, "Need help?"

"You bet," she said, sighing. She was so tired she could hardly move. Halfway home she had slipped the ring into the pocket of her jacket. Her fingers drifted to the front of her coat, checking to see if the bump still remained. It was best to keep the little box and its contents a secret.

George sat on a stool in the kitchen when she came in. "Betsy," he exclaimed with a smile.

"Miss me?" Betsy batted her eyelashes and smiled into his face. He stood and embraced her.

"Sure did. How was your trip?"

"Fine."

"I'm going to put your bags in your apartment. Okay, Aunt Betsy?" Sam said.

"Thank you, my dear. The universe will reward you for that."

"How was Philippe?" George asked, his eyes studying hers.

"Fine." Betsy dashed to the refrigerator and got a thing of string cheese.

"What do you mean, fine?" George asked.

"He was all right." She threw away the cheese wrapper.

"I don't mean to be rude, but I'm tired. The plane ride wore me out. All I want to do is sleep. Is that all right?"

Everyone nodded except George, who gave Betsy a questioning look. He wasn't going to let her off that easy.

Once inside her apartment, she pushed the button on her answering machine. There were several messages, but two caught her attention. First, the bishop wanted to meet with her; the second was Philippe.

"Mon petite choux, I don't expect an immediate answer. Think about it. Take your time. But I do want to tell you one thing, if you must still be a Mormon, that's okay. Do whatever you want. I'm afraid you might not have known that. I'll call in a week or two for your answer. Thank you for the wonderful time in L.A. I love you, my dear. No one could ever replace you. I've changed. Trust me. Au revoir."

Betsy moaned as she tossed around in bed. Why was he doing this? Could he actually be for real? Or was he just lonely and didn't want to go to the energy to court a new girl? What was she supposed to do?

⁂

The next day at breakfast, George walked into the kitchen wearing his navy blue silk suit with blue, yellow, and red suspenders. "Nice suspenders," Betsy said as George walked behind her toward the fridge.

"Thanks," he said. Silently he got milk and corn flakes, sat kitty-corner from her. "Are you going to tell me what happened with Philippe?"

"Why do you think something happened?" Betsy asked.

"Because I know you and I know him," George said gruffly.

"Maybe I've changed."

"Maybe you haven't. Which is it?"

"You sure get personal." Betsy bit a corner off her burned toast.

"I talked. Now you talk. It's only 'cause I care."

"No fair, you can't use my line — "

"Stop stalling. Tell me what happened."

"Short version?"

"Get down to the bare facts, please. I've got a meeting to get to."

"He asked me to marry him." Betsy looked George straight in the eye.

He choked on the spoonful of flakes he had shoved in his mouth. After he finished coughing, he asked, "He what!"

"Marriage. You know, when two people live together like you and Karen."

"I know what marriage is. What did you say?"

"I didn't answer."

"You didn't — "

"Nope. Just got on the plane."

George set his spoon down on his bowl. "What are you going to say?"

"I don't know."

"You don't?"

"See, I told ya I've changed. I'll give him my answer in a couple of weeks. Believe me, you'll be the second to know." She stood. "I got yoga and cleaning to get to. See ya tonight."

❧

Wednesday night, two days since Betsy had arrived home, her warning button had beeped, warning her to tread lightly with Karen. She needed to halt the negative vibes she assumed continued to exist while she was gone. Her co-existence in this mansion positively fed her aura. She didn't want that cut off. A strong feeling hummed within her that this home possessed the key to her future endeavors.

Betsy redirected her focus from Karen to absorbing as much information about the gospel as possible. She refused to be suppressed in the beginner status for long. She flipped through *Gospel Principles* again as she waited for the appointment with the Bishop to start. She had every main principle of the book memorized. She paced in front of the office. The Bishop was taking forever.

When Betsy arrived, she had walked into the Bishop's office to find him conversing with a woman in tears. Betsy stared sympathetically at the sobbing lady and waited for her to leave. She remained, wiping her eyes, then finally looked at Betsy and said, "What are you doing in here?"

"I have an appointment," Betsy said, studying the woman's outfit. All silk — white. Pools of black mascara rested under her eyes, and a trace of it had leaked onto the woman's blouse. "That mascara's going to be a killer to get out," she said, pointing to the stain.

She cried harder.

"Sister Ashforth, can I ask you to wait in the hall? I'll be just another minute," the Bishop said.

Betsy left, but paused before closing the door and said, "Crying can be a good way to search your soul. Don't allow yourself to get distracted."

Fifteen minutes later, she still waited for the lady to stop soul searching on her time. Betsy sat, flipping the *Gospel Principles* book on the bench next to her. How much longer was she going to be? Betsy marched to the door and pressed her ear against the chilled wood. She couldn't hear anything and didn't sense any vibes.

The door opened. The lady's head tipped down. With swollen red eyes, she glanced at Betsy, then ran to the exit, banging the door shut behind her.

Betsy asked, "What's the matter with her?"

The Bishop sighed. "It's personal."

"Is she cheating on her husband?" Betsy leaned in to hear the answer.

Clearing his throat and adjusting his tie, he said, "The Bishop keeps whatever goes on behind his doors confidential. Whatever the problem is with that sister is between her and the Lord. You shouldn't be jumping to conclusions. Sometimes people cry because they're overwhelmed."

"So it's not an affair. Too bad. It would have made things more lively." Betsy staggered in and took the distraught lady's chair.

After the Bishop sat, she said, "I know why you called me in here."

The Bishop glanced at her. "You do?"

"Yep. You want to test my knowledge of the gospel."

The Bishop smiled.

"I've been reading a lot and learning many interesting things. It's amazing how much of it makes perfect sense. It kinda makes you wonder why other churches don't believe it. It seems like this is how it should be."

"It does make you wonder." The Bishop leaned over his desk. "What book do you have there?"

Betsy held it up so he could get a better glimpse. "*Gospel Principles*. I've finished reading this and *The Marvelous Work and Wonder*. I'm in the middle of *Mormon Doctrine*."

The Bishop smiled. "Sounds like you're coming right along."

"I'm ready for that test you promised. I want to take it and progress to a more difficult class. I hate being stuck at the beginner level."

"Test?"

"Yeah, you said if I knew enough about the church, I wouldn't have to go to the beginner class any more. You know, the one Brother Kirby teaches with this *Gospel Principles* book. Now I don't want you to get me wrong, Brother Kirby is a fine teacher. But I want to know as much as I can about the church, and he follows this book exactly. I've already read it, and I'm ready for more."

"I really admire your love of learning."

"I've always loved to learn. There's nothing I don't want to know and understand."

"That's great. I believe you know a lot about the gospel. That's why I want to know if you will accept a call."

"What do mean by a call?"

"I mean a calling. Do you remember reading in there about service?"

"Yes, it said it was an important part of becoming like Jesus."

"That's right, and I'd guess it also says something about getting opportunities in the church to do service."

"I wondered what that meant."

"Well, in order to run the church effectively, the Lord calls people to different assignments. Me, for instance, am called to be in charge of the people in this ward."

"I understand. No problem. So you want me to help out with the ward. I can do that. I'll tell you what. I'll lead the people in the music during Sacrament Meeting. How's that?"

"That's an important job, but someone else already has it — "

"Okay, I'll be the lady in charge of the Relief Society. I'd be perfect. I have so many great things I could teach — "

"You do have a lot of great things to teach, and I'm glad you feel that way because the Lord has called you to teach the eleven-year-old boys."

"What?"

"Will you do it?"

"Did God tell you to have me do that?" She slapped the table.

"Yes." He nodded, revealing his double chin.

"I don't get to pick what I want to do? I have to take whatever you say God wants me to do?"

"That's right."

"Well since God told you, I'll do it. I don't know how receptive they'll be to meditation at that early age. I don't know if they have the focus or the stress in their lives to really want to learn."

"Meditation?" the Bishop asked with a surprised. His eyes widened behind the glasses.

"Yes, and how to tap into the higher levels of communication with your soul."

"There's been a misunderstanding."

"What's that?" Betsy sat back in her wooden chair.

"You're to teach them the gospel on Sundays during regular meetings."

"The gospel? But I'm brand new."

"You just got done telling me you know a lot about the church. Now's the time to apply your knowledge."

"Boy, you didn't give me much time, did you?"

"To be honest with you, we've been having a really hard time filling this position. There's one special little boy in there who'll need extra attention. He's struggling and I feel strongly you're the person who can reach him.

"You can get him to open up. He was in a car accident about a year ago and damaged his spine. Now he's a paraplegic. To make matters worse, his mom died in the same accident. He deals with his pain through disruption. You'll do a good job with him and will help him feel life is worth living again."

Car accident. This had a familiar ring. Where had she heard this story? But her helping someone in need? The image of Karen's sour face popped in her mind. How could she help this little boy when she'd tried so hard to help Karen and had failed so miserably? She wasn't qualified to do the job. She'd make a bigger mess out of the situation than it was. She wasn't good at fixing up people's lives. "I'm sorry, Bishop, but I don't think I can do that."

"Why?"

"I'm no good with kids. I haven't been around them much except my niece and nephew, and I don't feel like I can help others find solutions in their lives."

"It'll come. Pray. That's always been helpful for me. None of us ever feel we're qualified for our jobs, but somehow the Lord grows us into them."

⁂

Karen smiled as she entered the last order. The job came more naturally than she had ever expected. Of course taking a couple of computer classes and watching computer training videos hadn't hurt. She'd learned quickly that to succeed in this company she needed to keep her mouth shut and hands busy — a tip her friend Amber told her on the first day. It had turned out to be true.

Amber entered her cubicle. "Are you going to go home today or stay here and work all night?"

"Finishing up the information on this order, then I'm heading out," Karen said.

"You're acting like you want a raise or something."

"I do"

"Need the money?"

"Naw. I like being in charge of my destiny. This is the first job I've got where I could make something of myself, and I plan on doing it."

"Go, girl. Go."

Karen laughed, then flipped off the computer. She grabbed her thin coat and headed through the maze of office dividers with Amber. "Am I really doing okay?"

"You're doing great."

"I feel like I'm goofing up all the time. I'm worried I'll get fired. This job really does mean a lot."

"You won't get fired. It's a matter of time and experience, and you won't be making many mistakes. You got to allow some space to be human."

"Human? I forgot what that is," Karen said.

Amber laughed. "Why don't we take an hour off for lunch tomorrow and go somewhere nice."

"I don't — "

"Come on. You won't lose your job over one lunch. They let you relax every now and then."

"Okay. Sounds fun."

"See ya then," Amber said, heading for her car.

Karen smiled. She liked Amber. If it was okay for Amber to be human, it should be okay for her too. She drove homeward. The past couple of weeks had been nice. A welcome relief after the stressful weeks of wondering if she would ever understand her job. After she figured out she could learn everything she needed to know and she could do the job, it became something to look forward to. It didn't have the dull repetition of grocery store work. Groceries were groceries, but the computer software stood on the cutting edge. It was the latest, the fastest, and the best of the world. This idea thrilled her, and the fact she dove right dab in the middle of it made it all the better.

Her psychologist observed her in surprise when she visited last week. He said, "You seem happy."

"I am."

"Do you worry about the Mormons anymore?"

"I try not to."

"Good. Maybe we're done with these sessions for a while."

Karen smiled. She wasn't completely off the medicine, but at least she didn't have to visit the doctor every week. The next scheduled appointment was in a month, and she'd prove she could handle life without the medicine. An extra bonus, Betsy was no longer talking about Mormons. Karen appreciated that. Her life shifted into place.

To make things even better, Mikey wasn't hanging around with Mormons or quoting their doctrine. The last thing she'd ever want to see happen was having one of her kids get caught up in something that could destroy their lives. Betsy was an adult and could handle herself, but Mikey was her child.

Karen did worry about Mikey though. She seemed to be alone a lot, and she wasn't talking much. Karen would have to ask her about her friends at school. She couldn't believe she didn't even know if Mikey had friends or not. She must have been too worried about her job. Well she didn't have to worry as much about that anymore, so now she ought to get back in gear of being a mom.

With Sam, she had no worries. He seemed happy and had a lot of friends. He had sense enough not to worry about religious dogma. His concerns were filled with his performance on the soccer field.

Karen flipped on the classical jazz station, allowing the light music to seep in as she drove. Moving to Provo hadn't been as bad as she'd thought.

Chapter 13

What could the Bishop be thinking? Betsy pressed harder on the gas pedal as she drove home. He had to be nuts, but if he said God inspired the calling, she didn't have much choice but to give it a shot. She edged her car into the driveway, then rushed into the house. From the distance she heard the muffled sounds of a television. She approached the noise.

Sam and Mikey sat in the dark, blue color splashing over them. "Hi, guys," Betsy said.

"Hi," they muttered.

"Is that all I get?" Betsy asked. "A dead person could give a more energetic hi." Still no reaction. "Got any more dirt for me so I'll believe Mormons are weird?"

"I gave it up," Mikey said, her eyes fixed on the set. "I don't care about the dumb Mormons anyway. If you want to do dumb things, it's your choice."

Betsy sat on the corner of the couch. "What about helping your mom?"

"The best way to help Mom is to stay away from Mormons and not talk about them," Sam said. He sent his sister a quick glance. She nodded, and they both looked back to the chase scene.

"I see." This was getting her nowhere. Might as well retreat to a bubble bath — at least the bubbles got all blown up over her presence. She stood. "Bye, guys."

"Uh." Teenagers' favorite word.

She'd climbed half the stairs when she heard her phone ring. Dang it. She kicked the heel shoes and dashed into a full-fledged run. The phone hummed as she searched for her keys. The answering machine had picked up. She managed to open the door and dived for the phone on the bed, flicking the on button. Breathless, she said, "Hello."

"Mon amour, I thought I'd miss you and have to sleep sad tonight for not talking with you."

Betsy's stomach dropped. "Philippe." He wanted an answer, but she hadn't decided.

"How is ma petite choux doing?"

Betsy groaned. She hated being called a little cabbage, even though the French found it endearing. "Fine. It's been a real busy day, and I just arrived home. Ooooh, I'm tired."

"Have you thought about my little box?"

"Yes, I've thought about it. It's kind of hard not to."

"Well — ?"

Betsy tapped her fingernails against the shell of the phone.

"You're nervous," Philippe said.

"Am not."

"You always tap your fingers when you're nervous or bored."

Glancing at her fingers, she groaned. He knew her. How was she supposed to fight that? He'd cheated on her. Cheated! She took a deep breath. "Philippe?"

"Yes?"

"I've been thinking about your question and I — "

"Yes, mon amour."

"I…I," she looked at her bed. One pillow flopped in the middle of the mattress to fill the empty space. "I can't — I can't answer yet. I need more time."

"I see," Philippe said softly. His tone held an edge to it. Was it anger? Or perhaps hurt? "How much more?"

"I don't know. We've tried it before. What's changed so much that it's going to work this time?"

"Me. I've changed," Philippe said. "I'll be the gentle breeze comforting you under the hot sun. In winter I'll be a warm quilt wrapping protection and simmering heat through your chilled body. Please give me a chance."

She sunk her head onto the hard pillow. What was she supposed to say? Should she trust him again? The unwanted memories came. *White Shoulders* clinged to his shirt. Smeared lipstick under his lower lip. The ringing phone that went dead as soon as she spoke. The odor of rum and smoke filling her bedroom when he tumbled in with the morning sun. He didn't smoke.

"Philippe, I'm really tired. Can I talk to you later?"

"Of course, mon amour. I'm sorry to have called so late, but I wanted to make sure you were all right."

"You're a caring man. Thank you."

"I'll be faithful now. You're the only person for me, ma belle. Bon soir."

"Bon soir." Betsy pressed the receiver button and continued to hold it down. There was something satisfying in emphasizing the hang up. Oh, Philippe was a talker…and a good friend. He understood her. But he was too suave and smooth. Their life together promised to be full of adventure. She could travel the world on the arm of a wealthy, elegant man. Every girl's dream.

❧

Karen gave a full-body stretch before she slipped into her nightgown. The evening was slowly wearing down, and she anticipated watching the news with her husband's arms wrapped around her. It would make the day complete.

The phone rang. She answered. "Is Mikey there?"

"Yes, one minute, please." Teenagers had no sense of proper telephoning times. "May I ask who's calling?"

"Agatha."

A wave of uneasiness flowed through Karen as she flipped on the intercom. "Mikey, phone."

She heard a distant, muffled, "Okay." Picking the phone back up, she waited for Mikey to answer.

"Hello?" she heard her daughter say in a sad tone.

"Mikey?"

"Yes?"

Karen pressed the receiver but then released it. Would it hurt so much to find out what was going on in Mikey's life? She hadn't been talking. Her daughter used to tell her everything. What had changed?

"Are you ignoring me?" Agatha asked. "Did I do something to upset you?"

"No."

"Are you sure?"

"Yeah," Mikey said. Her voice had a dark edge to it.

"Why are you avoiding me at school?"

"I'm not."

"You are. As soon as you see me coming down the hallway, you go the opposite direction. I can't find you anywhere at lunch. Where do you go? You don't have a car, do you?"

"No car, I'm still fifteen. I've been extra busy with homework, so I go to the library."

Good for Mikey, Karen thought. Way to stand up to those Mormons. But to be alone at lunch day after day for a teenager seemed depressing. How could she do this to her own daughter?

"Mikey, you're not being honest with me. I thought I was your friend." Agatha said.

"You are."

"Trust me enough to talk to me. I promise I won't laugh or make fun."

"I don't know what you're talking about," Mikey said.

"You seem angry or nervous or something. If you don't like being with me, you can tell me."

"I like being with you."

"Then what is it? Is it because I didn't want to finish sewing your shirt and made you do all the unpicking?"

"Nooo," Mikey said weakly. "I'm not mad about that. It's just that — "

"What?"

"I don't know how to explain it."

"Try."

"It's because you're Mormon."

Karen sucked in her breath. She'd done this to her daughter. She'd made her a social recluse because of her own fear and hatred of religion. Karen should hang up now. She'd found out what she needed to know. But how would this information play out with Agatha?

"So?" Agatha asked.

"So, that's not good."

"You haven't been talking to me because I'm Mormon? I won't trouble you anymore. I guess I'll be going."

"No, wait," Mikey said, her voice cracking. "It's not that I care if you're a Mormon or not."

"You just said it was because I was Mormon."

"What I meant was my mom is sick."

An emotional knife jabbed at Karen.

"Again? Is she okay? How long has she been in the hospital? Why didn't you tell me?" Agatha's voice flowed with concern.

"It's not like that. She's acting like she's going to get sick, but she's not ill now."

"Oh," Agatha said, sounding confused.

"I mean the reason she became so sick last time was because she thinks Mormons are devils."

"Devils?"

"Yeah, devils who are trying to destroy us."

"Oh."

"It seemed like my mom was going to get sick again, and I didn't want her to be worse, so I've been staying away from you 'cause you're Mormon."

"Then why are you talking with me now?"

"I miss being with you. It's lonely."

"I'm not a devil."

"I know," Mikey whispered.

"Do you? Every time I come around, you act like I have the cooties."

"You guys captured my aunt."

"Captured?... I heard she was baptized, and I've seen her around the ward."

"If you Mormons are good enough to trap my aunt, then I bet you can get anyone."

"Look, Mikey, I don't want to capture you. I want to be your friend. I like being with you. I thought you liked hanging out with me. We can forget this religion thing and just be friends, can't we?" Agatha seemed to be catching her breath, then said, "You're my only chance of being a real good friend with a movie star, and I don't want to blow it."

Mikey laughed. "I've missed my favorite fan too. The library is just not the same as performing for you."

"I bet not."

"And I miss learning how to sew...Hey, I have an idea. My mom got a job now so I could go over to your house without her knowing, and we could finish those shirts. What do you say?"

"What about your mom? I don't want you to lie," Agatha said.

"I'm not going to. I won't tell my mom unless she asks. Besides, she never said I couldn't be with you. I just know she'd extremely dislike it."

"Well if you're sure about it, how about tomorrow?" Agatha asked.

"Deal."

Karen hung up the phone. Sleep wouldn't come easily tonight.

Chapter 14

Thursday night the Bishop called Betsy to be a Primary teacher. Friday, the Primary president, Mrs. Jefferson, met with her for a quick training meeting. Saturday, she prepared her lesson, and Sunday was her first day in class. She sighed as she rubbed on one more coat of blue eye shadow. Was she ready for eleven-year-old boys? What did she know about boys? Kids for that matter. Or even the gospel. She'd only been in the church a few short weeks. The Bishop wasted no time in having her jump into the world of participation. She would willingly help out, but with little children?

Sacrament meeting rushed by in a heated run, and before Betsy could blink, Mrs. Jefferson smiled at her. "I'm so glad you accepted the call," she said. "It's a big relief to find someone willing to take this class."

Betsy slipped on a confident smile. "No problem." They remained silent as they wove through the crowd.

The Primary president stopped in front of a classroom door. "Here we are."

"Are you sure you want me to teach? You know, I've only been in the church a few weeks," Betsy said.

"The Bishop has complete confidence in you. Good luck." Down the hall she dashed.

Betsy's hand was on the doorknob when she heard a young male's voice say, "Okay, guys, we've got to think fast. The new primary teacher should be here any second."

Betsy moaned. Kids with terrorist hearts.

Another kid asked, "Why? What we've been doing has worked perfectly."

The first guy answered, "Because the Bishop's got to be catching on by now. Five teachers in three months is enough to make the most dense person realize this class is hard…Come on, think," the first boy demanded in a loud tone. He sounded like a man running a tight ship in the navy, not a boy in a church class.

Who was that kid, and why was he so bossy?

Another boy asked, "What do you think we should do, Dudon?"

Dudon. The mini-Hitler was named Dudon. What a strange name for a kid. These Provo Mormons sure had a thing for awful sounding names.

Dudon said, "I think we should..." He paused, and Betsy firmly pressed her ear against the door. "Try our basic philosophy which is..."

The class chanted in a loud whisper, "Ignore, ignore, ignore."

"And?" Dudon asked.

"Talk," they said loudly.

"Yes! I want to hear it one more time. This time louder."

"Ignore, ignore, ignore, talk," repeated the class.

Betsy straightened the sequins on her dress and whispered, "I'm impossible to ignore. So much for your plan, little sweeties." She put her hand back on the knob and was about ready to open the door when she heard a new voice.

"Now, would this make Jesus happy?" Silence. "Well? Would it?"

Betsy heard a growl. Dudon said, "Thank you, Sister Cox."

A couple of the boys giggled at the namecalling, but the objecting boy ignored the teasing as he continued with his little sermon. "I mean it, guys. It's not good to act up in class. Jesus wants us to learn as much as we can, and we're only cheating ourselves."

There was a roar as the boys started talking and laughing, shunning each other by using peer pressure. The little boy continued his plea. "Guys!" his voice squeaked.

Betsy decided it was time to stop the sermon and begin her first mission assigned by the church. She barged in, batting her eyes and pursing her lips. She'd might as well make the first impression as bad as possible. "Ah, um, is this the eleven-year-old class?"

The kid with Dudon's voice answered, "No, they're in the classroom next door."

Betsy scanned Dudon. He sat perched in the middle of a wheelchair like a king on his throne. His long brown hair fell over the wide forehead into deep brown eyes. He stared back at her. He was an attractive boy. "I think I found the right room," Betsy said in a controlled voice.

"You have," said another boy.

Betsy looked for the speaker and located a boy who resembled a skeleton with thin skin draped over his bones. "You must be Mr. Cox."

His small grayish-blue eyes gazed in wonder. "Yeah, Brett Cox."

"Nice to meet you," Betsy said, holding out her hand.

"Man, she's got claws," another boy said.

Betsy turned and looked into the boy's freckled face and said with a halfsmile. "The better to strangle little boys with." She laughed wickedly. The boy's gaze grew larger. Betsy forced her eyes away. "We'd better get started."

Dudon's hand shot in the air, waving as though he were creating a wind.

"Yes?" Betsy asked, rolling her eyes.

"Which president of the Church is the best tasting?"

Betsy glanced around at the boys' expressions and saw a smirk on every face but Mr. Cox's. Dudon was up to something. "Who?" she asked, raising her left eyebrow.

"Brigham Yum."

The class laughed as she stood there blinking. "Oh, I see we have a jokester."

"He's always telling them," Mr. Cox said. "He thinks he's so cool, but he's not. He's just a cripple."

Betsy blinked in shock as Dudon glared at Cox. That seemingly nice boy had a mean streak. "I *will not* have any negative thinking in my class room, and that includes put-downs."

"Just stating the facts," Mr. Cox said through a clenched jaw.

"All right, let's fight it out. Now," Dudon said. "I'll show you who's crippled." His face reddened.

"That's enough, or I'll make all of you meditate. I sense unhappy vibes in this room."

The boys continued to issue threats.

"Okay. On the floor! Lotus position. Down," Betsy said.

The boys continued. Betsy walked over to Brother Cox, wrapped her hand firmly around his shoulder, and said, "On the floor."

The boy gazed up helplessly as Betsy stared back. He settled on the floor.

"Okay, I'm going to have you do a half lotus because the full one is too advanced for beginners. Extend your legs straight in front of you and have your feet touch each other."

"I'm not doing this," Brother Cox complained.

"Yes, you are. I won't have tension in my classroom. You guys have negative electrons floating between you, and you're going to have to learn how to have positive ones as well. I'll teach you until you can do the mental and physical exercises of relaxation in your sleep."

"I promise there won't be negative things floating around any more," Brother Cox said, pale-faced.

"All right, get off the floor," Betsy said. She turned her attention to Dudon. "How about you, young sir? What's your verdict?"

"There's no way you can get me to sit on the floor."

"There's some simple mental exercises that I could teach, though." Betsy smiled sweetly. "The first thing you need to do is close your eyes and picture nothing."

"That's okay. I'll behave, but Brett's going to get it after class."

Betsy ignored him. "Is it true you like riddles?" Betsy felt lucky that the lesson manual actually had riddles in them. That'd be the perfect way to reach this kid. Well, at least to capture his attention. From what she could judge, he was the leader, and if she could get him to listen and participate in class, then the others would follow.

"Love riddles. I read them all the time," Dudon said, his eyes perking with interest. "My favorites are Rick Walton's. His are real good and they drive adults crazy. I bet he writes them just to make adults mad. I'd really like to meet him one day."

"What kind does he write?"

"All kinds. Baseball, basketball, cowboy — you name it — he's done it."

"Has he done pioneer ones?" Betsy asked.

"Yep. Why?"

"Cause I was going to tell you some riddles the pioneers told as they were crossing the plains," Betsy said.

"Ah, you don't know any."

"When Brigham Young left Winter Quarters, what did he see on his right hand?"

"Fingers," Dudon said, yawning.

"Is he right?" asked a boy who'd been quiet for the whole class period.

"The answer was four fingers and a thumb," Betsy said.

"Close enough," Dudon said, then smiled.

"Isn't," Brett said.

"Who cares what you say?" Dudon said with a cold voice. "I got one for you, Teacher."

"Okay, shoot."

"How did happy dogs cross the plains?"

The room was silent until Betsy asked, "How?"

"In waggin' trains." Dudon slapped his leg and laughed.

"Good one. And that reminds me, does anyone know who was in the first company of pioneers?"

By the time Betsy had finished explaining who was in the first company of pioneers to leave Winter Quarters, a lady poked a head of fluffed hair into the classroom and said, "Five minutes."

"For what?" Betsy asked.

The lady was already out of the room, so she had to repoke her hair in. "Till you dismiss for Sharing Time."

"What's that?"

"That's when the kids come into the primary room and practice singing."

"Do I go with them?" Betsy asked.

"Sure do. It's right around the corner. The kids will show you." Then her head disappeared for good.

Dudon laughed and elbowed the guy next to him. "Yeah, we'll show her where it is, won't we Jason?"

Jason caught Dudon's vision and smiled. "Sure will."

Twelve minutes later, Betsy and her class of boys had found the primary room, and only Dudon and Jason weren't there. They had disappeared, saying they needed to visit the men's room. Betsy could tell that this calling was going to be challenging.

After church ended, Betsy swam through the crowd toward the closest exit. When she pressed the metal bar of the door, she heard a deep baritone voice say her name. "Sister Ashforth?"

Betsy turned to the distinguished-looking Mr. Chadwick. Jeff, the widower she'd said would one day be a Bishop. His streaks of gray glistened in the sun. Her heart puttered an extra pound. "Yes?"

"How did teaching go?" His bronze eyes peered into Betsy's.

"Fine, for the first day, I guess. I'm sure it'll get better." She clutched her lesson manual a bit tighter.

"My son wasn't too much of a problem for you, was he?"

"Your son?"

"Dudon."

Dudon was *his* son? That'd explain where the kid got such good looks. "Oh, he tried to be rowdy, but I whipped him into shape."

"Whipped him?"

"I didn't mean it literally. He's kind of active, isn't he?"

"Boys will be boys." Mr. Chadwick smiled.

"Boys will be what you expect out of them," Betsy said, then wished she hadn't spoken.

"Have you any kids of your own?"

"No."

An awkward silence fell between the two of them until Mr. Chadwick made up an excuse and dismissed himself. As he walked away, he turned around and said, "I do appreciate you teaching the class. It's not an easy one." Then he disappeared out the side door.

Mrs. Jefferson had come up to her right after Jeff and asked, "Are you still alive?"

Betsy had planned to quit the job right there, but said, "Just barely."

The primary president smiled. "It'll get better. Here, I have a book for you that might make things a little easier. It's a teacher's handbook. It'll help you become a more effective teacher. I've found it very helpful."

"Thanks," Betsy mumbled, and before she could say anything else, the smiling primary president had disappeared. After that she glanced up the hallway, only to spot an angry-looking woman with little Mr. Cox tugging on her sleeves, pointing directly at her.

Great. She'd forgotten that with boys came parents — a slight oversight. The woman marched down the hall as Betsy waited for the bomb to explode.

"There's the one who tried to strangle me," Brett said, pointing at Betsy.

"Are you the one that taught my son Brett's class today?" Brett's mom pointed at Betsy.

"Sure am." Betsy smiled casually. "I'm their new teacher."

"They've called you and everything?"

"Sure have. This is my first job in the church. I'm pretty excited."

"You're a convert?" The lady's voice grew louder.

What was wrong with that? Betsy thought, then said, "Just a couple of weeks."

The lady's nose crinkled. "How dare they call someone who doesn't even know the gospel to teach young impressionable minds! These boys are at a critical stage in their lives. Does the Bishop know about this?"

"He told me to do this," Betsy said, feeling on the offense.

"I meant does he know you're a recent convert?"

"Of course," Betsy said.

"I doubt that." The lady glanced over Betsy suspiciously.

Brett tugged on his mom's blouse. "Mom, don't forget about the strangling part."

The lady looked from her son to Betsy. "Oh, yes. What's this I hear about you threatening to strangle the boys in your class?"

"What about it?"

"Is it true?"

"Of course."

"Of course? How dare you admit to such a sin so lightly? You're unfit to be teaching those boys! I can't understand what the Bishop was thinking. They need to release him. He's been in too long. He's really losing his marbles. I'm going to talk to the Stake President."

"What kind of Christian are you anyway?" Betsy asked, then shrugged and walked away. Why did she even try with that class? Was it bad that lady was going to talk to the Stake President?

She noticed a display and wandered over to see it. The table was filled with crafts for Thanksgiving and Christmas. Betsy had never been one for crafts, but her sister-in-law would definitely go apes over these, especially the painted Christmas tree and Santa. Karen was a sucker for anything to do with holidays. If only she could get Karen to see how cute these decorations were, maybe she'd come to Homemaking, and then she'd know the Mormons weren't devils.

Betsy glanced over to where she and Sister Cox had argued and thought maybe they are devils. Maybe Karen was right.

Mrs. Thomson, Agatha's mom, came up to the table and smiled. "Cute, aren't they?'

"Sure are," Betsy said. "I was thinking if I showed these to my sister-in-law then she would have to make them."

"Bring her over here to the display table. I won't be putting it away for another minute or two."

"My sister-in-law isn't a Mormon. Remember she'd never set foot into a church building if she could help it?"

"Oh, that sister-in-law. How's she doing anyway?" Sister Thomson began taking down the display.

"Not so good, but maybe you could help me," Betsy said.

"Like how?"

"What if you come over to my house to ask me if I want to sign up for crafts, and you just happen to have these crafts with you. Then I could run and show her how cute they are. It might be enough to whet her appetite. Could you do that?"

"I have a real busy day today, you know, with my kids and all, but I'll see if I can manage."

"Oh, please. It would mean so much."

"If it means that much. Sure, why not? I can't get away until around five. Would that be okay?"

"Perfect," Betsy said, smiling at the genius of her plan. This one even had the possibility of working.

⁂

Thoughts of making her children social recluses plagued Karen during the night. Was Mikey really being negatively influenced by her or was she, as a mother, overgeneralizing? Was Sam affected too? Kicking at her sheets, she decided to climb from bed and find out.

She wrapped her robe around her, slipped into her worn blue slippers, and sloshed down the hall to Mikey's room. She stopped at the closed door and knocked.

"Just a minute," Mikey called, using the voice she'd always spoken in as a child when she hid something. What now? Karen's lower lip slipped under her big front teeth as she waited. Seconds seemed to drag on, and finally she twisted the door knob open. There'd be no more secrets from Mom. "What's going on in here?"

Mikey stood by the side of her bed with her blouse half unbuttoned, fingers tugging at the fabric as she fumbled to button. "Nothing." Her eyes were wide, and a blank expression covered her face.

"Were you changing shirts?" Karen asked as she sat on the rocking chair.

"Yeah."

Karen looked at the light green and white checkers that brought an added sparkle to Mikey's coloring. The sleeves tapered down half her arm, in a stylish design. "Why? It's cute."

"I thought I'd wear it tomorrow."

Karen squinted her eyes, then recognized the fabric. "Isn't that the shirt you were making with Agatha?"

Her daughter didn't reply.

"Is it?"

"Yeah."

"Why didn't you want to tell me?"

"'Cause, Mom."

"Have you been hanging out with Agatha a lot?"

"No. Promise. Just to finish the shirt."

The silence was strained, and Mikey squirmed under her mom's gaze. "I won't see her again." Tears slid down her face.

Karen hadn't overgeneralized this time. "Oh, baby cakes, this is my fault." She embraced her daughter.

"I tried not to play with Agatha or any Mormons to make you happy. Every day I eat lunch alone in the library, but, Mom, it gets so lonely. They really can't be that bad, can they? Agatha's a nice girl. If you got to know her, you'd think so. She believes some strange things, but she promised me she wouldn't suck me up into her group or even talk about it unless I wanted to."

Karen stared at her daughter's wide eyes.

"She really is a nice person," Mikey insisted.

"Did you sew the whole shirt by yourself?" Karen asked as she fingered the material.

"Agatha sewed it as I talked. She said she'd teach me how to sew pillows first if I wanted to learn."

Teaching her daughter a new skill wasn't a bad thing. "Maybe it's time I went over there and met her mother. It isn't very neighborly of me to have never said, 'hi.'"

"You did meet her once. Remember? She brought the homemade bread."

"Was she the one wearing the pants with the frayededge?"

"Yeah."

"And all the kids?"

"Yeah."

"She's got to be crazy to have all those kids, but perhaps she's not that bad. I could give it a try."

"Oh, thank you," Mikey said, squeezing her mom tight. "You're the best." She smiled, but the grin faded into a look of fear.

"What is it, child?"

"Will this make you upset again? I don't want to make you get sick."

Karen nestled Mikey's face inbetween her palms and said, "No."

"But they're evil. I'd much rather not get anywhere near them and have you get better than have Agatha as a friend."

"Don't worry. I'll handle it."

❧

Karen leaned forward in the alternate leg pull. She had to pull herself out of this depression one way or another and shake her mind of her daughter's fear-filled eyes. It was difficult knowing she was the cause. All hers. The psychologist had warned her that if she didn't control her unrealistic fears, her children would absorb them. Now her daughter was living in fear. She didn't want to mess Mikey up, but what choice did she have? She couldn't help how she felt. Deep down she knew the Mormons were another one of those religious cults. Charissa had belonged to a group like that.

Karen had been so upset over her friend's death that she'd refused to attend the funeral. Maybe she should have gone. She had heard it would have given her closure to see the body dead in a coffin. Every year on the commemoration of the date, her conscience pricked her to at least go the grave site, which she normally did. It had happened so long ago, and she still ran from it. The time had come to stop the race. She'd call her mother and find out what had really happened. Surely her mom knew more than she'd ever told. Karen's insides burned with uneasiness, but despite the ill feeling she knew it was right. She promised herself she'd make the call after dinner.

She changed her extended leg and stretched. Someone came up the stairs. Too heavy of a step to be one of the kids, and George had left for work to finish a project. It must be Betsy home from church.

Karen didn't have to wait long before her sister-in-law walked into the room and smiled.

"Hello," Betsy said. "I see you're doing some yoga. How's it coming?"

"I'm getting better. My body is growing used to it so it doesn't hurt as much."

"That's great."

"How was church?"

"Good," Betsy said. Her eyes drooped shut as she yawned.

"They sure keep ya there for a long time. How long do they need to brainwash?"

"They do seem to keep us forever. I'll have to ask why. It's done me in. Hey, if it's all right, I'm going to go rest a while. Then I'll prepare supper."

"I'll cook it," Karen said.

"No, I will. Let me get a little rest; then I'll be good as new."

"No, you've done enough," Karen said. She meant it. Everyone acted as if she were a queen so special they had to dote on her.

"I've been trying to help out."

"And you've done a great job, but it's my turn. You relax. I'll do the cooking."

"Sounds wonderful," Betsy said, "but are you up to it?" She kicked off her shoes.

"Positive." Karen rose to her feet.

"But — "

"I can handle it."

"Okay." Betsy slumped out of the bedroom.

*

Betsy flopped on the bed after slipping off her dress, too tired to slip on jeans and a T-shirt. Thankfully, Karen was doing better and preparing supper. Betsy doubted she had enough energy. The primary boys had sucked her strength. Sister Jefferson had told her right before the singing began it was her job to keep the kids quiet and participating for the whole hour. Not an easy thing.

Actually, she had failed to control the kids, like she had failed with Jeff. Handsome, single, and she had stood there lecturing like a know-it-all fool, and she'd never even been a parent. Stupid.

She had wanted to be a parent once, but Philippe said they had plenty of time. They didn't. And husband number one hadn't stuck around long enough for them to even talk family.

An image of Jeff's pained face flashed in through her mind. Oooh. Her and her mouth. Falling from grace with Jeff was probably for the best. He was too nice and normal to be her type. Philippe was more her speed. Wasn't he?

Yawning, she glanced at the clock. She had a little less than half an hour until Sister Thomson would stop by and show Karen the crafts. Betsy jolted out of bed. What if it caused a relapse? She closed her eyes; sickness sloshed around her insides. She'd created another mess, and now was the time to confess to minimize the damage.

Throwing her clothes on, Betsy treaded down the stairs. Karen hummed in the kitchen. Did she have to tell her sister-in-law she was going to force another Mormon on her? Yes, or risk a relapse.

Karen buzzed around. Betsy dragged herself to the cabinet and took the dishes to set the table. "You sound happy."

"Why not? I've decided I've had enough of being scared, and I'm not going to let Mormons control my life. I'm going to face them headon."

Betsy set her plate down. "Good for you. I'm glad to hear it." She placed cups on the table and listened to Karen's high-pitched hum. "Can I ask you why?" she asked, watching Karen closely from the corner of her eye.

Karen sighed. "I talked to Mikey today. Did you know she has no friends 'cause she's too busy hiding from the Mormons?"

"No," Betsy said.

"My fears are becoming hers, and it's not healthy. I decided to discover once and for all if they really are as bad as I thought."

Betsy continued to watch her, then softly asked, "Are you sure?"

Karen nodded as she rubbed her fist against her chin. "Yeah, I think so. They can't be bad if *you* joined them, can they?" She laughed nervously and glanced at Betsy.

"No, they can't," Betsy said. "Okay, so I've been known to join a couple of groups that were a little off."

"A couple?" Karen said with a smile.

"A lot. But," Betsy paused and stared at Karen, "but this one's different. Trust me. This group has the truth."

"You keep saying that. I'll have to believe you haven't lost your mind and you know what you're doing."

"How ready are you to trust me?" Betsy asked.

Karen searched Betsy's face. "Why?"

"I've done something I probably shouldn't have."

"What?" Karen asked, her voice becoming tense.

"At church they had this display of crafts that the sisters get together and make once a month."

"You've already told me about that."

"I know. Anyway they have some really cute stuff for Thanksgiving and Christmas. You'd love it."

"What did you do?" Karen snapped.

"I didn't like you being so afraid of the Mormons. It's not healthy for the mind or the soul..."

"And...Get on with it."

"I...knew how much you loved doing crafts — "

"And?"

"You see, this lady was putting up the display, so I just happened to ask her to drop by and show them to you."

"You did what?" Karen asked loudly.

"I thought if you saw how nice and normal this person looked, you wouldn't think Mormons were devils."

"And you thought you would entrap me with crafts?"

"Holiday ones."

"What kind?"

"Stuff you hang on the walls. You know Santa Clauses, Christmas trees, and Thanksgiving cornucopias."

"Are they ceramic?"

"Yep. They have everything." Betsy decided not to mention the small fee to cover the cost. She'd gladly pay it herself if Karen would bite at the bait.

Karen laughed.

Betsy looked up surprised. She thought she was ready for any kind of reaction, but she hadn't expected this. "What's so funny?"

"I worried about the Mormons entrapping me, but I never dreamed they'd use you and crafts. The combination is hilarious."

"Why?"

"Face it, Betsy. You're not the vision of a perfect homemaker who sits around making adorable knick knacks."

"You aren't either," Betsy said.

"I fit the picture better than you."

Betsy laughed. "That's true."

"To think you stooped so low — "

"Stooped?" asked Betsy. But before she could answer, the doorbell rang. Her glance darted to the microwave. Five o'clock exactly.

Karen looked over at Betsy and asked, "Is that your little craft friend?" She rubbed her hands together.

"I told her five." Betsy glanced away from Karen's eyes. "Do you want me to get rid of her?"

Silence filled the room until the door bell rang again. "I never agreed to have them in my home. I still have standards." Karen drifted into thought, and the bell rang again. "I guess my fears did come true. I did set up a ricochet effect, demanding there would be no Mormons in my house. You just couldn't leave a dare alone, could you? You're still a kid and thrive on them. You won't stop pestering me until I let one in, will you?" Karen's eyes grew large as she studied Betsy. "Well, I'm going to stop the pestering and meet this…one."

"Are you sure?" Betsy asked.

Karen nodded.

Betsy ran to the front door and caught Sister Thomson just as she'd walked down the sidewalk. Mrs. Thomson turned around and smiled. "I thought no one was home."

"Sorry," Betsy said. "Come in."

"Thank you. This is a beautiful home."

"Thanks. We like it. Let me get Karen. She's agreed to meet you."

"Oh, good."

Betsy rushed hastily into the kitchen. "Karen, are you ready?"

"No," she said, then brushed passed Betsy on her way to the front entry.

Betsy followed.

Karen approached the lady with her hand held out. They shook. "Agatha's mom. You're the craft lady?"

June nodded and looked up at Betsy. "Yep, I'm one of them. I heard you might have an interest in our projects."

"I don't know. When is it?" Karen tucked a lose strand of hair around her ear.

"This Wednesday at the church."

"If I come, would I have to stay the whole time?"

"No. You could leave any time." June shifted from one foot to the other.

"How do I know this isn't a trap?"

Sister Thomson shoved her hand in the pocket of her coat. "A trap? What do you mean?"

"How do I know you're not sucking me into your church?"

"Suck you in?"

"Yeah, with all those brainwashing techniques and stuff."

"Oh...I don't know. We just have a brief lesson at the beginning; then we do crafts all night. That's it. Nothing else." June looked over at Betsy as if searching for clues as to how she was doing. Betsy nodded.

"So if I miss the first part, then I'd miss the brainwashing stuff."

"I guess so."

"After the lesson you only do crafts?"

"Yes."

"What do you talk about?"

"Girl talk. You know about how difficult our husbands and kids are. That kind of stuff."

"Can I see what you're making?"

"Yeah," said June, tugging the bag off her shoulder. "Sorry, I forgot about it." She pulled out a small Santa with a red hat and toys surrounding his feet. The old man held a chubby child in his arms, and both wore huge grins.

"That's cute," Karen said. Then her eyebrows lowered. "Are you doing any without kids?"

"Of course," June said, eyeing Betsy. This time Betsy gave no response, so Sister Thomson glanced back at Karen and smiled.

"Can I come after the brainwashing session?" Karen asked.

June swallowed. "You bet."

Karen smiled. "Thanks, I'll try. It's been nice seeing you again."

After several tries to slip her purse back up, June said, "Um, one thing. I wouldn't call the lesson a brainwashing session. It's an uplifting thought. It wouldn't hurt you to hear what they have to say."

"Thanks," Karen said. "I've left dinner on the stove. I've got to go." Turning on her heel, she left without another word.

Betsy smiled at June. "Thank you. I appreciate this. You don't know what a big step this is for her."

"Why is she so afraid?"

"When she was a little girl, one of her friends was killed by a religious cult groups. She thinks all religions are evil, especially ones like ours that try to convert the world."

"Oh."

"Well, I hope she comes."

"I do too. Sign us both up for everything just in case. She needs the peace the gospel would bring her." Betsy returned to the kitchen and noticed Karen circling the room like a zombie. "It'll be fun, you'll see."

"Yeah," Karen said.

"Come on, smile. It will."

"If they suck me up, Betsy, I'll never forgive you. Never."

Chapter 15

Betsy bundled up in a thick coat with a wool blanket tucked around her as the fresh mountain breeze blew over the porch, wrestling the edges of the book pages. The sun had set, and she'd recently stood to flip on the porch light. The purple sky hovered on the tips of the mountains, hugging her with its beauty. Night grew darker as the sun sank deeper.

She glanced across the lawn and saw a dark thin figure drawing near. The shadow slipped closer with flowing elegance. Entranced at the grace, Betsy watched, placing her hand on her spot in the book. The shadow approached on the sidewalk. The person's jacket flopped open with each step. At last he came close enough for Betsy to make it out. "Jeff!"

"Hello," he said, smiling sheepishly. He handed her a wildflower. "I came to apologize. I overreacted today."

She sniffed the flower as she rubbed the stem between her fingers. "You're right. I don't know the first thing about being a parent."

"I do feel sorry for my son. It's hard not to. It's rough on a kid his age to lose his mother and legs in one instance."

Betsy nodded. "Come and sit."

He sat on the porch step. His dark brown eyes darted up at hers, then across the landscape. "Sometimes I wish I could just be in the solitude of nature."

"Sounds wonderful."

He smiled. His white teeth glowed in the darkness. "You like nature too?"

"It's a great way to tap into the center of one's self. There's messages in it. We need to pause and listen to it. Do you agree?"

"I don't know." He glanced at his hands. "I was never one much for nature until…until my wife passed away. Too busy. You know, had a career to advance and all. When she died, my life seemed useless. She was what counted and now she's…I like to be with nature 'cause I feel somehow it brings me closer to her. These are my times to commune with her, if only in my soul. Is that silly?" He searched Betsy's face.

"No...if she can relate to you, it makes sense it would be in those quiet reflective times."

"Perhaps it's my lonely self playing tricks, but I can't bear thinking I have to completely give her up in this life. Oh, listen to me. I'm rambling. If she heard me, she'd say, 'Jeff Chadwick, you straighten up right now and stop this moping. It's unbecoming on a man, and you're a man's man.'"

Betsy laughed. "She does have a point."

"What?"

Betsy rocked in her wooden chair. "It's time for you to start living your life. Think about your son."

"He's handling this thing better than even his old pop."

"Maybe you're not giving him any other options."

He sighed.

"Maybe you are," Betsy added quickly. "I wouldn't know. I've never been a parent. Only help my sister-in-law out now and then. And let me tell you, I don't do such a great job. My niece and nephew get embarrassed when I'm around and try to stay as far away from me as possible."

"That's typical. All teenagers do that. You should have heard my son go on and on about my tie and how it announced to the whole world I had no taste, and he'd rather die than be seen in the same building with me."

"The pink and purple tie you wore when I first met you? The one with all the dots on it?"

"Yeah."

"I love that tie. It's a piece of art. Kids these days don't have an appreciation for real beauty."

Jeff smiled, revealing a small straight line down his chin. "You're right. They don't. I'm glad to meet someone who can appreciate the finer things in life."

Betsy grinned. "That's me. I'm a magnet pulled to beautiful articles of clothing. Perhaps that's why I met you."

"Perhaps. If you're so talented at shopping, maybe you'd help me? I need a new tie, and I can't seem to find one that's not boring. I want something with class like my last one."

"Sure. My gravitational skills toward wonderful art pieces need sharpening anyway." A butterfly of happiness swept through her.

A confused look darted across his face. "That'll be great. How about Saturday afternoon?"

"Sounds wonderful." She couldn't help but smile at him. She felt like one of those silly teenagers all over again.

He grinned and stood. "Well, see you then."

❧

The night faded as Karen lie in bed, staring into the blackness. She'd agreed to go to one of those Mormon meetings. What was she thinking? George had laughed hysterically when he found out. "Got you with crafts, huh? They're clever."

She shot him a whole machine-gun load of dirty looks; he continued chuckling, until he paused to ask, "Why are you really going?"

This took Karen by complete surprise. She stared in amazement at her husband's perception; then a few stray tears escaped. "For Mikey. I realized she has no friends and lives in fear because I think the Mormons are evil. If her life's going to be miserable, I'd better make doubly sure I'm right."

"Be careful," George said.

Karen searched his serious face. Boy, he was full of shocks. "Why the sudden concern?"

"That's uncalled for. I'm always worried about you. Just have a hard time showing it."

"Uuuuh," Karen stumbled for words. He admitted he worried about her! He had a hard time showing it. She couldn't believe that. What a kind man! She grabbed her husband and squeezed him tight, feeling she rode an incredible wave of love.

"I'm happy to see you become a strong person and face your fears head on," George said.

Karen's grip around him loosened. "What did you say?"

"That I'm proud of you for facing your fears."

Karen's arm dropped to her side. "But you were embarrassed before?"

"I didn't say that."

"Didn't have to."

George tried to back pedal from there, but the damage was done. He thought she'd been a chicken through this whole thing. How could he think that? She was his wife. The person he was supposed to put on a pedestal, not find fault with.

Three hours after the incident, Karen decided she'd show George, and he'd regret ever thinking she was a chicken. It may not be very mature, but she'd make him eat his words. In three days, she'd walk into one of their churches and talk with their people. Of course she'd go late and miss their brainwashing session.

Stress tensed her muscles throughout her body. Why was she doing this? Mikey. She needed to be an example of facing things headon.

The next morning, the restlessness of the night became apparent as she longed for sleep. She even gave in and took a break. In the common room, a fluffy couch invited her to enjoy a short catnap. She had barely stretched out and shut her eyes when she heard the voice of her friend Amber chatting with another co-worker, Mary. Karen didn't know Mary well. She seemed like a nice girl. The two girls discussed the boss.

"What do you think is wrong with him?" Amber asked.

"Stress," Mary said.

"Maybe he got in a bad fight with his wife last night, and he's still upset," Amber said.

"Doubt it." Mary shook her head.

"Why?" Amber asked.

"They made him a bishop," Mary said, with a voice of importance.

"You're kidding?"

"Not."

Karen sucked in her breath. A sharp pain shot through her chest. Was her boss one of them? She sat up and yawned. "Do you mean the bishop over the Catholic church? Isn't he going to have to quit work here to do that?"

The two ladies laughed. "Nah, we mean a Mormon bishop," Mary answered. "That'd be funny. Can you see Mr. Rawles running around in one of those white robes."

"He's a Mormon?" Karen asked. Her back stiffened. She thought *relax,* but it didn't do any good.

"Yep."

The ladies were calm and able to understand the lingo. They must be part of the cult too. "Are you two Mormons?" Karen asked.

"Yep."

"Oh," Karen whispered. Her miserable morning worsened. Her leg cramped.

"Is there anything wrong?" Amber asked.

Karen looked up. The two ladies watched her intently. "No." The ladies' confusion lessened, but waited for further explanation. "I didn't know everyone was Mormon around here."

"They aren't. Some are. Some aren't."

"If Mr. Rawles finds out I'm not, will that mean I won't be able to move up in this company?" Karen asked.

"Of course not," Mary said.

"Not unless they want a lawsuit," Amber said, crumbling up her potato chip bag. "And being a bishop, I doubt Mr. Rawles wants anything more to worry about." She shot for the trash can and missed. Groaning, she retrieved her trash.

"Ain't that the truth," Mary agreed.

"I'd better get back to work," Karen said.

"Me, too," chorused the other girls, and, reluctantly, everyone returned to their cubicle.

The calls poured in and Karen kept working, but thoughts about Mormons sank into her mind anyway. Why were they everywhere in Utah?

An hour after lunch, Karen received an e-mail informing her that Mr. Rawles wanted to meet with her at four o'clock. Her heart stopped beating for a brief moment as she pondered why. Mary and Amber had heard her admit she wasn't a Mormon this morning, quick enough for the news to spread to the big cheese's ears. Would he fire her?

Karen fiddled at her desk, trying to decide what to do. She remained that way for several minutes until she glimpsed Amber visiting the little girl's room. Now was her chance. She followed her coworker into the rest room and made funny faces in the mirror until Amber came out of the stall.

"Hello," Amber said.

"Hi," Karen replied.

"What's the matter?"

Karen looked into Amber's traitorous face. "I just received an e-mail. Mr. Rawles wants to meet with me."

"I'm sure it's nothing to worry about." Amber put her hands under the running faucet.

"Did you tell him I wasn't a Mormon?" Karen crossed her arms over her chest.

"No, why would that...You don't think that would make a difference, do you?"

"There are an awful lot of Mormons working here."

"There are a lot of Mormons living here." She wiped her hands on the towel.

"Explain."

"The Mormons settled Utah because the mobs drove them from the east in the 1800s."

"Oh, so you don't think Mr. Rawles would fire me, do you?"

"If he did, I'd leave too. You're one of the best employees he has." Amber patted Karen on her shoulder. "Don't worry."

Karen sighed, relieved. But Mary could squeal.

She returned to her desk, and the hours faded quickly as her work became more and more demanding. It seemed like everyone across the county had eaten lunch and taken a pill drugging them to buy software. The calls rang one on top of the other, draining her.

The clock struck four. Karen continued talking with an elderly customer from Wisconsin.

"Yes, Ms. What tapes can I get for you today?"

"I'm still thinking. I just hate making decisions like this, don't you? It seems like kids of today don't take the time to consider the value of money and how careful you need to be with every dime. If they would've lived through the depression, it would be a different story."

"I'm sure it's different. Can I get you the beginning tape or the whole set?" Karen's eyes were fixed on the clock, which now read five after.

"If I buy the package, I get the discount?"

"Yes."

"But if I only buy the beginning, I might need the others. But maybe I won't."

"Let me tell you what's in the first tape to help you with your decision," Karen said, her stomach knotting as the clock continued to tick away. At last the woman made her decision, and Karen was on her way to the boss' office.

Once inside the big chief's domain, she saw Mr. Rawlins perched behind the desk covered with papers and books. He chatted on the phone as his plain blue eyes watched Karen enter. He signaled for her to sit. She waited; he talked. "No, don't do that. That'll be a mistake. It would cause confusion with the writers. A better way to organize that is to..." And on he went.

He spoke with certainty as his young face listened intensely to the person on the other end. He must be in his early thirties, and he built the company from the ground up. Impressive.

A few more minutes passed, and then he hung up. "Mrs. Ashforth, I called you in because I wanted to thank you for the hard work you've been doing for the company..."

"But," thought Karen. Her muscles ached from flexing.

"Amber and Mary have been talking about you..."

Karen held her breath. Amber was a double-timing, back stabbing...

"I've decided to give you your first pay raise."

Karen blinked. "What?"

"It'll only be a dollar more an hour, but the next time you'll be up for a promotion."

"You're giving me a raise even though I'm not Mormon?" Karen asked in a daze.

"What does being a Mormon have to do with it?"

"I thought…" Heat rushed to her face. She didn't want to say any more.

"You thought what?" Mr. Rawles leaned on his desk.

"It's silly."

"Tell me."

"I heard you were made a bishop, and I thought you would want to give everyone in your congregation jobs, so you'd kick out the non-Mormons."

"If you stay employed here or not will have nothing to do with your religious beliefs; it'll have everything to do with the way you perform. I promise you."

Karen sighed. "That's good."

"I'm sorry you got the wrong impression."

"I am too."

"Thank you for coming." He stood.

"Thank you for the raise."

"Keep up the good work." They shook hands, and Karen returned to her pile of messages.

⁂

That evening Karen strolled to her car. Her heels clicked against the concrete in a short, slow pace, which spoke of a confident business woman. Feelings of success uplifted her as she slipped into the car. The radio blared a commercial. She switched it off, not wanting to ruin the mood.

The car cruised around the sleepy town in its golden hour. Everything glistened with color. The last of the fall flowers had reached their peak. Grass stood dark green, nourished by recent storms. Karen inhaled a deep breath. She'd gotten a raise! She'd achieved success in the business world. Even in her dreams she hadn't dared think she could, but now it had come true. This was where she belonged. Forget nursing. It was too much fun being involved in the rapid evolution of computers. A smile spread across her face. She'd found her place.

Halfway home, Karen realized this positive feeling in her life was what she'd been waiting for. It gave her the strength to face her past.

It was time to call her mom and learn about the Magdalene cult. She'd put it off long enough. Successful business women didn't let their pasts scare them, but confronted their challenges head on.

Once home, her heart sounded like rolling thunder. She knew the noise wouldn't stop until she made the call. Her fingers pressed the cold numbers on the phone. The line connected with the receptionist. "Fern Watson's room, please."

"One moment."

The clock ticked on Karen's desk. She slumped to her bed and sat down with a plop. The phone rang several times. A tired "hello" greeted her ears.

"Mom."

"Who is this?" her voice cracked.

"Your daughter, Karen."

"Hello. It's been a long time since I heard from you."

"I wanted to check on how you are." She scooted herself back along the mattress.

"Doing great. I'm dating this real sexy guy, and he's been stealing all my time."

"Mom!"

"I'm alive, aren't I?"

"Yeah, but you're a mother."

"I'm not dead, sweetheart."

"All right. Tell me about Mr. Perfect." The next twenty minutes Karen received the whole life history of the man, including every pet he owned and how they died. Married twice, he was a double widower. Now, Karen felt sure his ambition was to move onto a third marriage. Didn't sound so bad, and he kept her mom busy. She needed that.

"What have you been up to?" her mom asked.

"I wondered if you can help me."

"What's that?"

"I wanted to know more about the cult Charissa's mother belonged to."

"The Magdalene Members. I don't know much. Let's see. The leader's name was Daisy Carter, but she changed it to Mary Mage after she had a vision to do so. But I'm getting ahead of myself. Let me start from the beginning. She was married to this guy… The name escapes me, but anyway they couldn't have children. After a few years of trying, Mary started losing it. She'd growl at children when they walked by her house."

"Growl?" Karen asked.

"Yeah, you know like an angry dog."

"You're kidding?"

"I'm telling you she was whacked," Fern said. "Her screws were bouncing all over the place, crashing into each other.

"All the neighborhood kids would avoid her place like the plague. She was basically harmless until she discovered her husband's affair and the children that came from it. Then she freaked."

Karen wiped the moisture on the palm of her hand onto her skirt. "What did she do?"

"First, it was little things. She kicked her husband out, cut her hair short, and talked about how awful men were — the basics of a divorced woman. But that must not have been enough for her rage because she gathered women together who felt the same way. They'd harp together about how unfair society was. These meetings continued until she claimed she saw Mary."

"The Virgin Mary — the mother of Jesus?" Karen asked.

"No, Mary Magdalene. People said Daisy called her The Prophetess Mary..."

The title, the Prophetess Mary stuck in Karen's mind like a scratched record, playing over and over. She'd heard that reference before. Where?

Then an image came of a dark misty room with women dressed in brown robes, huthering together. They were in a daze at Daisy's words.

"The Prophetess Mary spoke to me. She said I had been called to lead the faithful followers to salvation," Daisy said, then paused to look her followers in the eyes. A sound of awe vibrated through the room. "The Prophetess Mary then revealed to me that I was the chosen one.

I'm the woman she'd been waiting for because I have John the Baptist's blood pumping through my veins."

Karen squinted her nose with this memory. She heard her mom pause in her speech, so she asked, "Was Daisy a Hebrew?"

"Heaven's no. She was as English as they come. Why?"

"I just seem to remember hearing Daisy claim to have a direct blood line to John the Baptist."

There was a pause on the other end of the line. "One thing you got to remember, poodems, is a lot of what Daisy said made no sense. People will believe anything if they have a strong enough desire to."

"Yeah, I guess that's true," Karen said quietly.

"People have a strong need to want to belong and fit in. Look what Hitler was able to do by manipulating that desire."

"It's so sad people could become so vulnerable." Karen's stomach knotted. "But you'd think people would wake up when she said a ton of confusing things."

"That's why she isolated them. It's part of her way of manipulating brain control. She made them give up their families and friends."

"What do you mean?" Karen asked.

"They weren't allowed to speak to them, see them, or have any other contact."

"You're kidding?"

"Nope. It gets worse. They couldn't read magazines or books, no TV. Nothing. That's how she was able to maintain mind control."

"Crazy." Karen fingered her bedspread.

"She eventually told the group what to think. Their minds became her property."

"Sick." Karen lay down. How could someone control another person like that? Why would they want to?

"The more she controlled, the more extreme she became for power, until at last she declared Mary Magdalene had told her that a holy person had to die to prevent corruption from infiltrating the group. John the Baptist and Christ of old had done so."

"But both those people were men, and Charissa's a girl. Wouldn't it reason that the target should be a male?" Karen asked.

"It would reason, but since the group was all females, and only daughters were allowed to remain with the women followers, it had to be a female. Daisy reasoned that society was undergoing an evolution under her direction from a patriarchal society to a matriarchal one."

"Right," Karen said with bitter sarcasm.

"To acceleratethis transformation, the sacrifice needed to be a firstborn and have a parent as a faithful follower."

"Charissa."

"Yes," her mom's voice cracked. "It was my understanding Charissa's mom begged for her daughter to have the privilege. She was so off-based."

Fern fell into a coughing spell as Karen stared into nothingness. "Excuse me. I need some water."

Charissa was the chosen one. Her mom wanted the privilege! How sick could someone's mind become? How could other people fall for this crap? It all seemed so stupid.

"Sorry, dear, I'm back. That's all I can think of."

"I remember the group looking at me and pointing as though they were considering me for the sacrifice."

"That's awful. I can't tell you how horrified I was when I discovered this stuff was happening at the house in which my baby had been hanging out! I spent years agonizing over it. I'm so sorry, my child. If I would have known, you'd never have gone near that place."

"Mom, I know that. But if they needed a faithful follower, why would they have considered me?" She wiped her forehead.

"I heard there were a few members who thought any girl would do. But, Mary or Daisy, whatever you want to call her, insisted it be a follower to make the ultimate sacrifice."

Karen's eyes closed as swooping darkness enclosed her. Her best friend killed because some sick woman wanted to get revenge on the world because of her lack of ability to have children. Senseless.

"Karen? Are you there?"

"Yes," she whispered.

"Did I tell you too much? I shouldn't have told you."

"No. I wanted to know.... I needed to know."

"Why?"

"I had to face it. I had to know why I lost my friend and what sort of religion it was."

"A sick one. Not like the normal kinds you're allowed to question. Mary was the indisputable leader. If people challenged that they were made to believe something was wrong with them."

"Thank you for telling me. I have a lot to think about. I better go."

"You sure you're okay?"

"Yes, I believe I am. The truth has somehow made me feel sick yes, but free. Do you understand what I mean?"

"I do."

❧

Two days had passed, and Homemaking night had arrived. Betsy bubbled with excitement; Karen had decided to come. Betsy had made additional plans to surprise her sister-in-law. She had told her the meeting started at six-thirty. It really began at seven. If they were a half-an-hour late, Karen would arrive just in time for the happy thought. Things had worked out even better than she'd planned. If Karen heard the word of God, she'd be more impressed. Betsy hummed as she cleaned the house.

The phone rang. "Hello," she sang into the machine.

"Is Ms. Betsy Ashforth there?" came a voice with a sharp, jagged tone.

"Speaking."

"This is Mrs. Johanson. My son, Brett, is in your Sunday school class."

"Yes?"

"I heard about your lesson, and I don't approve of you threatening the children. I don't think it's funny when it comes to witchcraft."

"Witchcraft?" Betsy asked dumbfounded. "What are you talking about?"

"Didn't you say you were going to force positive feelings through yoga and meditation?"

"Yeah?"

"See, you admit to teaching kids witchcraft. I won't allow my son to attend a class where they learn the devil's tricks. They're supposed to be having lessons on the gospel, not bizarre philosophies."

Betsy dropped onto a stool. "But learning how to relax and project a positive thought pattern is a good thing."

"I don't want to hear any justification of your actions. I want you to fix the problem. If I hear you've taught any more wild lessons in the church classroom, I'll withdraw my child from your class. We'll go to a different ward. Do you understand?"

"I hear you," Betsy said, biting back words. It was pretty plain this woman wouldn't listen to a thing she said.

"I'm going to have the Bishop keep a close eye on you. You're a dangerous woman. A devil in sheep's clothing. I'm warning you, if you hurt any of the children, you'll never get away with it."

With that, the woman hung up. She shrank to the floor. Witchcraft? She'd never been accused of that before. It was pretty clear she wasn't up to this job. She simply didn't have enough knowledge about the way things were supposed to happen. She'd call the Bishop and resign. She'd never meant to upset people.

Maybe she should have a talk with the Bishop about her membership, too. If working on positive thought power and meditation wasn't something the Mormons believed in, then she should know. Maybe she'd quit. This tugged a sad string on her heart. She liked the warm feeling she received when she went to church, and she liked knowing the answers. It was the truth. But positive thinking and meditation were so dear to her and so much a part of her existence. Could she give them up?

She hadn't felt so gloomy since her big battle with depression after Philippe's betrayal. The church had the truth, and positive thinking had to be part of their belief system. Had to. Suddenly, Betsy's visions of being the Relief Society president and leading the women to happiness shattered. This church was a different type of noodles than what she'd expected. They had a new set of rules, and she didn't know if she wanted to learn or follow them. Would believing in positive thoughts and meditation keep her from getting saved?

Betsy flipped the phone book open and found the Bishop's work number. After the third ring, a girl with a chipper voice answered.

"Is Mr. Hawthorne there?"

"Who's calling, please?"

"Betsy Ashforth."

"Hang on, I'll see."

The Bishop must have given some teenybopper a job, Betsy thought. He was a good man.

"Betsy, what can I do for you?" the Bishop's asked.

"I don't think I should teach primary," Betsy choked out.

"Why not?"

"I don't seem to be fit for the job. I got an angry call from one of the mothers. I'm sure you've heard."

"People are people, and I hope you won't let their closed-minded treatment push you away," the Bishop said. "The Church is true. The people try hard, most of them, but we all fall short. I hope you'll allow room for mistakes like you want God to do for you."

"But aren't you worried I'm going to pollute these young minds?"

"I have complete faith in you. You'll search out what the right and proper things are and be a big asset to the kids."

"But...I threatened to teach them to meditate in church. What does the Church think about that?"

"I'm sure you'll know what's right. Meditation is great if not carried too far. You should be careful not to deny the power of the Holy Ghost or faith in Jesus. But you're a truth seeker and will figure it out. The Lord will make you equal to your task."

She sighed.

"I wish there were more intellectually strong women like you in the ward."

The Bishop was right. She had no choice but to keep plowing ahead, but no more meditation and energy flowing lessons? It seemed too controversial. Besides, what would Jeff think if he found out she'd been teaching Dudon those kinds of lessons?

Why did she care what he thought? It wasn't like her to base any action on others' opinions. Why start now?

Chapter 16

Karen slumped to the back door, carrying her dress shoes. Since her pay raise, she'd been extra busy proving she'd earned the promotion. The door squeaked as she opened it; her head screamed in pain. She needed an aspirin and rest so she could make it through that dang craft meeting that night. She crept into the kitchen, only to be greeted by Betsy.

Her sister-in-law sat at the table with her hand on her forehead, moaning.

"Bad day, huh?" Karen asked, hoping this meant she'd want to stay home tonight. She could use extra sleep.

Her sister-in-law looked up, wrinkling her nose. "Huh?"

"I asked if you had a bad day."

"Not too bad."

"Is anything wrong?" Karen asked.

"Just tired." Betsy batted her make-up covered eyelids, yawning.

"If you're too tired to go tonight, I'll understand."

"Oh, no, you don't! I'm not that tired. But I have to hand it to you, it was a nice try. You'll be ready to go at six-thirty?" Betsy asked.

"Seven. Remember I want to miss the brainwashing stuff. It would take about half an hour, right?"

"Probably less." Betsy frowned.

"Seven then. I don't want to take any chances."

Karen turned to leave, but then paused. "Betsy, there's something I must know about the Mormons before I go."

"What's that?"

"Is the church controlling?"

"That was my big hang-up about them before I joined. But the more Mormons I've met, the more I discovered how strong-willed and independent they are. They encourage education and finding answers for yourself.

"You'd understand how individuals are respected if you knew the way the Bishop treated me just a few minutes ago.

"I've been struggling with my church position, feeling discouraged and wanting to quit. I called the Bishop. He listened to my concern and didn't belittle me afterwards or say it was all in my head. Instead, he had faith in me. He said the Lord would make me equal to my task, but I could quit if I choose too. I declined. He said he wished more intellectually strong-willed women like myself lived in his ward."

"He did?"

"He did. You might say it was because he didn't want me to quit, but I doubt it. I'd cheat myself if I did give up. He's been supporting me and giving me the courage so I can face my own battle. I see no control taking place there. It was totally my choice."

The phone buzzed. Karen sighed. Who could it be? She hated the telephone. She'd spent too much time on that machine at work, but the phone's nonstop ring continued.

"Want me to get that?" Betsy asked.

"No, that's okay," Karen said, answering the phone. "Hello."

"Is Karen Ashforth there?"

"Speaking."

"Hi, this is Mrs. Thomson."

"Yes."

"I was calling to remind you about Homemaking tonight. We'll be starting at seven."

Karen raised her eyebrow as she glanced at Betsy. "Thank you. I appreciate your calling."

"No problem. See you there."

Karen hung up the phone. Turning toward Betsy, she said in a loud voice, "You lied to me."

"What are you talking about?" Betsy asked.

"That was Mrs. Thomson to remind me Homemaking's at seven. You knew how I felt about missing the brainwashing session, and you charged right ahead and tricked me so I'd be there."

"I-I-I — "

"I don't want to hear your excuses. If the church you belong to teaches you to lie and manipulate people into doing what you want them to do, then I want nothing to do with it. Nothing. You hear?" Karen popped two aspirin in her mouth, took a handful of water, tossed it in, and swallowed. "I've had it with your lies. I used to think I could trust you. I was wrong." She marched up the stairs.

How dare Betsy trick her? Mormons were evil. Just look what they'd done to her sister-in-law. She used to be honest. Hadn't she? She flopped herself on the bed in hopes sleep would come, despite the anger brewing inside.

Angry thoughts tossed around. Just when she'd drifted off into la la land, the door squeaked opened.

"Mom?"

"What?" Karen asked in a grouchy voice. She closed her eyes tighter, then opened them to see Mikey. "What is it?" She took a special effort to sound nice.

"I wanted to thank you for going to that craft thing tonight. It means a lot to me that you're willing to find out firsthand what the Mormons are like."

Karen remained silent. What was she going to do? She could leave Betsy in the dust, but here was her daughter, the person she wanted to be a good example for, especially since she'd been so awful lately. "Did Betsy put you up to this?" She raised an eyebrow.

"Aunt Betsy? What does she have to do with it?"

"Just checking." Karen yawned.

"Mom, I also wanted to tell you that you don't have to do this if you don't want to. I can find other friends besides Agatha. It's no big deal."

Ouch, thought Karen, as she lay in silence. Mikey was better at dishing out the guilt than Betsy. She must have learned from the best and improved. "Don't worry, I'm going and I'll be fine." She smiled to prove her point.

"I'm serious. You don't have to. If you feel tense, I want you to stay home. Promise me you will."

"I'll be fine."

"Promise me."

"All right, I promise."

"If you feel any stress at all, don't go."

"Any."

"I love you." Mikey kissed her mother on the cheek.

After Mikey left, Karen cursed herself. How did she get in such a situation? Why had she said she'd go? How could she not, when her daughter was preparing to martyr herself so her mother wouldn't experience discomfort? Why did Karen promise she'd stay home if she felt an ounce of stress?

She couldn't stay home. Not after knowing it would break her little girl's heart. But there was no way she was going to make it through the situation without being very tense and stressed.

What was she going to do about Betsy? She didn't want her sister-in-law to feel she could lie to her continually and have things work out. Karen clenched her fists. She'd sneak away and go to the meeting by herself. That would be better anyway. It would make her judgment of the Mormons a more objective opinion, and she'd wouldn't have to talk to Betsy. Since she told Betsy she wasn't going, she hoped her sister-in-law wouldn't go either.

Karen forced herself out of bed to freshen up. She normally didn't wear make-up, but this was a special occasion, and she wanted any booster possible.

A knock sounded on her door. Dropping the mascara, she ran to the bed and threw the covers over herself. "Come in," she said in a tired voice.

Betsy walked in. Karen tugged the blanket farther over her face. "Hi." Betsy said, peering in shyly. Strange for her.

"I came to say I was sorry," Betsy said.

"For what?"

"Upsetting you. I also wanted you to know Mormons didn't put me up to it. It was my own scheme."

"So? You're one of them."

"That's true, but lying isn't something they believe under any circumstance. I was wrong. I did it, though, 'cause I care."

"How does deception show care?" Karen asked, still hiding beneath the blanket.

"You're not going to understand, but I honestly believe The Church of Jesus Christ of Latter-Day Saints has the truth. If you would listen to the principles with an open mind, then you, too, would find the comfort I discovered. The knowledge would make you happy like it has me."

Karen didn't know what to think. Lying, truth, feeling good... Religions on whole seemed strange.

Betsy backed up. "Sorry, I didn't mean to hurt you. This was my idea, not my religion's. The principles are truth, not the people." Betsy closed the door behind her.

Karen shut her eyes and listened to her sister-in-law's steps fade. Betsy was defensive of this new religion of hers. She opened her eyes to peek at the clock. Six-forty-five. She might as well see what their brainwashing session was like. If she put up a strong enough defense, there was no way their talking could control her.

She forced herself out of bed, keys jingling in her hands. The phone rang. "Hello?" she whispered.

"Karen, is that you?" George asked.

"Yes."

"You don't sound so good."

"I feel a little under."

"You're not planning on going to that Mormon church then, are you?"

"Still planning on it."

"Don't go," George said.

"Why?"

"'Cause I don't want you getting sick."

"I'll be fine. I'm just tired. That's all."

"Why don't you stay home?" George asked.

"Why don't you be honest with me? You're afraid I'm going to have another breakdown, and you're too chicken to admit it." George had picked the wrong time to mess with her. Anger at Betsy still bubbled through her blood. Silence. "Aren't you going to say something?" Karen snapped.

"What? You make it sound like a crime that I care about my wife."

She didn't respond.

He continued, "Okay, I admit since you had your little episode, I haven't known how to act around you, so I treated you normal, thinking the medicine took the edge off and that was how you wanted to be treated. But then you seemed like you were going to lose it, so I got real cautious. Good grief, Karen, I don't know what you expect. I try to do everything you want. This isn't easy."

"I guess not. Sorry, dear. I didn't know I was causing you so much frustration."

"I'd like to know if I'm helping you or not," George said.

Karen bit her lip, fighting back tears. "Oh, sweetheart, you do. You're a great support. I wouldn't have made it without you. I know it's been hard with the stress of your work, family, and everything, but I really do appreciate it."

"You do?" he asked mildly.

"Of course."

"That's nice to hear. And I appreciate you too. I want you to be happy. That's all I care about."

"Oh, George, I love you and appreciate your worry. It means a lot."

"Thank you."

"We need to discuss these things more often," Karen said.

"You're right, dear. Let's go out this weekend and do more talking."

"Great." Karen said her farewell and hurried to the church.

She made it to the meeting five minutes early. A few cars dotted the parking lot. Should she go in or go back home? An incredible urge to return home flooded her, but memories of Mikey's tortured face haunted her. She had to do this.

She crawled into a side door and paused. Where should she go? A couple of ladies brushed past her and smiled. She followed them into a little room with chairs set out and a table decorated with lace and fake floral arrangements. Someone played the piano. Several older ladies huddled in a group, talking.

Karen scanned the room for an empty seat away from everyone. The chair next to the door remained vacant, so she slid into it. A perfect location for a get away.

As the minutes passed, more and more women streamed into the room, until people had to climb over her to reach chairs. Ten minutes after seven Mrs. Thomson rushed in, dumping tons of supplies off by the side wall. She spotted Karen and smiled. "You came."

"Yeah," Karen said.

"I hoped you would. Save the seat next to you and I'll sit by you. I have to do a couple more things and I'll be right back. That's if you want me to."

"Sure." Karen smiled, not certain how to respond. She was glad she'd be sitting by someone she knew, if only remotely.

A middle-aged woman in a striped blue and white dress stood in front of the group. Her hair rested at shoulder length and curled up. Definitely a fifties look, Karen thought.

"I'd like to welcome you all out to Homemaking. I'm glad so many of you came." She smiled, indenting the deep blue eye liner underneath her dark brown eyes.

Heat radiated from Karen. The brainwashing had begun. She'd promised Mikey she wouldn't come if it made her uncomfortable. She'd told a big lie because this made her very uneasy.

"Sister Wahlquist will give us our visiting teaching message after our opening song and prayer." The greeter sat and an eighty- or ninety-year-old lady struggled up to the front of the room.

"The hymn, 'Lord, I Would Follow Thee,' is found on page 220."

A person a couple of chairs down passed a hymnal to Karen. Karen struggled to breathe. Relax, she told herself, as she gulped.

Right then Betsy barged into the room. She looked at Karen and said too loudly, "There you are. I've been searching all over for you. I can't believe you came."

"Shh!" Karen said, sliding over to make room.

Betsy sat, leaning over to whisper, "Are you okay?"

"I'm glad you're here," Karen answered.

Betsy patted her hand as the group sang.

> Sav-ior, may I learn to love thee,
>
> Walk the path that thou hast shown,
>
> Pause to help and lift an-oth-er,

Find-ing strength be-yond my own.

Sav-ior, may I learn to love thee — Lord,

I would fol-low thee.

Karen's breathing had eased, although she wondered if the leaders of the church manipulated the followers to do their will under the pretense of following the Savior.

Mrs. Thomson slipped around Betsy's and Karen's knees to the empty chair, smiling. The line "pause to help and lift another" raced through Karen's mind. Was that what Agatha's mom was doing? Helping her? Heaven only knew what Betsy had told her. Karen guessed Betsy had mentioned her fears of the Mormons.

Betsy lifted her hand from Karen's and smiled. She bowed her head, her purple hair falling slightly forward, and whispered, "Prayer."

Karen closed her eyes, but her thoughts raced. Betsy surely tried to lift her spirits, even though she'd gone about it completely wrong. The idea of stopping and helping another person wasn't so bad. There seemed to be an ideal that would build virtue. But to blindly follow seemed dangerous and was what happened to those people who got caught up in cults.

A girl stood. She looked in her early twenties, and before she talked she flipped her long flowing hair. The hair sparkled as it bounced. Oh, to be twenty again.

"Sisters, I'd like to encourage you to get out and do your visiting teaching. There are many blessings and rewards that come from serving God's children."

Karen glanced at Betsy. "What's visiting teaching?"

"It's where two women go over to another woman's house to make sure she's doing well and to give her an uplifting thought. They're supposed to visit her once a month. Also they're advised to help her in any way they can. It's a way for everyone to look out for each other."

"Oh," Karen said, impressed. She listened again to the talk.

"In Galatians, which is found in the New Testament, it says in chapter fourteen verse thirteen, 'By love serve one another.' How does this apply to visiting teaching?"

An older woman raised her hand, and the teacher nodded. The elderly lady spoke. "It means we should truly love the sisters we visit."

"Exactly," the teacher continued, "and in order to love them you must know them, visit with them, and serve them. I'd like all of us to think about serving our sisters we're in charge of and think of how we can lovingly serve them. I say this in the name of Jesus Christ, Amen."

The twenty year old stood and gave a five-minute talk on the importance of having a two-year supply of food, then sat.

"That was the brainwashing session," Betsy whispered. "Pretty sneaky, I' d say."

Karen smiled faintly, lost for words.

⁂

The exhilaration of the creative power had gushed into Betsy's blood stream, pumping with tremendous power. She reacted to this surge of energy that came from being exposed to craft-making in action. After Homemaking, she drove to the hardware store a few minutes after they'd closed and banged, until a cross-looking sales clerk opened the door.

"Thank you, my child." Betsy pushed her way in. "I'm overcome with the muses and must reorganize the bland patterns of my kitchen. It's screaming at me right now."

By this point, Betsy had made it to the cart and shot it straight for the paint section. The young boy gave Betsy a helpless look when Betsy turned to see him following. "Hurry up, boy," Betsy said. "You don't want to be up all night, do you?" The boy's pace quickened. Betsy arrived at the paints and immediately stopped. Closing her eyes, she took a deep breath. "My being, what brilliant colors. Ahh!"

The boy jumped at Betsy's screams and then glanced with big eyes toward where she pointed.

"You have deep purple. Wonderful and look... There's shocking pink. How about sunflower yellow? I must have yellow." The boy walked over to a gallon of paint. "Oh, not wimpy yellow. I want brilliant, bright. I want yellow you can't miss. The stuff that says, I'm here."

The boy found a different gallon. "Not as bright as I'd like, but I don't expect you'd mix paint at this time of night, would you?" The boy shook his head. "Orange. Do you have a dark orange?"

"Crossing-guard shade?" the boy asked.

"Yes!"

"Is that all?" The boy looked at his watch.

"It'll make a good start."

The boy sighed. Betsy raised her eyebrows.

"Sorry," the boy muttered.

Once Betsy arrived home, she allowed the sparkling energy to burst upon her white kitchen that had been begging for color for so long, until she collapsed into an exhausted sleep.

Chapter 17

The next morning Betsy woke, lying on the floor in her apartment, to screaming. She moaned as she twisted around under a tarp. "What in the universe?" Another moment she broke loose the tangle the fabric had on her. She must have fallen asleep while she was in the midst of her painting frenzy last night. Betsy smoothed her own hair down and yawned. "What's going on?"

"Your kitchen's been attacked by vandals!" Mikey pointed at the streaks of orange, pink, purple, and yellow.

Betsy laughed. "That was me," she said. "Isn't it exhilarating? My creative juices really gushed last night."

"You did this?"

Betsy glanced around the room, admiringly. "Don't you love it?"

"Not really."

"Philippe would," Betsy muttered.

"What?" Mikey looked irritated.

"Nothing. Did you wake me for a reason?"

"Where's Mom? Did she have another attack?"

"Goodness no, child. Why do you ask?"

"She went to that Mormon church last night, didn't she?"

"Yes." Betsy noticed Black Bear dangling from Mikey's hand.

"I waited up for her, but she never came home. She's not in her bed." Mikey had shadows under her eyes, and her hair was wildly tangled.

"Oh, I hope she's all right," Betsy said. Agatha's mom was supposed to give her a ride home because I had to fly to the paint store. It was an emergency."

"So you don't know if Mom even made it home?"

"Relax, dear, I'm sure we'll find her." She grabbed Mikey's elbow and led her from the room. They heard a grunting sound and turned to see Karen lugging a big box up the stairs.

"What are you doing?" Betsy asked.

"Setting up my craft room."

"See?" Betsy laid a hand on Mikey's shoulder. "There's nothing to worry about."

"Worry about what?" Karen balanced the box on her knee and pressed the load against the banister. "Oh, the Mormons. No fears, I had a good time."

"What! With Mormons? Are you kidding?"

"Crazy, huh?" Karen laughed.

"Mom, they've sucked you into their vortex!"

Karen sighed, readjusting the box. "Maybe, but I don't think they're as bad as I thought."

She pushed the box farther onto the carpet, ending the balancing act.

"What about them being a cult?" Mikey asked.

"They aren't forced to believe or do anything they don't want to," Betsy interrupted. "The Church encourages learning, so I doubt it's possible."

"I give up! The Mormons are wonderful." Mikey rolled her eyes.

Her mom put her arm around Mikey's shoulders. "Not wonderful. I didn't say that. But not as bad as I thought." With her fingers, Karen pushed the corners of Mikey's mouth up, forcing a smile. "This means I won't get so uptight when you want to do stuff with Agatha."

Mikey's eyebrows raised. "You sure about this?"

"I am."

"But, I'm scared someone in our family will get hurt if we get too close to any religious group," Mikey said.

"I know, but we have to face our fears headon," Karen said.

Betsy beamed while Mikey sneered at her aunt.

"Great," Mikey said. "So much for my movie. I don't have enough to make any of this work. I'll have to scrap the whole thing or do a movie on the conflict between Aunt Betsy and the Mormons."

"What?" Betsy placed her hands on her hips.

"Can't have Aunt Betsy involved in anything without controversy." Mikey favored her aunt with a cheesy smile.

Betsy sighed.

"But that would mean I'd have to go to church for research. I don't know if I'm up for that. Too many people have already gotten sucked away."

"Mikey," Karen said. Her mouth dropped open.

"It's okay," Betsy said. "She's just speaking her mind. Can't fault her for that."

"And she might be right," Karen said, looking a little nervous.

Mikey rubbed her toe on the carpet. Betsy hugged her neice. "Don't," Mikey said, walking away from the embrace.

"Stop pouting and go do something with Agatha," Karen said.

Mikey's chin lowered. "Are you sure?"

"They might have some sneaky tricks up their sleeves, and I don't want you becoming one of them, but I see no reason to fear," Karen said, then clapped her hands together. "You'd better hurry or you'll miss the school bus."

Mikey dashed down the hall.

Betsy helped Karen with the craft box and headed toward her room. Mikey charged passed, flying from the door. Betsy's gaze followed her niece through the bay window. Light delicate snow flakes floated around her niece's head. Mikey's arm shot out as she twirled her face heavenward. Laughing, she grabbed at the flakes.

Betsy laughed too. That child would become cold soon. She'd better grab her coat. Running to the apartment, Betsy slipped her feet in pink flats. Coat in her hand, she set out after Mikey.

Her shoes squeaked with each step against the snow. Who would have ever thought snow would make such noise? It had been so long since she'd seen it. The white world caused her to smile. She paused long enough to snatch a handful for herself so her fingers could rub. The coldness seeped into her hand as the flakes melted.

Mikey saw Betsy and waved. "It's as pretty as the ocean."

"Yes," Betsy agreed.

Slipping on her coat, Mikey said, "I feel like I've won the Oscar. First Mom says I can hang out with Agatha, and now it's snowing."

"You're pretty lucky."

"I can't wait to tell Agatha. I'm going to see if I can make it to her bus stop. Maybe the snow will make the bus late."

"That'd be great." Betsy struggled to keep up with her on the slippery sidewalk.

"My first white Christmas," Mikey said.

Betsy smiled.

"Oh you better watch out. You better not pout, I'm telling you why — Santa Claus is coming to town," Mikey sang into the crisp mountain air.

Agatha sneaked on the scene, laughing at Mikey's rendition. A gust of mountain wind rushed against them. They shivered and giggled as breeze blew against them. Mikey stopped singing. "Guess what?" she said to her friend.

"What?"

"My mom went to the craft thing you had at your church. She said she doesn't think you're as evil as she once thought."

"Really?"

"Yep. As of now, I can be with you any time."

"Cool." Agatha smiled. "So do you want to come over after school? We could make matching sweatshirts. It would be fun."

"That would be so cool. "

"Totally," Agatha said and laughed.

Betsy waved good-bye to the girls, returning home. She stepped carefully, fearful she might fall. Winter had begun.

❧

Friday evening Betsy paced around the house in zigzag circles. First she walked into the kitchen, turned to leave, then back into the kitchen to put a cup in the dishwasher. Around and around she went.

"Stop," Sam said. "You're making me dizzy. What are you so excited about anyway?"

"Nothing," Betsy said, checking her reflection in the glass of the microwave. "I'm an aging beauty queen."

"What's that smell?" Sam asked.

"Roses. Like it?"

"I don't see any flowers." Sam turned his nose away from her.

"My perfume. What do you think?" Betsy waved her wrist in front of Sam.

He scrunched his nose and leaned back. "It's definitely different. Where are you going?"

"Shopping." Betsy tugged on the side of her skirt.

"For what?"

"Ties."

"You're getting all decked out to shop for ties?" Sam looked at her like she had three holes in her head.

"Yep."

Karen walked into the kitchen. "Any ideas for dinner?" she asked, heading for the cookbook cupboard.

"Spaghetti," Betsy said.

"Yuck, we always have that," Sam said. He stuck out his tongue.

"Perfect. Do we have any sauce?" Karen asked.

"In the soup cupboard on the top right." Betsy patted her bangs.

"Mom, Betsy's getting spruced up to buy ties."

Karen shot her sister-in-law a full body stare. "You do look good. You always put the movie-star beauties to shame."

Betsy grinned.

Karen asked, "Going with any one special?"

Betsy patted her hair. "Maybe."

"It's a man, isn't it?" Karen asked.

Betsy's hands fell to her side. "No lectures."

"Just a little one?" Karen asked.

"I'm helping this guy out. Nothing more."

Karen took a big sniff. "I smell that. You're going to be married within the year."

Betsy's mouth fell open. "Am not. I won't be married by New Year's!"

Karen turned to open the can. "I know. Have fun on your date."

"I'm not going to jump into marriage on the first date."

"Um hum, so it's not Philippe?" Karen said, pouring the sauce into a pot.

"No. And I'm not rushing into things like I normally do!" Betsy folded her arms across her chest.

"I'm not saying anything," Karen said. "I'm just glad it's not Philippe." She took the pot off the burner. "New Years Eve I'm going to say, 'Told you so.'"

"HA!" Betsy said as the doorbell rang.

"Looks like the Romeo you're not going to marry is here." Karen batted her eyelashes. Then she burst into a fit of laughter.

"I'll be," Betsy said, leaving the room. She ran to the mirror, softened a hair, wiped at the lipstick below her lip, then dashed from the room.

⁂

Betsy breathed deeply. "Hmmm, *Polo,* always been my favorite perfume. Dreamy yet masculine."

Jeff smiled, running his hand through his thinning hair. "I'm saving the tie for you to pick out."

They walked to the car, and Jeff rushed to the passenger door to open it. The perfect gentleman. She slid onto the seat, watching him walk calmly around the front of the vehicle. He wore Docker pants and a pale blue dress shirt.

As she watched him, she thought of an accountant. Boring! Yet there had to be something interesting lurking inside, waiting for her to draw the real him out. Hadn't he said she reminded him of his former wife? Perhaps his grief suppressed his wild, crazy side. His taste in ties as well as her suggested something exciting lay hidden underneath the surface. This idea intrigued her.

Jeff's smooth skin reddened as she watched him. He continued to drive, but fell silent. His fingers tapped the steering wheel.

"Is this your first date since your wife died?"

He coughed several times. When he recovered, he said, "Yes." He clenched his square jaw.

Betsy leaned over and patted his hand. "I'll go easy on ya. Promise."

He sent her a weak grin, then stared ahead of them. A couple of minutes passed; then he said, his voice cracking, "Sorry."

"Perfectly understandable."

The muscles in Jeff's neck strained.

"She must have been one heck of a lady."

"She was."

Betsy sighed. What had she gotten herself into? This man was still broken-hearted and probably would never notice her. But then, they were just friends with anyway. Did she want more? They stopped at another signal. A red Porsche whizzed passed them. What about Philippe? She had to decide soon. He'd be calling any time, and she'd put him off long enough. Remembering the two dozen roses he'd sent her yesterday, she smiled. Such a romantic. Life would never be dull with him.

Betsy glanced at Jeff and at his full lips. What would it be like to kiss those lips? She mentally slapped her face. Straighten up old girl. This man grieves over his wife. He has a son. A challenging one at that. You're here to be his friend, nothing more. If you want romance, you have Philippe. The light turned green, and they rounded a curve up a mountain. Jeff seemed like the loyal type. He still had his wife constantly on his mind. Security was an appealing quality. She'd lived the adventurous life already with Philippe, and that had led to pain. Would Philippe prove a painful choice a second time or exciting? If something bloomed with Jeff, would it be peaceful or dreadfully boring? How could she choose?

⁂

Betsy poured over the manual for primary. Two days until Sunday, and she still didn't know how to reach Dudon. He acted as though he didn't need to hear the gospel, but Betsy felt he needed it more than the others. Since he was in a wheelchair, he had to prove something to everyone. He had to be extra cool to be accepted, she reasoned.

The topic, showing gratitude to Heavenly Father and Jesus through keeping the Sabbath day holy, added stress. Dudon may feel he had nothing to be grateful for. She needed to compose a list of his blessings, so she could spend the hour convincing him of his Father in Heaven's love. First off, she'd talk about the physical blessings he did have. Then the fact that he had the Church and a parent who loved him. His smarts were another gift.

Closing the manual, she sighed. She'd been lucky Karen had gone to Relief Society despite her big mistake. Adding to her fortune, Karen seemed to have had a good time and even rushed home to hang up the Thanksgiving craft. Karen had completed all of them in record time. Betsy stared, dismayed at her own effort. She had splashed a little paint here and there. The buttons she painted down Santa's jacket resembled big yellow stains. Crafts weren't her forte.

Leaving her apartment, Betsy searched for Karen to discover what she planned for dinner. Christmas music drifted down the hall, bringing a feeling of coziness to the Thanksgiving season. Betsy followed the tune and found Karen in her new office buried under a pile of scraps, paint, and glue sticks. "What's this? A craft production line?" Betsy eyed the mess scattered throughout the room.

Karen laughed. "No. But please feel welcome to come into my new craft room."

"The craft bug has bitten."

"Sure has."

"What are you doing with it all?"

"I'm taking them to the mental ward at the hospital for Christmas."

Betsy's hand flew to her rouged lips. "Really?"

Karen shot a dot of glue onto the fabric to secure the black button serving as a Santa Claus' eye.

"That's so neat. What a good idea. Can I help?"

Karen's face looked scared.

"Don't worry, I wasn't thinking about actually making anything. More like helping with transporting them and buying supplies," Betsy said.

"Oh," Karen said. She seemed relieved, and Betsy felt hurt, but ignored it.

Betsy and Karen worked out dinner plans. Betsy left Karen singing with her CD, "Joy to the World." Smiling, Betsy considered Karen crazy for planning to make at least two hundred crafts for the patients. She'd have to spend all her free time from now until Christmas to come close to the goal. Crazy, but a happy crazy. Betsy couldn't help wondering if Karen's church experience had influenced her sister-in-law. Grinning again, Betsy decided that naturally the church influenced Karen even if she didn't realize it. The gospel was making her a better person.

❦

Primary time arrived, and Betsy dashed around the classroom, preparing for the lesson. She glanced at her watch. Two minutes before the boys streamed in. She offered a quick heartfelt prayer, pleading to her Maker to give her the knowledge to reach these young ones.

Dudon entered first. Jason held the door open as the boy wheeled himself in. He glanced over at Betsy as if searching for her Goliath's forehead so he could shoot. "Hello, Sister Ashforth," he said.

Betsy had barely made it off her knees. She straightened her skirt and looked directly into Dudon's blue eyes. "Hello there, I'm glad you came."

Dudon snickered. "Yeah, right."

"No, I mean it."

He wheeled his chair to the far corner. "When will the confused people be resurrected?"

"When?" Betsy asked.

"During the last daze."

Betsy smiled. "You're a walking riddle encyclopedia."

"Sure am. Which president of the Church had a tough time in the summer?"

"Which?"

"Lorenzo Snow."

Betsy smiled again. "I see."

A few more boys drifted in. Brett said, "Oh, you again. I thought you wouldn't be coming."

"Why's that?" Betsy asked.

"Because, um, of what…Mom said to you."

"I've got a surprise for you boys." Betsy slapped her hands together.

"What's that?" they asked.

"I'm not so easy to chase away. In fact," Betsy stared directly at Dudon, whose gaze darted toward the door, "I refuse to leave. So until the Bishop tells me to hit the highway, I'm yours."

Dudon's upper lip curled in disgust.

Betsy ignored the sneer and called Brett to say the prayer. He walked to the front of the classroom with his arms folded and head bowed. His chin came close to his chest. He offered a three-minute prayer and sat with his arms still folded.

Betsy cleared her throat. "Dudon, can you remind the class what last week's lesson was about by telling a joke?"

Dudon raised his eyebrows.

Betsy kept a straight face and stared. The exchange lasted for ten seconds; then Dudon said, "Okay. How did the happy dogs cross the plains?"

"In the waggin' trains," Jason blurted out.

Dudon's eyes narrowed. "How did you know?"

"You told me during Sharing Time last week?"

"How about...What did the pioneers use to buy food?" Dudon glanced around with a smirk. "Hum?" The class remained silent. "Winter Quarters," he said, folding his arms across his chest.

"Thank you, Dudon. I'm glad you remembered we talked about the pioneers and the struggles they went through to establish the church in the Salt Lake Valley."

"No prob," he said with a smile.

Betsy started out with the teaching manual attention activity. A child thought of something he was grateful for, and the other children tried to guess what it was by asking questions. Most of the boys jumped right in and participated. A couple smiled when they guessed right, but Dudon scowled. Betsy noted the mental wall rising the second he heard the word "grateful." She'd give the wall a chance to weaken before she tried to utterly knock it over.

The last boy guessed the answer. All eyes were on Betsy except Dudon's. "Dudon, will you please read a scripture?" She handed him a Book of Mormon. "It's in Mosiah 18:23."

He turned the pages, sighing after every few flips.

Finally he read, "And he commanded them that they should observe the Sabbath every day, and keep it holy, and also every day they should give thanks to the Lord their God." He slammed the book shut.

"Thank you. Can anyone guess what the lesson's on?"

The boys answered, saying thanks and keeping the Sabbath holy.

"We already know about keeping the Sabbath day holy," Dudon muttered.

"That's great," Betsy said. "Then you can be an extra help to me. Can you please tell the class what you know about it and how you apply it to your life?"

Dudon watched his hands. "It's where you only do boring church stuff all day long, and you can't do anything fun."

"Okay. Why would the Lord ask you to do boring church stuff?"

Dudon shrugged.

"'Come on, I expect a better answer than that." She took a step toward the wheeled-chaired boy.

"Cause Heavenly Father wants us to learn stuff."

"Yes. What does He want us to learn? Can anyone answer this?" Betsy glanced around the classroom. All eyes remained on Dudon.

The silence grew thick and uncomfortable. Betsy thought about answering the question, but decided against it because she suspected Dudon's defensive wall might be cracking. If it wasn't cool to mouth-off, then he might have to save face by impressing the teacher. Acceptance from the other boys seemed very important to him.

Finally he spoke. "He wants us to learn about Him."

Betsy smiled. Dudon did have a depth of understanding. "Yes, He does. And why do you think the subject of keeping the Sabbath day holy and the word gratitude were written in the same verse?"

He shrugged and the rest of the boys avoided Betsy's gaze. The boys watched Dudon to see if the teacher had stumped him. He glanced at Betsy, at the boys, then at last answered.

"Because showing our gratitude to God is what the Sabbath is all about," he said.

"That's right."

Dudon relaxed against his chair and took a listening pose.

"I'd like each one of you to tell me two things you're grateful for."

Jason said, "That I finally got my own room." Similar responses continued until it came to Dudon. He sat very still. "Dudon?" Betsy asked.

He didn't move. Betsy wanted to speak to him again, but had a strong impression not to.

He looked at Betsy with a tear in his eyes and said, "I'm grateful for my life. When I got in the car accident, I almost died. I was really sick right before they did the surgery. The doctor said he thought I was too weak to survive a major operation. But my dad gave me a blessing. He said I'd live." Dudon's eyes misted over. "The Priesthood saved me that day."

Betsy continued to stare. She had thought he would be bitter at God for losing his two legs and his mother. But instead, he was grateful for his life, and from that confession, Betsy had no doubt this boy had a strong testimony of the existence of God. As she suspected, his wall of defense was only a cool act to be accepted by his peers. Nothing more.

The rest of the class time continued well. Betsy ended the lesson with a quote she'd found in a Relief Society manual from Elder Mark E. Peterson.

> Our observance or nonobservance of the Sabbath is an unerring measure of our attitude toward the Lord personally and toward his suffering in Gethsemane, his death on the cross, and his resurrec-

> tion from the dead. It is a sign of whether we are Christians in very deed, or whether our conversion is so shallow that commemoration of his atoning sacrifice means little or nothing to us.

Betsy bore her testimony that she knew these things were true because of the warm feeling she received praying about them; then she dismissed class. As the children raced out of the room to Sharing Time, she stayed to gather her things. She turned around and saw Dudon waiting. "Why haven't you left with the rest of the class?"

"I want to know where that quote came from."

"Which one?"

"The last one."

Betsy flipped opened the Relief Society Manual. "It says you can find it in the Conference Report of April 1975 on page seventy-two or in the *Ensign* of May 1975 on page forty-nine."

"I need a copy."

"I'll make one for you."

Dudon nodded and went to go.

Betsy said, "Wait."

He flipped his wheelchair back. "Yes?"

"I appreciated your thoughts today. They were touching. Thank you for sharing."

He shrugged. Betsy hurried over to open the door for him, and he rolled away to Sharing Time.

❦

Jeff leaned against the white wall outside the primary room, his hands shoved in his pockets. Betsy walked to him and fingered his tie. "Good taste."

He smiled shyly down on her. "Thanks." His shyness was cute. It was rare to find that kind of innocence mixed with so much life experience.

"Haven't you seen Dudon? He left a couple of minutes ago. I stayed to help clean up."

"I saw him. It wasn't him I was waiting for."

"Who then?" Betsy gazed into his brown earth-rich eyes, then away. His stomach hung slightly over his belt. She smiled, stifling the urge to reach out and pinch his love handle.

"You, of course. You want to walk home?"

"Sure," Betsy wished she didn't have her high heels on.

They headed out of the building, and Jeff proceeded to go out of his way to walk on the outside of the curve. This made Betsy grin. She enjoyed being treated like a lady; plus it was nice to walk home from church with a man. Something about it represented the white-picket-fence life. Perhaps she could use this soothing calmness in her life. She couldn't tramp all over the world forever.

"Sorry about the other night," Jeff said.

"Why?" Betsy dangled her hand by his side.

"I wasn't paying the kind of attention to you that I should have," Jeff said, taking her hand into his.

"That's okay. I understand about your — "

"She's gone. She must have known I was lonely because I feel like her spirit has brought us together. I've been an idiot for not recognizing it."

Betsy stopped walking. "What?"

"You're a lot like her. Off-the-wall. You both love loud and crazy colors and patterns. She knew we'd make each other happy, so she led us together."

Betsy laughed. "That's kind of far-fetched."

"Not if you knew my Cindy. Nothing too much for her. Believe it or not, I know she wants me to marry you."

"Marr — "

"Don't worry. I'll go slow. This isn't a proposal — yet. We need to get to know each other better first." He grabbed her hand as they strolled up the hill.

Betsy gripped his fingers, not knowing what to think. Electrical currents jolted her. A silence filled the air after Jeff's declaration, yet the quiet was nice. The sun pressed the top of their heads as the wind cooled them off. December.

Betsy had a lot to think about, but ever since they rounded the bend and she could see her house, her thoughts focused on who marched up and down the sidewalk by the front door. The person was male and dressed in a suit. Please be the Bishop, she prayed.

The closer they came, the more she suspected it wasn't the Bishop. The man saw her and approached. "Philippe," she said, dropping Jeff's hand.

"I take it this is my answer," Philippe said, pointing at her hand. "You could've at least called. I traveled the world for you." He handed her a bouquet of wild flowers.

"Philippe," Betsy cried.

"Who's this?" Jeff asked.

"I doubt she's told you about me." Philippe said as he held out his hand. "I'm Philippe, Betsy's second husband and trying to be third.

And you are?"

Jeff blinked. "Jeff. I'm also fighting for the honor to be her third. Third right?" he asked, looking at Betsy.

She nodded without looking at either of them.

"I think it's time for you to make a decision," Philippe said. "I've waited long enough."

"Let's go in the home." Betsy glanced around to see if her neighbors were outside. Both men stared at her. She marched ahead and into the house without turning to see if they followed. Inside, she pointed at the couch in the living room. They sat, eying each other uneasily.

What could she say? She tapped her fingers on her lap.

"Are you going to make a decision?" Philippe asked.

Betsy cleared her throat. "To make the record straight, Jeff hasn't asked me anything. We're friends."

"Hand-holding friends," Philippe said with bitterness.

"As of twenty minutes ago, yes."

"So you've decided not to marry me then?" Philippe asked. His eyes cast downward.

"I guess I have." Betsy sighed. Her actions had decided for her.

"Why? Was it because you couldn't forgive me?"

"No...I think it's because of my new lifestyle."

"Ahh — " Philippe said.

"Mon cherie, don't get me wrong. You're wonderful, exciting, and full of adventure. But Jeff here has shown me there's another world, promising security and the belief of God. I'd like to try that out with someone if I can find the right person." She briefly eyed Jeff, whose presence calmed her.

"I see." Philippe stood. "If you change your mind, you know where to find me."

"Yes." Betsy kissed his cheek. She whispered, "I'm so sorry."

He whispered back, "Au reviour, mon petite choux. Keep the ring. My parting gift. Just please get married soon. The alimony's killing me."

Betsy laughed through her tears as he left. Once she settled down, she looked into Jeff's expectant face. "Don't forget we still need time to get to know each other," she said.

Jeff smiled. "Phew," he whispered.

Chapter 18

Christmas season arrived, and Karen had stayed up countless nights making her Santas for the hospital. Only three more to go. So much for Betsy's doubts that she couldn't make it. She sang as she worked on the next Santa. The patients were going to love them.

Mrs. Thomson had called her and invited her to the ward Christmas party. When Karen asked if it was held at the mental ward in the hospital, Mrs. Thomson had laughed.

"No, we call our congregation a ward."

Karen was beginning to really like Mrs. Thomson, so she agreed to come.

"Great. I'll love talking to you," Mrs. Thomson said. "And then you could tell me how you managed to get all those crafts done. They're so adorable!"

"You want my secrets, huh? I'll have to give it some thought before I spread it to the whole world." Karen smiled. They could become good friends. "You know, I'm impressed that your church encourages service to others. It's amazing how much better it makes a person feel when they actually do it."

"I've always been a big fan. Call me simple-minded, but I've believed if I follow the Lord's way then I'd be happy," Mrs. Thomson said.

"I don't think that's simple-minded." Karen measured a red ribbon with her finger, preparing to cut it. "It isn't easy to believe in God."

"Sometimes it's not, but it's harder not to. Because alone a person is left with no faith. That would make it harder for someone to have reason to live when life gets hard."

Karen held her scissors in midair.

"Hello?" Mrs. Thomson asked.

"Sorry. Maybe that's what my problem's been. I'd like to learn more about it."

"I could set you up with the missionaries anytime."

Karen swallowed. "I don't know about that."

"I'd be with you the whole time. Just listen to what they say. See if it makes sense. If it doesn't, no big deal. Promise."

The scissors fell onto the carpet. "But — "

"What are you worried about?"

"Brainwashing," Karen choked. "Will they let me ask questions?"

"As many as you want. Our church firmly believes you can find out things for yourself. That's one of our underlying principles."

Karen's grip tightened on the phone. "If that's the case, I'll give it a try."

❧

The Ashforths spent a cozy Christmas around the fire, wrapped in the new quilts Karen made. Christmas music echoed out of their new stereo system, George's gift to the family. Mikey hung the phone up. She'd been talking to Agatha, whose family had a real neato Christmas too. Their friendship had bloomed to best friends. Mikey now had a wardrobe of clothes Agatha had made for her under the pretense of teaching Mikey how to sew. She'd gotten good at unpicking seams.

"Can I go over to Agatha's and see what she got for Christmas?"

Karen sighed. She'd liked having the family gathered around. "In a minute. I've got an announcement to make."

"Oh, man," Sam said, halfway out of the room. He returned to the couch. "Hurry, I want to go play soccer. Mark's going to meet me at the school."

Karen ignored him. "I want to apologize for the way I acted when we first moved here. I overreacted a little."

"A little?" George huffed.

"I should've found out what the Mormons were like before I freaked out. My fears convinced me they were like the cult that killed my friend. I didn't think about Mormons as Christians."

"Sometimes when we have the most violent reaction to something," Betsy said. "It's because our subconscious knows the thing will dramatically change our lives forever. It'll be hard, but these things are best for us — "

"What are you trying to say, Mom?" Sam asked.

"I've been taking the Mormon discussions and learned about forever families and how we can be together forever in the next life. I've been praying about it."

Betsy gasped and put her hand to her mouth, her hand shaking.

Karen continued to talk, "The gospel's the truth. There's no denying it. I've decided to be baptized."

Tears poured from both women's faces as they ran to each other and embraced. "Really?" Betsy said. "This is too good to be true. I can't believe it. Why didn't you tell me you were taking the discussions?"

"Because I wanted to find out for myself. No outside pressures."

Betsy's hands dropped to her side, and she glanced at her brother, who smiled. "Is this all right, George?"

He shrugged. "I don't care what Karen does as long as she doesn't expect me to become a Mormon and she's happy."

Betsy lifted an eyebrow.

"I already talked to him about this," Karen explained.

Betsy waved her finger. "And you two kept it from me! How dare you."

"I wanted it to be the final Christmas gift," Karen said.

"Oh, I'm so happy for you." Betsy kissed her sister-in-law on the cheek again.

Karen smiled. She'd searched for happiness in all the wrong places: the ocean, a big home, job, medicine. None held the answer. She now knew the solution; happiness came from having faith in God and generating His love to others. If she'd sprayed insect repellent all over the Mormons, she would've missed out on the happiness she now experienced. Funny how things turned out.

"Mom, when are you moving out?" Mikey asked.

"Move?"

"You said if I became a Mormon you'd kick me out of the house. Does that mean if you become one then you go?"

Karen laughed. "Oh, Mikey, I'm sorry. Will you forgive me?"

"Yeah."

"Is it okay if I become a Mormon?"

"If it makes you happy."

"It will. Believe me it will."

"This doesn't mean I have to become one, does it?" Mikey asked.

"Of course not, but I don't know how you're going to avoid it."

"Ohhh, watch out. Now the Mormons will really be after us," George said. He grinned as Karen play hit him in the stomach.

"We'll just have to see," Karen said.

"Can I go over to Agatha's now?"

"I need to meet Mark," Sam said.

"All right, go on." Karen said. "As long as you know I want to be with you forever."

"Sweet," Sam said with a big fake smile.

❧

Betsy and Karen chattered as they prepared dinner a couple of days after Christmas. The phone rang. Karen answered and handed it to Betsy. "For you," she sang.

"Hello?"

"Sister Ashforth, hi, this is Sister Jefferson. I wanted to thank you for the great job you're doing with your primary class."

"I'm just doing my job."

"No, you're doing much more. You're reaching the youngsters. I got back from visiting teaching Dudon's grandmom. She said the change in Dudon was incredible. He doesn't mope around on Sundays. He took that thought you gave him and carved it into wood, which he set on top of his desk. He'd die, though, if he knew I told you. So don't tell him I said anything. The carving was gorgeous. He must have spent hours on it."

"It's a good thought," Betsy said.

"Not only that, but he talks about the gospel."

"The gospel's a pretty exciting thing," Betsy said.

"I want to thank you for doing such a great job. I have to admit I had my doubts when the Bishop suggested this job for you. Actually he demanded you take it. He promised you would be caughtup in the doctrine. He thought you'd be the perfect one for Dudon, and he was right! Thank you."

With a wide smile, Betsy hung up the phone.

"Good news?" Karen asked.

"The best. The best. Nothing beats the feeling of helping God make a difference in someone else's life. Nothing."